Faces *in the* Firelight

Faces
in the
Firelight

written and illustrated
by

John L. Peyton

McDonald and Woodward Publishing Company
Blacksburg, Virginia
1992

McDonald and Woodward Publishing Company
P. O. Box 10308, Blacksburg, Virginia 24062-0308

Faces in the Firelight

All rights reserved
Composition by Marathon Typesetting, Roanoke, Virginia
Printed in the United States of America by McNaughton and Gunn, Inc.,
Saline, Michigan

99 98 97 96 95 94 93 92   10 9 8 7 6 5 4 3 2 1

First printing March 1992

Library of Congress Cataloging-in-Publication Data
Peyton, John L., 1907-
    Faces in the firelight / written and illustrated by John L. Peyton.
      p.   cm.
    ISBN 0-939923-19-X : $14.95
    1. Ojibwa Indians—Fiction. I. Title.
PS3566.E982F33   1992
813' .54—dc20   91-39539
                                                CIP

The Tribes

Anishinabe (plural: Anishinabeg — The First Men):
The Ojibway or Chippewa.
Abwan (plural: Abwaneg — The Roasters):
The Dakota, Lakota or Sioux.
Muskego (plural: Muskegag — People of the Swamps):
Those Crees living in the low country southwest of Hudson Bay.
Saganash (plural: Saganashag): The whites.

The Men and Women

Iron Feather: An Anishinabe hunter.
Otter Woman: His wife.
He-Rises: Their son.
Shanod: Their older daughter.
Smoke Drifting: Their younger daughter.
Sound of Waves: Daughter of Shanod and Ice Stone.
Sturgeon Man: Father of Iron Feather.
Tamarack: A Muskego.
Crooked Lightning: An old warrior.
Dawn Sailing: A captive Abwan.
The Turtle: Her husband.
Loon's Foot: Their son.
Red Sky Woman: Wife of Loon's Foot.
Little Toenail: Their son.
Woman of the North Wind: Foster mother of Dawn Sailing.
Blackduck: Husband of North Wind.
Madeyn: An orphan.
Jamieson: A white trader.
Willow Woman: His wife.
Undertooth: A sorcerer.
Ice Stone: His son.
Tom Stone: Son of Ice Stone and Shanod.
Joe Mashkegwatik: Son of Tamarack and Shanod.
Shakes-His-Wings: Friend of He-Rises.
Wood-that-Sizzles-in-the-Fire: Brother of Willow Woman.
Threetit Anna: Loon's Foot's second wife.
Blue Flag Woman: A huntress.
Cedarstick: An American Anishinabe.
Louise: His wife.
Charlie: His brother-in-law.

The Spirits

Nanabush: Demigod and trickster
Manido (plural: Manidog): A powerful spirit.
Missepishu: The lynx that lives under the water.
Pauguk: Death.
Peboan: Winter.
'Tschgumi: Lake Superior.
Matchi Ayawish: A dangerous animal, brought back
to life by sorcery.
Windigo: A cannibal.

It should be noted that a spirit may be a person, an animal, or an inanimate thing as well as a supernatural being. 'Tschgumi refers to the body of water and also to the spirit that rules over it.

Glossary

Andeg: Crow.
Amik: Beaver.
Kokoho: Owl.
Makak: Bark container.
Manidoke: Power.
Manomen: Wild rice.
Mukwa: Bear.
Muskeg: Swamp.
Pikogan: Cone-shaped lodge.
Tikinagon: Cradle board.
Totosh: Woman's breast.
Wabeno: Shaman, healer or sorcerer.
Wabooz: Rabbit.
Waginogan: Dome-shaped lodge.

1

His skin was warm in the pale October sunlight. He squirmed, lively as a brown caterpillar shining up from the cool, gray-green caribou moss.

His mother had freed him from his cradle board to roll and gurgle in naked ecstasy while she scraped a moose hide laid across a slanting log.

He was not crawling yet, not big enough to get himself into serious trouble. All the same, Otter Woman looked up often from her work to make sure that her baby was where he belonged.

The fresh hide was heavy, but she had carried it up to a rocky knoll overlooking a curve of the river. This was a good place to work, far enough from the wigwam to keep the scrapings from getting tracked into it, but still in sight of the rack where the meat was drying.

So when a pair of Canada jays dropped silently down upon the thin gray strips, Otter Woman was instantly in motion, shouting as she ran, and waving the bone scraper. Four-year-old Shanod, who had been helping with the hide, came stumbling down the slope behind her.

The black-masked robbers ripped off swift beakfuls while they measured the approaching vengeance. At the last prudent moment they soared to a branch well out of reach but not too high for quick return, whence they looked down with unruffled insolence on the panting woman.

She drew back her arm to throw the scraper, thought better of that, and was stooping to pick up a stone when she felt a tug at her skirt. Shanod was jerking with one hand and pointing toward the hill with the other.

The boy had somehow worked his way over the fungus-covered ridge of a fallen tree, then rolled, wriggled, and hudged across the moss carpet. Otter Woman stared up at him, hardly believing that he could have moved so far so swiftly. But there he was, poised on a rock shelf that overhung the river. As she started toward him, he pushed farther, slid on the slanting stone, and disappeared. There was a splash, then just the benign murmur of the water.

Otter Woman turned and ran, her square body crashing through the dense brush along the bank. She tripped over a down timber, fell heavily, then, up and running again, she burst into the open at the landing. She flung the canoe in a wild splash to the water and leaped into it. Its wooden frame groaned under the impact but it shot out from the shore.

Peering down over the side she could see only waving green water-weed.

She paddled several frantic strokes and stopped, her blade ready and dripping, as she looked again into the water, out across it, and then down its length. For terrible moments she saw just the quietly speeding river. Then, at a distant curve, a glistening little black head broke the surface.

The paddle churned white foam. The bow split the current with a sound like boiling water.

The head disappeared.

Otter Woman surged around the bend to see only the reflection of spruce, birch and sky wavering on the placid surface.

But she was gauging more accurately the quiet rush of the Minnisabik. She coasted now, and backed water a little, keeping in sight the stretch of river where, if the boy should rise another time, he would be most likely to appear.

There! A swirl, with a dark spot at its center, disturbed, for a moment, the mirrored picture of the shore. She forced her paddle almost to the breaking point.

The head came up again — close, but a little downstream. Otter Woman swung the canoe broadside to the current and reached far out toward the feeble commotion.

Too far. Water poured in over the gunwale. She leaned back, righting the canoe. The child sank.

Then she was ready, her paddle backing against the current, holding her position a stroke or two upstream. If he would rise one

3

more time!

Straining, her eyes caught the movement. He was coming up again through the amber water. Instantly she was over him, waiting. Her fingers locked in his hair. Her other hand went under his arm, thumb clamped against shoulder. She swung him into the canoe, drove it, with desperate power, to the bank and went to work on the limp little body.

✦ ✦ ✦

That was how they came to name the baby. When I met him many years later the Indians still called him He-Rises-to-the-Surface, Mwashkamagad in Ojibway. But that was too hard for civilized white people to pronounce. To us he was Old Moosh.

The century was young then, and so was I. The surgeon, the judge and the mining engineer, friends of my family, had somehow accepted the bother and responsibility of taking me on their annual fishing trip. I wondered why these men would call Moosh "old." They all seemed ancient to me.

I was standing on a rock ledge where a cool breeze brought the smell of pines and riffled the surface of the river below. Our gear had been offloaded beside the railroad track and "our Indians" had carried it down to the log landing. Moosh was making sure that the packs were properly distributed and that each canoe was balanced, for upstream travel.

I had been told about the near drowning in the first year of his life, and I could see that he had suffered other misfortunes since. His left forearm was strangely warped above the wrist and two fingers were missing from his left hand. The coarse woolen cloth of his trouser leg sagged into a depression where a piece of his thigh had been torn out. He had pulled the brim of his greasy felt hat down over the right side of his face. As he squatted, holding the canoe steady for me, he looked up and I saw that right side. Brow and eye and cheek were gone in one great shining scar, as grotesque and irreparable as the gash that a landslide leaves on the mountain.

I stared, mouth open, until he smiled and motioned me into the boat.

In the weeks that followed I noted that his one remaining eye never failed to find the grown-over blaze that marked the portage, or the safest, least punishing passage across stormy water. None of us white men understood how he could remember each bend and boulder

4

in the rivers and every detail in the changing shorelines of the lakes.

So "Old Moosh" may have been an honorary title, bestowed in recognition of his experience and seniority as head guide. There may have been something a little condescending in it, too — an amiable attempt to maintain a proper master-and-man relationship. His patrons could hardly be blamed if they felt some such need, because once the canoes had left the settlement, the important decisions had to be left to him.

Not that he was bossy or impertinent. On the contrary, after quietly offering advice, he would do just the opposite if so ordered. But his employers were prudent men who had traveled with Moosh before and had observed the unfortunate consequences of such reversals. They knew how to repair and punish people and how to get iron ore out of the earth. He knew the woods and the water.

As the youngest and least capable member of the party, I had been assigned to his canoe. This was made of bark and without seats, according to the custom of these people. To get right down on the ribs and planking, either kneeling or sitting, is a stable and efficient position for paddling, but painful to a white boy's bones and buttocks.

I had not yet learned how hard the world is. The small discomfort seemed unbearable. I complained. Moosh folded a thick blanket for a cushion.

Even with that red woolen padding beneath me, I soon began to hurt again and told him so. At the next portage he found a flat piece of driftwood, shaped it with a few easy axe strokes, and propped it against a thwart as a backrest. That felt just right. From then on I sat most of the time at idle ease, facing backwards and looking at Moosh.

In calm weather, even without my help, he seemed to have no trouble staying ahead of the heavily loaded canvas canoes. Often we had to wait for them to catch up. My privileged position was more than just comfortable. It turned out to be an important part of my education. I was, literally, sitting at the feet of the master. Only once did an inquiry of mine come up against the barrier of Indian silence.

The river had foamed down out of a gorge in the hills and had split into the channels of a flat delta. We were drifting in the dying current, some distance ahead of the rest of the party, waiting to show them the best passage into the lake ahead.

That was when I asked Moosh to let me look at the knife that hung in a moosehide sheath from his belt. He took it off, laid it on the flat of his paddle, and passed it over the packs to me.

The handle was carved in the shape of an animal, with forepaws drooped flat against the body and snarling muzzle protruding downward behind the grip. An ancient and persistent stain flared red around the eyes.

I could imagine some old artist muttering witch words as he cut that piece of antler by firelight on a winter night. He might have had in mind a bear but he was not making a realistic representation of that or any other creature. Instead, he had abstracted his sculpture into some unfamiliar thing that charmed and excited me — and frightened me a little. He had expressed a certain menace, the dark mystery of the forest.

I had often seen Moosh doing camp work with this knife. Now, as I held it in my hands it seemed long and heavy for such humble tasks. More like a weapon or a sacrificial instrument, and somehow not characteristic of its owner.

"This wasn't made for opening cans and peeling potatos. Certainly not for skinning. . . . And not really for butchering game either, was it? Or for filleting fish?"

He did not answer.

"The decorations along the sheath are different from those I've seen on other Ojibway things. Those were curvy designs. Like trees or flowers. These straight edges and zigzag lines have to mean action. Lightning, maybe. Or jagged rocks grinding."

"It is the quillwork of the 'Bwaneg. You call them Sioux. They were our enemies, and yours."

He paddled several strokes before he spoke again.

"But the Anishinabe knife came from an enemy, and the 'Bwan sheath was the gift of a dear friend."

"You could get a lot of money for these things."

"They will be buried with me."

I could see that there was a story connected with the knife and that I was not going to hear it. Not then, anyway.

But when I asked him about an even more personal matter, he spoke freely. He seemed amused rather than offended by my fascination with his deformities.

Each day as we lead the procession over the water, in camp while I helped him clean fish or pluck partridge, and at night when we were sitting alone by a fire, he answered my questions about his injuries and about the events that led up to them.

Later, in other canoes and by other fires, I learned of different and more general misfortunes. These had multiplied in the years since the first French trader, with one hand outstretched to offer gifts and the other raised in what he hoped would be recognized as the peace sign, walked cautiously up from the beach toward the silently watching people.

The woods Indians have been changing from that moment on. He-Rises' family were quite different from their ancestors of those earlier times. They were even more different from their present-day descendants.

The northern Anishinabeg lived on the triangle of worn pre-Cambrian stone that extends, like the shell of a giant turtle, from Lake Superior to Hudson Bay and the Atlantic. The account that follows is the story of a fateful year in the lives of He-Rises and his sisters, as it was told to me on the rocks and water of that great Canadian shield.

2

A little breeze, faint, but sharp as a hand-honed arrow, flowed silently out of the north, crossed the frozen muskeg, and found its way between the spruce trees. It swayed the boughs, shifting the spots of moonlight that filtered down to the face of the snow. Nothing else moved.

From far away in the forest came the crack of a freezing tree, loud as a rifle shot in the vast silence. Then there was no sound except an occasional rumbling groan, a distant thunder, as ice froze, broke, and heaved deep beneath the lake's surface.

But in the shelter of a windbreak, a snowbanked tangle of standing and fallen trees, a dim light glowed, disappeared, and glowed again. It came flickering up from the blackened smoke-hole in a cone of bark and timber that protruded above the drifts. And after a while, if you were listening closely, you might have heard a little girl's soft laughter.

There were people down there, warm and at ease in the great cold, hungry but not starving. And not in the least downhearted. They were used to hunger.

The pikogan, their winter lodge, was built of heavy poles covered with birch bark, buttressed and reinforced with forked timbers, insulated with layers of moss, earth, and spruce boughs, and now under the added protection of the deep snow. It was a rough looking structure, but strong. Strong enough to have resisted the savage winds that had torn at it in the early winter and to hold up the weight of ice and snow that had settled upon it since.

Inside, its frame was hung with mats of woven cedar bark. These deflected any incoming drafts toward the opening overhead, keeping the lower level warm and fairly free from smoke. Within their rounded wall was spread another circle of balsam boughs, covered with more mats and with sleeping robes made of caribou and beaver skins.

Two men were stretched out on this resilient bedding. Iron Feather, the father, lay completely relaxed, sunk deep in fur and greenery. His eyes were closed, his lips parted a little and one arm was flung out, the slender hand palm-up on bare earth.

He-Rises, the other man, was fifteen. A boy becomes a man early when the lives of his family depend on his skill and endurance. He knew that he, too, should be lying in a state of full repose, gathering strength for the next day's effort. Instead, he twisted and turned a little, tense with the guilt of failure. He was hearing again the twang of the bowstring and the whir of wings, and watching the dark form of a spruce hen speed away in a trail of white flakes sifting down from snow-laden branches. It was the only game that either of them had seen all day.

"I should have taken two steps closer. She was watching me with a kindly eye. She would have waited."

He had intended to speak only in his thoughts, only to himself. But the intensity of the feeling forced those last few words out through his mouth.

Otter Woman looked up from the battered kettle and spoke quietly without stopping the circular motion of her spoon.

"Rest now, my son. Don't trouble yourself with a bird that has flown. You and your father have hunted well in this hard winter. The pot will need to simmer only a short time more and then we will all eat a little."

The kettle contained half a rabbit, some wild rice, lichen-moss scraped from pine trees, a few dried blueberries, and plenty of water. It was, indeed, sending out alluring sounds and smells. And, propped beside the fire, a disk-shaped little loaf of bannock, firm enough now to stand outside the frypan, was turning just the right shade of brown.

Shanod was mending a torn parka and pulling, from time to time, on a bark cord that swayed her baby's hammock. She had been given a white girl's name, Charlotte, and she wore a white woman's dress, but both had been softened, altered, and eased. Her black hair was matted now, and a little straggly, but her calm, fine-boned face might have qualified her to model for a madonna.

Sturgeon Man bent stiffly beside the fire, pushing up unburned wood, or drawing it back to keep a mild, even heat under the kettle. He wore his white hair long, in the old style, not cropped shoulder-length like his son's and grandson's.

Ten-year-old Smoke Drifting had her mother's blunt features and flat cheekbones. Her small figure was already taking on square proportions. She would be a good woman, some day, with axe, paddle and tump line. Now she was weaving a foot-covering of twisted rabbit skin. Her stubby brown hands and Shanod's slim fingers worked swiftly and with certainty. Moosehide parkas, leggings, mitts and moccasins must be repaired tonight for the hunters to put on at morning.

Earlier generations of the Anishinabeg would have been dressed in deerskin, but that material had been getting hard to come by. And for those who live in a country of rain, mist and snow, cloth has some advantages over leather. It dries faster and is warmer when wet.

To a hunter, though, a rent torn in a garment by the stiff twigs

and branches of the winter woods could bring frostbite or quick death. So the men still went out in moosehide leggings, mitts and moccasins, and in parkas of caribou skin. Under these, and now around the fire, they wore garments of coarse wool. This would have been considered cheap stuff in the white man's world, but it commanded a good price in pelts at the trading post.

The women's dresses were made of cotton print, with long skirts, short waists, and bright ribbon at the throat. Shanod had cut and hemmed vertical slits in her blouse, tied shut with tape when not open for nursing. Smoke Drifting's garment was made of flour sacks.

These cloth garments were wrinkled from being slept in, and stiff with old dirt. The weave showed clearly in dark grease spots. During the summer, the Anishinabeg bathed and washed their clothes often. As often, anyway, as the average white settler of that time. But when they had to chop through a foot or two of ice to get at the water, they used it sparingly.

The lodge smelled of wood smoke, balsam bedding, cooking grease, unbathed bodies, and a hint of diaper moss. Clothing and foot-wrappings, soaked with sweat and snow, were drying above the fire. Several small but musky mink pelts hung farther from the heat. These combined to make a rich and assertive odor.

To the hardworking men and women crowded together in this busy little space, smells were unimportant compared to keeping warm enough to live, on reduced rations, through the dark cold.

Whatever Otter Woman's dinner may have lacked in quantity or ingredients, it was eaten with swift enthusiasm. The empty kettle was scraped and finger-rubbed and greasy fingers were licked. The last crumb of frybread was tracked down. The outdoor work was done for that day.

The winter night would be long. Shanod put fresh wood on the fire. In the renewed light and warmth the younger members of the family looked expectantly toward the grandfather.

The weird beings that moved through the forest and the water in summer were far away now, or locked under the ice, where they could not hear their actions related. It was time for the old to continue the education of the young.

For the Anishinabeg, story-telling was more than entertainment.

It was the means by which one generation handed on to another the joys and sorrows of the ancestors, religious instruction, pride in past achievements, and determination to act with wisdom and courage in the future. It led the young listeners toward a code of behavior that would have to be observed without urging, scolding, reward, or punishment.

Tonight's story was of Nanabush, who remade the drowned world, and brought fur and fire to chilled humanity. Such a benefactor might be thought of as a god, but this one was different from the ordinary run of gods. He was not above sly trickery, and sometimes he made ungodly blunders, passing suddenly from the sublime to the ridiculous. There was that unfortunate occasion when he got into a dispute with his own rectum.

The argument between the demi-god and the insolent orifice became increasingly bitter until he finally silenced it by sitting in the fire.

At this point the audience broke into quiet laughter. But they had received a message of some importance to young people who might later bring danger of injury or death to themselves and others if they allowed reason to give way to the quick pride of anger.

The merriment changed to wide-eyed silence and the listeners leaned forward. The grandfather had lowered his voice and was looking warily around. He seemed to fear that something out there might have escaped its icy enclosure, might even now be listening. Might, if it heard its name spoken, tear through the bark and mattings to stand before them grinning, slobbering and grasping.

Then, with hands floating in the smoky firelight, he told of the malignant dead that lie in the depths of 'Tschgumi. And he told of Windigo, the cannibal, who robs graves and burial scaffolds in the summer, and who, in times of winter famine, comes looking for some isolated camp.

The garments were mended, the weaving completed. The storytelling stopped. The people lay back, wrapped in furs and blankets, their feet toward the fire. Sturgeon Man rearranged the smoldering wood, stacking and banking it to burn slowly. He would wake to tend it as needed.

The flame subsided to a dim but comforting glow. That small heat at the center of the lodge and the thick blanket of snow above it held the cold at bay, but not the silence. There was only the heavy breathing of the sleepers and an occasional whoosh and thump as one log burned through and dropped another into the coals.

3

Late each autumn, Iron Feather's family paddled up the Minnisabik to its headwaters and camped there, getting in as much meat and fish as they could in the cool, good-keeping weather. When the river froze they went on over its diminishing ice road and then, by trails through the swamps and between the ridges, to their hereditary winter territory. In this country of hills, lakes, and muskeg, far from any other Indians, they faced old Peboan, and had always been able to keep him at bay until the strengthening sun brought back warmth and plenty.

Sturgeon Man had taught his sons to hunt this winter forest as had his father and grandfather before him. The men and boys had dragged many toboggan-loads of frozen meat down the trails that spoked in toward the pikogan, and many hides had been scraped and dressed by their women. The fact that four generations of the family were alive and together proved that this was good country and that these were good hunters.

But this winter was not good. The summer had been dry so that the rice was thin and poor. During the moon of little spirits the family had lived well enough on the carcasses of beaver and other fur-bearers, and on the fish that they took from nets set under the ice. Then the weather turned cold, a deadly cold. It froze the entrances to the muskrats' little push-up houses, and the rats died beneath them. The mink and marten became inactive. The ice grew too thick for trapping beaver or netting fish.

He-Rises and Iron Feather left the lodge each morning in the biting predawn chill and hunted until the gathering darkness left only enough time to find the home trail. On still days, when each footstep crunched out a warning, Iron Feather would sit between snow-capped boulders on some ridge or summit, his gun across his knees, while He-Rises, with Ma-eengun, the wolf-faced lead dog, combed the woods below. Or the father might stand beyond a cedar island in the muskeg while the son pushed and crawled through the curving branches and wind-tilted trunks, making noise enough to scare out anything that might be hiding.

There was no other sound. No moose, caribou or stray, wandering white-tail deer came bursting out of cover. The snow surface changed — powdery on the bitter mornings; fresh, dazzling, and sculptured after a storm; soft at noon when the days lengthened. But it showed no hoofprint, nor any tell-tale blowhole with hoarfrost whitening the weeds or twigs around it and a little mist rising out of it above a sleeping bear.

Sometimes, as he pushed through the snow-covered forest or waited in the cold watches, He-Rises thought of Shakes-His-Wings. He too would be with his father now, somewhere off there in the rough hills to the east. But they might have been hunting together.

The two young men had been close friends, an unusual relationship for He-Rises, who did not make friends easily. Shakes-His-Wings had suggested that he might come with Iron Feather's family so that they could be brothers for the winter. But He-Rises had not spoken of this offer to his father and nothing had come of it.

He could not understand now why he had acted like that, or rather, failed to act. He hoped that they would meet again in the spring sun at the sugar camp.

As the winter lengthened, He-Rises and Iron Feather ranged far from the pikogan, too far to get back at night. Sometimes they would sleep in a snow cave, dug out of a drift with snowshoes. Or they might lie curled close up to a little fire, sheltered by a snow-covered windbreak of poles and spruce boughs.

Walking out from such a camp for wood, He-Rises caught a glimpse of a timberwolf, thin, but looking big as a deer. And later that evening he heard the hunting call not far back in the forest. Ma-eengun growled, and moved in close to the fire. Wolves knew better than to attack men, but they might seize and eat a dog if he were to stray into the darkness.

As he sat with hands spread to the heat, He-Rises thought back over the year's work, wondering what he, or others in his family, might have done wrong. They had not killed more than they needed, nor wasted meat, fish, fruit or rice. They had thanked the manido of each animal taken and had handled its bones with respect. Iron Feather had drummed and chanted the songs that had, in the past, been effective in bringing the game to them. Yet all these things had failed. He-Rises wondered whether they would be able to hold off Pauguk, the death skeleton, until the thaws came.

"Do you think that this is just another hungry winter?" he asked his father. "Or are the old spirits giving way to some new power?"

Iron Feather squatted in silence for a while before he answered.

"Your mother talked with the black-robe at the settlement. He told her about his jealous and unforgiving God. He roasts his captives over a slow fire, drawing the torture out longer than even the most loving and careful 'Bwan squaw. Such a spirit would be harder to evade than our manidog.

"I have several times made him offerings of tobacco and sung him prayer-songs, begging him to forgive any offense that we might unintentionally have given him, and to send us at least a small deer.

"I have wondered whether these ignorant Indian prayers do more harm than good. I have come to think that they don't make much difference one way or the other."

The hard winter continued, but some god, red or white, had not been altogether merciless. While the two hunters searched in vain for the big game that would have assured the family's survival they continued to pick up a little small meat.

Sometimes Iron Feather would motion with his gun toward a tree. He-Rises, looking hard, would make out the rounded shape of a grouse, with head erect, watching. He could usually bring down such a sitting bird with an arrow, saving the father's shot and powder. Another day it might be a porcupine, very good eating in the fall or early winter, but poor and bony now. Once a white owl, come south from the arctic prairie, flew silently through the dim evening light and settled on a branch, an easy target. Each of these was carried back to the lodge, much better than nothing.

And Wabooz, the life-saver, the kindly rabbit-spirit, never entirely forgot them during this long, cold winter. His people — the big, white, long-legged, broad-footed, snowshoe hares — were not plentiful. But every so often he would send one of them bounding in front of the hunters, or along the hard-packed little trails where the women set their snares.

17

Rabbit lacks the fat that people must have for energy and to withstand cold. There had not been much real meat for this family of seven. But they were alive, they still had a little something to eat every day, and the winter was passing.

Otter Woman had been careful. The lodge was her domain. What meat the men brought in they turned over to her. She processed and stored it, with the help of her daughters. She distributed it in whatever ways she thought best, just as her mother had done before her.

She still had a cedar bark bag half full of rice, a little flour tied in the bottom of a sack, and a makak, a bark box, that held quite a lot of bear grease — whiter and richer than cream, a lovely treat, issued only in tiny tastes. Part of a beaver carcass and four whitefish hung, frozen hard, in the high cache out of reach of the dogs.

The dogs, yes. They were very thin, but edible. They would be needed for the spring journey. They might yet enter the kettle but not before all other food was gone.

Otter Woman had calculated closely, cutting a notch in a stick each night and a deeper notch for each new moon, giving the hunters a little more than the others because their strength had to be maintained. She knew her husband and her children. None of them would give up, and each would do what had to be done, regardless of cold and hunger. But she was not sure about Sturgeon Man.

"You must help me watch the grandfather," she told Shanod. "Old people know that they can't help much with work and that they are eating food that may make the difference between life and death for the others. Sometimes they will stay behind at an abandoned camp-site, or just walk from a winter lodge into the snow. And that is a good thing to do when it is necessary. It is better that an old person should die than a child.

"But now the days are getting longer and the moon-stick is filling with notches. There is still a little meat and rice. We are all going to come through this winter alive.

"I have told him those things and he smiles and says that it is good. But my grandmother walked away without our knowing.

"When he goes out for firewood, go with him. Or else happen along the trail soon to help him bring it in."

"I will do that, my mother. But he often leaves the wigwam during the night."

"I have the wife's place by the door and I sleep lightly. I know when he goes and when he returns. If he should remain too long outside I would wake Iron Feather and he would follow."

4

Whatever may have been going on in Sturgeon Man's mind, he gave no outward sign of suicidal intent. Each night, when the evening meal was finished, he was ready with a story. This was not always about magic, monsters and ghosts. It might come from one of the Aninishinabe epics, an account of the brave, brutal and glorious deeds of men now dead.

"We came here long ago," said the grandfather. "We came from the Eastern Ocean. The Iroquois followed us as wolves follow the caribou, killing stragglers and cutting off small groups. But on the shore of 'Tschgumi the ancestors turned and destroyed them."

Shanod responded politely with a low, sighing "oo-oo-oo." The others joined her, continuing the sound and drawing it out to show that they were properly impressed and that they appreciated the telling. Sturgeon Man went on.

"When the Sauks and the Foxes attacked the island village our people were too few to fight them on land. We trailed the raiders across the big water, closed in on them when the strong wind blew, upset their canoes, and broke the heads of those who did not drown."

Sturgeon Man leaned over an imaginary gunwale, swung a phantom warclub, brought it crashing down on the skull of a swimming specter.

"And even now, when the storm spirits move over that part of the lake, you may see them tossing far out there in the waves, pale canoes paddled by painted ghosts."

The old ones had fought well, too, against trained European soldiers. They had sent a contingent down lakes and rivers and then overland all the way to the bushy ravine in Pennsylvania where the advancing British regulars and their colonial auxiliaries had been met, shattered, and driven into panic flight. The names of Braddock and Washington would have meant nothing to Sturgeon Man, but he knew the story of that long warpath and short fight.

And he could tell how Anishinabe men and women, by guile and by fury, overwhelmed the redcoat soldiers and took the strong fortress that commanded the Straits of the Turtle.

"Those were the people that we came from. You must not forget what they did. Their fires still burn in our wigwams and their smoke hangs over us."

But what particularly fascinated this audience was the familiar account of Sturgeon Man's experience as a warrior. Smoke-Drifting called for it now.

"Tell us again, grandfather, about your own war. Your war with the 'Bwaneg."

"They were savages, backward in many ways, but fierce and deadly killers. They still are. We had better guns than they did and more shot and powder from our trade with the whites. We kept pushing them west. To the edge of the forest. And then farther. We took this country from them, but it was not easy."

The heaviest fighting had taken place in the hardwood areas, rich in fish, game, rice, and sugar maples, that lay to the south. Dwellers in the cold boreal forest could not ordinarily afford the luxury of war.

"Up here we were too busy keeping ourselves alive to take much time out for killing other people. But even here, the 'Bwaneg returned.

"When I was about your age, He-Rises, I stood beside what they had left of a wigwam just a little down the river from the Wabigoon camp. The bark was still smoldering, and people were dragging out the dead. They had been gutted like deer and scalps, ears, and genitals had been cut off. And the hands of the babies. When I looked at those I was sick.

"I walked back along the trail trying to forget what I had seen. I heard something move in the underbrush. It was a dog. He had an arrow through him, the head on one side, the feathers on the other. He was the only one from the lodge that was still alive.

"Those days were different from these. The men were braver then. And the women were more beautiful."

He stopped quickly, and looked across the fire at Shanod.

"Anishinabe women are always beautiful. But they were beautiful in a different way.

"And the young men. In those times, when an enemy came into our country and harmed our people, the young men were not willing to sit in the wigwams and do nothing."

As Sturgeon Man sat now in the snowcovered lodge, telling the story to his grandchildren, the vengeance ceremony that he had experienced in his youth was still clear in his memory.

It started with drumming, a soft, relentless thunder that called on men to come together. The deep vibrations were soon repeated in chanting and the beat of dancers' moccasins.

A woman came running out into the firelight. She had torn her clothing, sawed off her hair with a knife, and slashed her arms and face.

"You have seen what they did to my son, my daughter-in-law, and my grandchildren."

She threw back her head and gave a long wail. Then she hunched forward and swung around, looking out under her ragged hair from one to another of those in the circle.

"Now, you men! You young men of the Anishinabeg. Which of you is going to kill me a 'Bwan?"

Sturgeon Man, with many others, answered her by smoking the red-feathered war pipe, striking the painted war post, and taking his place in the war dance.

✦ ✦ ✦

It was known that the old hunter, Crooked Lightning, had fought the Abwaneg when he lived in the flat country beyond the white man's medicine-line. They said that every man was a warrior there.

The young men asked him to be their leader. His southern drawl was so heavy that they could not always understand what he wanted them to do, but he made his preparations well. He sent out messengers carrying the red buckskin hand, the invitation to a war party. Many wanted to come but Crooked Lightning would take no one who was not well armed. This was in the good years when the white men paid well for beaver, and guns were plentiful.

Blue Flag Woman came to him carrying a sawed-off musket.

"With this gun I killed a bear and with it I can kill a 'Bwan. My brother will be one of your war party. I can shoot as well as he or any man. I will come with you."

Crooked Lightning rubbed the sparse hairs on his chin and looked unhappy.

"I have heard of you and of your hunting. I am sure that you would shoot 'Bwaneg as well as you have shot deer and the bear. But these animals shoot back. They might kill you instead."

"I am not afraid to die."

"I will not take a woman on this long journey."

"I can walk as far as my brother can, and farther. I do not have to tell you, uncle, that there have been great woman warriors among the Anishinabeg."

"I know that well. I fought beside one of them myself. But those with us were experienced fighters, men of firm will and strong self-control. To them she was a comrade, just as though she had been a man. We knew that if any one of us even thought of her womanness, misfortune would befall our war party.

"They are young men who will go with me from this place. They know nothing about war and they think much about women. You might cause jealousy and quarreling among them."

"I will go with you to meet enemies, not lovers. I will give no one of your men cause to be jealous of another."

"You would do worse than that, no matter how good your intentions. The sight of you would pollute their thoughts. They would be thinking about you and the mystery of your body. That must not happen in a war party. It turns the spirit power not only against the offenders, but also against their companions.

"So stay here and provide the meat that will be needed while we are away. I cannot take the risk of having you with us."

She stood looking at him, searching for something else, maybe some kindly weakening in his eyes. Then she swung the short gun over her shoulder and went away, walking boldly as though she did not care.

When a strong force had come together, Crooked Lightning led the fleet of canoes down many lakes and rivers to the southwest. The women paddled beside them all that first morning, shouting contempt for the Abwaneg and singing kill-them songs. The new warriors were pushing hard to go swiftly over the water and get at those hated ones.

Canoes bearing other men kept coming out from points, bays,

and river mouths. They had received the message of the hand and were camped along the route, waiting to join the war party.

They passed through many lakes and streams until these flowed together in one river that brought them at last into a big lake. Not so big as 'Tschgumi, but very big. They couldn't see the other side.

When they did reach that far shore, it was flat muskeg beyond the sand beach, and here the waterways ended. Everyone was happy to be on ground again, even this trembling earth. They had been paddling for a long time.

They followed the old war road through a broad bog with intervals of forest. The weather was hot, with rain always in the sky. Not much was coming down, but enough to keep this swampy path soft. In the low places it was all a man could do to lift one leg out of the sucking pull of the mud and push it back in again ahead of the other.

Every so often somebody would go down deep and have to be dragged out with a pole or a line. That would have been funny on a soft portage in their country, but not in this place.

So late in the summer the flies and mosquitos had eased at home. Here they buzzed and bit as though spring flowers were blooming.

On the third night that they camped on this trail, one of the young men stood up beside the fire and spoke to the others.

"I never thought that the world was so big nor that the 'Bwaneg lived on the other side of it. The rice will soon be ripening. If we keep on walking west much longer we will be late for the harvest and our families may starve next winter. Also, my moccasins are wearing thin and I am tired of this kind of war.

"I will go home to the lakes tomorrow. I advise the rest of you to come with me."

In the morning many people turned back. But more went on with Crooked Lightning. They were still a strong war party.

They came up into a higher country, with tall grass, scattered swamps and lakes, and wandering belts of timber. This was a no-man's-land where the hunters of neither tribe were safe. Nobody hunted it much. The animals had fattened and multiplied. The young men camped, made meat, ate what they wanted, and cached the rest for the return trip. Then they walked on to the west.

One evening Sturgeon Man, with some of the others, crouched in scanty brush and peered out at a small circle of skin-covered tipis on the edge of the prairie. Looking back he could see the tree line. It

stretched out to the south and the north like the shore of a great lake.

Crooked Lightning, keeping low and silent in the long grass, came in beside him. He was speaking in signs and whispers.

"The scouts who found this encampment have said that its hunters are away. This is good.

"At the first light of dawn, I will give the signal shout. Several men will be waiting to scatter the horse herd. The rest of us will rush the village. The boys there, and the old men, will fight. The 'Bwaneg will always fight. But this time probably without guns, or without many guns. The hunters will have them, and most of the ammunition.

"Shoot carefully and then go in fast. We should be able to overrun all who will try to stop us without losing anybody of ours. Then we must wipe out every person in the camp. The men first, then immediately the women, and then the children. By that time it will be light enough to find any that escape into the grass.

"Sleep now and be ready at daylight."

He started to leave, then turned back.

"Do not delay about the women. They are unsafe."

He slipped away to the next group, going as quietly as he had come. There was no sound after that from any of the Anishinabeg, but Sturgeon Man could hear the Abwaneg moving about and talking.

The women were bending over the cooking fires and the children were playing or scuffling a little, waiting for the food. After they had eaten, most of the people went into the tipis, but three old men sat for a long time by a fire. When it was quite dark Sturgeon Man crept in close.

One of the elders had a big nose and a long, flat face. He must have been saying funny things. He kept moving his hands and sometimes pointing. Then the other two would take the pipes out of their mouths and laugh. Sturgeon Man could understand nothing of their strange, throaty language, but they did not look very different from old men by the fire at home.

He came back to the others and waited there through the night, too excited to sleep.

When the stars began to fade he heard the war-shout. There was a thunder of hoofs as the horses stampeded. People were running out of the tipis, most of them naked from the sleeping robes, not dressed a little as sleepers would have been in the north.

All around him the Anishinabeg were shooting. Sturgeon Man fired with the others. He knew that he should pick out one man, but he just aimed at the mass. Then he threw down the empty musket, drew his knife, and ran forward.

A tipi had been knocked over in the rush, a pile of hides and poles. He was running as hard as he could and it was right in his way. As he bent to jump over it a man with shaggy white hair rose out of it, swinging a stone-headed war club. He was the one with the big nose and the flat face, but he was not joking now. That evil old man was trying to kill him.

Sturgeon Man tried to stop, skidded into the wreckage, and fell. He rolled over, his hand slipping on the leather lodge covering, not able to get up quickly enough. He saw the stone swing down at his head.

There was an explosion from behind him. The Abwan fell across him, knocking him flat on the ground again. Sturgeon Man struggled up, but the old man was not trying to kill anybody now. He was jerking a little and bright red blood was coming out of his chest. Another Anishinabe had held his fire.

Sturgeon Man got to his feet and stood there, glad to be still alive but uncertain what to do next. An arrow sang low above him.

The Abwaneg, boys and elders, fighting with bows, spears, and axes, were holding back the Anishinabeg like a mass of broken ice that heaves and cracks and groans as it stops the swelling river for a little while before it is swept away.

Beyond them he could see women running. They were carrying babies and herding the other children ahead of them, pushing and dragging the smaller ones for speed.

He knew that something had gone wrong. The enemy were not many and they had no guns. But they had not been wiped out in the first rush as Crooked Lightning had ordered. Others, like him, must have fired without really aiming.

He couldn't find his knife, but he picked up the war club. Some of the young men had dropped back to reload their muskets. He joined them as they hurried into the fight again.

He saw an old Abwan turn and look behind him. Now there were no more women or children in sight. He called something to the others. The ice jam broke. An Anishinabe flood roared through the empty village.

Those of the enemy still on their feet were running. Some of them were holding up others who stumbled, or carrying bodies whose feet dragged in the dust. Those who went last were moving quickly, but turned a little to keep watch, with weapons still ready. They disappeared into the long grass and low hills.

Crooked Lightning was running after them, calling for everybody else to follow. Sturgeon Man and several others started to, but not swiftly. The rest just stood and watched.

The old man came back, very angry.

"Have we come so far, then, to kill so few? Will you let yourselves be beaten by kids and grandfathers?"

They stood there, breathing hard from the fighting. No one answered and no one moved.

Crooked Lightning swung his arm in a violent gesture of contempt.

"I used to hear it said that the men of the spruce forests were not warriors but bush rabbits. I didn't believe it then. Now I know that it is true. A southern Anishinabe war party would not stop while a single 'Bwan stayed alive."

It was a while before someone answered.

"The 'Bwaneg are devils. We caught them naked, asleep, and almost unarmed. But even the women knew just what to do. Those old men must have fought in many battles. If we follow them they will probably lay a trap for us. They might kill us all."

Another spoke quickly. "Gagonce is dead, Gwekabi's arm is broken, and several have been wounded. But I don't think that we have been beaten. See, we have taken scalps."

They had the hair of four males, of one woman who had been cut off from the flight, and the scalp of her new baby. That one was like gosling down. And the horse-chasers had brought in a captive, a girl a little younger than Sturgeon Man, who had been tending the herd.

"We have enough for a good victory dance. And enough to show the 'Bwaneg that they can't just come up and kill our people in the north and go back without getting hurt themselves. We hit more of them than we have scalps. They carried away dead and wounded.

"It would do no good to walk farther into that strange country, all grass. See how the wind blows waves over it as though it were water. There is no way to know what kind of evil spirits may be waiting for us in such deadly emptiness."

Crooked Lightning was still very angry. Seeing the captive did not make him feel any better.

"I told you to kill all of those. You well know that they bring misfortune to a war party. Cut her throat now!"

"The fighting is finished, uncle. We have had our misfortune and our good fortune. We are going home and we will take her with us."

The old man gave a sour little snort.

"The fighting may not be finished yet. We are a long way from the canoes. And do not think that this one is like an Anishinabe woman. These are vicious. All of them. Whenever we have allowed one to live she has made bad trouble."

A man had been leading the captive with a rawhide line around her neck.

"She is not big enough or old enough to be dangerous. She will do whatever I want her to do. See, she has already learned to obey the cord."

He twitched it and she stepped quickly ahead.

"I will watch her myself to make sure that she does nobody any harm."

Crooked Lightning spat on the ground and turned away.

Another of the men called after him. "There is no need to worry, uncle. We will kill her if she gives us any trouble along the way. If she gets to the rice camp the women will finish her off at the ceremony."

Crooked Lightning did not look back.

A healer bound up the wounds. The dead one was wrapped in a blanket and slung from a carrying-pole. Some took what they wanted of the scattered village possessions, but there wasn't much that they could use.

Sturgeon Man went back and found his knife and musket. He was thinking about those hunters, wondering when they might be getting home. Maybe others had the same thought. Anyway, they soon started back to the east, and they walked fast.

Sturgeon Man ended his story, but the full story had not stopped there. He had never told them all of it. He might, some other time. Or he might not. That would be enough for tonight.

Soon the others were sleeping and he sat alone beside the fire. From time to time he put on a little wood and whispered a few words to himself, stirred by old memories of war and woman.

5

Late in the night Sturgeon Man dropped into a heavy sleep. Gray ash covered the fading embers. Cold came inside the lodge and woke Iron Feather. The opening overhead was dark, but he knew that morning was near. He touched his son's face. They put on their outer garments, took their weapons, and left the lodge.

Shanod was accustomed to wake at their departure. Kneeling, she pushed together the blackened points of the sticks the fire had left and blew on them, bringing them first to glow and then to flame.

The baby lay in a little hammock, suspended from two of the lodge poles. Above her hung a net, a willow hoop strung with red yarn netting, carefully woven to catch bad dreams. Dreams that could frighten a child or perhaps bring real misfortune to her. In the center of the circle was a hole. Good dreams were calm and wise. They could find that opening and get through to the little sleeper. But who knows, or can remember, what dreams come to the net of a one-year-old?

In the bright new light she opened her eyes. They were like the eyes of her father, Shanod thought.

Ice Stone had brought his heavy cargoes of fur to the lakeshore trading post for the past two summer gatherings. He was the son of a powerful shaman, much feared by the people of the mountainous country north of 'Tschgumi.

In those cold hills, Shanod knew, witchcraft flourishes like the black spruce. She had been told that Undertooth, her baby's grandfather, worked his evil charms while sitting on the broad, pale, skin of a tundra grizzly, a killer that had destroyed three men before a storm of spears and arrows brought it plowing down into the trampled heather.

She suspected that the witchman father had given Ice Stone a love medicine. It was the only excuse that she could think of for her own sudden surrender.

The Anishinabeg of those days did not take such matters lightly, at least so far as the girl was concerned. Unlike the other woods Indians, they had a double standard of sexual morality, perhaps acquired from their puritanical enemies, the Abwaneg. Adventures outside of marriage were considered bold, exciting, and only a little wicked for a man, but shameful for a young woman.

Talk of Shanod's disgrace spread fast through the trading, fishing, and berry camps. Most of the women were inclined to a rather uncharitable view of the culprit. Some of them would pronounce their criticisms quite audibly as she or her relatives passed by.

This kind of pressure had its effects. A man might be ashamed to take a wife with a child not his own. Especially a girl-child. A boy would grow up to bring in meat and fur, but a girl was just another person that would have to be fed where there were too many hungry mouths already. So it sometimes happened that a girl would disappear or die mysteriously shortly after birth. When this resulted from the mother's action or intentional neglect it was called "throwing the baby away."

Shanod's girl, Sound of Waves, had never been in danger of anything like that. The young mother had simply faced the situation down. Any man who wanted her would have to take the daughter along with the wife.

She had hoped that Ice Stone would be that man. She had been sure that, when the people gathered again at the post, and when he saw this delightful little girl that he had fathered, he would want to move into her lodge and accept them both as his own family.

That had not been his response. Tall, powerfully built, and a good hunter, he was continuing his successes with women and had no wish to tie himself down yet to any one of them. He had greeted Shanod cheerfully, but had politely declined her father's invitation to join their party. He had conscientiously observed the ancient rule against sexual relations with a nursing woman, even when Shanod hinted that she might be willing to make an exception. And he had said nothing about marriage.

Shanod, a mother without a husband, would have been considered fair game by the "lynx hunters," young men less respectful of the old taboos. But now the bold hunters had become cautious. Ice Stone had told some of them that he intended to take Shanod again when he felt so inclined, and perhaps even marry her. In the meantime, he suggested, it would be well for the others to stay away from his woman.

There was a hint of a threat in the way he spoke to them that was unusual among the Anishinabeg. They recognized, however, that his strength and skill with weapons would make him a dangerous adversary in his own right. And that, beyond the immediate menace, some really dreadful calamity might be visited upon any rival suitor by the notoriously malevolent father. It had been a quiet summer for Shanod.

The disgrace had fallen even more heavily on He-Rises. No one had expected him to do anything about it. Ice Stone would have laughed at a challenge from him. But he had felt keenly the injury that had been done his sister and the insult of her rejection.

Now Shanod cleaned the little girl, nursed her, and packed her in dry moss to sleep a while longer. She drew on long, moose-hide leggings, wrapped herself in a robe of woven rabbit-skin, and pulled a worn blanket-parka over her head. She pushed aside the weighted bearskin that covered the door and clambered up the steep, hard-packed grade to the surface of the snow.

The night seemed very black as she bound on the snowshoes, but when she stepped out on them her eyes had grown used to the darkness and she could see the white paths that ran out from the lodge.

The eastern sky was growing light behind dark treetops by the time that she arrived at the first of the long circle of snares. The noose remained spread, ready, and empty. So did the next. Well, you could not blame the wabooz people for staying in their snowy little lodges on so cold a night.

She had reached the curve in the snare-trail farthest from her own lodge when she heard the cry. At the sound she stopped, tense, listening.

It came again closer and clear in the morning stillness. And then almost overhead. "Caw! Caw!"

That harsh call was sweet to the girl's ears. Peering up between twisted branches she could see a black form that perched and strutted high above.

Then it went flapping off and Shanod was running over the drifts to the next snare and the next. They were all empty, the butts of their toss-poles pointing to the sky. But she was happy as she hurried back to the pikogan. She was carrying news that would be more welcome than a sackful of rabbits.

"Great-grandmother Crow has come back! She stood right over me and spoke to me! She will bring us the spring!"

Sturgeon Man was starting out for firewood while Otter Woman harnessed the dogs to bring it in. The grandfather leaned on his axe

and looked back, smiling like a benevolent turtle. Smoke-Drifting straightened up from spreading the sleeping robes to air. They could all feel Peboan's frozen grip beginning to loosen.

Not that they could yet see any promise of change in the desolate landscape around them. A wind was coming up, tearing at the ragged tops of the spruce trees and fogging out their lower trunks with whirling ground-drift. The snow level would almost certainly rise in the days ahead before it would begin to subside. But now that black Andeg had returned, the time for travel could not be far away. Soon they would go back over softening snow and melting ice to the rich food and renewed friendships of the sugarbush.

The timing of that move would be critical. The risks of cold and blizzard must be weighed against the danger of unseasonably warm weather that could bring an early breakup of the rivers. Until they reached the canoes, the ice road would be their only way out.

But these people, to whom wind, temperature and precipitation were so important, usually had a pretty good idea as to what to expect. They believed that some individuals were kept informed by super-natural powers, and many white men who lived among them were also convinced that this was the case. If it was not so, then they had at least developed a strong feeling for weather, a subconscious recognition of the faintest preliminary symptoms of a coming change.

Iron Feather would know when the time was right. His family were not worried about the hardships or dangers of the journey into spring.

6

Time passed, and another storm howled over the pikogan. For three days snow flowed in white rivers south through the forest. It drifted into a solid, domed mass behind each spruce. Its weight sagged the strong timbers of the lodge wall and almost covered the dark cone.

Then, at night, the wind died. Iron Feather pushed up to the surface to study the solid gray sky. Snow was still falling, but no one was surprised when he gave his decision.

"We will go now."

There was no discussion, no further orders, no differing opinion. Everyone except Sound of Waves was suddenly busy. Otter Woman, Shanod and Smoke Drifting soon had the few implements and the small remaining food supply wrapped in the sleeping robes and tied with rawhide into packs. They took the bark coverings from the lodge poles and rolled them into compact cylinders. Winter gear and many of the steel traps were stored in the cache.

The toboggan was long, made of thin birch slabs, with prow rounded up and flattened into a high, graceful curve. Sturgeon Man beat it free of snow and laid out the harness in front of it, placing each moose-hide collar in tandem position. Iron Feather and He-Rises loaded the sled, starting at the bottom with heavy bales of pelts, tightly bundled and bound in birch bark. They laid the packs on top of these, then passed the rawhide line back and forth over the cargo, lashing it down hard to stay in place even in an upset.

During these preparations the three big dogs were barking joyfully, jumping and straining at their tethers. They were so thin that their hip bones seemed ready to push through the skin, but they could

37

hardly wait to get pulling. Maybe they remembered the fishgut feasts at last summer's lakeshore gatherings. Two part-grown pups were joining in the uproar, but with less assurance.

The grandfather slipped the lead collar over Ma-eengun's head, lifted and inserted his front leg into its opening, then went on to do the same for the other two old dogs. He would like to have had two more in the harness, but the pups were still wooly, not big enough to pull. They would run behind on this journey.

Iron Feather started well ahead of the others. He was carrying an old Northwest flintlock. It had been made for the Indian trade, and made the way the customers wanted it — short, light in weight, and of heavy caliber. Its recoil was fierce but the simple mechanism was dependable at even the lowest temperatures and was easily repaired in the woods. The trigger guard curved wide to accommodate a mittened hand. A brass snake coiling along its left side guaranteed its British manufacture and quality. Elsewhere it would have been a museum piece. Here it was the family's provider and protector.

He had heard that the Abwaneg had attacked the whites and been defeated, that the warriors had been killed, imprisoned, or driven far away into the western mountains.

So he had heard, and he hoped that it was true. But other optimistic rumors about the destruction of the Abwaneg had proved false. And there was always the chance that the man ahead might see game. So it was thought best that he walk upright carrying only a light pack and with weapon ready, rather than with head bent under a pack strap.

Otter Woman was not limited by the need for any such precautions. She tied the thongs of her tump line around the heaviest of the burdens, knelt with her back to it, brought the broad center of the strap across the top of her head, leaned forward, and struggled up with the cargo riding low against the small of her back. She stood then with feet braced wide apart while Shanod boosted a wooden box with her knee and slid it in between the taut sections of strap. A smaller pack went in above the box. The snowshoes squeaked in protest. Otter Woman took several staggering steps, then found her balance and strode off at a good clip in Iron Feather's tracks.

Sound of Waves had been wrapped in fur and tied firmly in place under the up-curve of the toboggan. Shanod bent over her and tucked a scrap of woolen cloth around the child's head to keep out the blowing

snow. Then she took on her back a heavy burden, but less than Otter Woman's, and followed the parents down the trail.

Auntie Smoke Drifting tipped her head sideways as far as her strap would allow, to look down at the baby. Dark Asiatic eyes stared solemnly back at her from under the fringe of black hair.

The loaded toboggan had settled, freezing a little into hard-packed snow. The team's first attempt failed to budge it. He-Rises pushed, lifted and swayed it from behind, calling to the dogs. They barked their answer and lunged against the collars. The flat bottom broke free and they moved smartly into the snowshoe trail.

Sturgeon Man stood for a moment, looking back at the familiar clearing. The circle of dark earth and flattened greenery where the pikogan had stood was almost covered with snow. So were the timbers, stacked on their skid poles. All would be waiting for the family's return when the rivers froze.

Iron Feather set a quick pace, bending forward, lifting the toes of the snowshoes high at each step to clear the surface. The shoes sank deep and the fresh snow swirled in a mist around the rhythmic beat of his legs. By the time the others had their burdens in place he was out of their sight.

His tracks led over snow-covered ice wherever possible, following channels in the muskeg at first, then a frozen stream. He crossed high ground only when it was necessary to pass from one watercourse to another.

The team strained up the side of each of these ridges, with the girls pulling on the traces to help them, and He-Rises pushing in back. At the summit, the toboggan tilted forward and dropped into a swiftly accelerating slide. He-Rises dragged his snowshoes, holding hard to the tail rope, pulling back with all his strength while the dogs ran faster and the sled dog curled in his tail to keep from getting bumped from behind.

Often the toboggan tilted threateningly. Wherever the trail slanted over uneven rock formations, Shanod and Smoke Drifting stood by, ready to help wrestle it back into position. Even so, Otter Woman had several times to drop her load and come running back to help avert an upset.

Late that afternoon the snow stopped, the sky cleared and night came on starry and cold. They were glad to reach the sheltered place, where, under an overhanging rock ledge, Iron Feather was digging with a snowshoe to open a patch of moss and earth while erecting a wall of snow.

Here the men unharnessed the dogs, and brought in wood. The women quickly set up a lean-to, a sloping framework of poles roofed over with bark. Iron Feather got flint and a piece of an old file out of a pouch. Sparks dropped into dry punkwood.

By this time Otter Woman and Smoke Drifting were cutting spruce boughs to carpet the shelter and He-Rises was setting a line of snares. Shanod was waiting with dry pine twigs and then larger kindling. A welcome little flame sprouted and flourished. Its heat, reflected by the snow wall, drove back the shadows and warmed the grandfather's hands and feet. He sat, head drooping, with a blanket wrapped over his shaggy coat. He would not be expected to tend the fire that night.

Each dog bolted his small portion of thawed fish, searched hopefully for more, then dug out sleeping space in the snow and curled up, nose protected by bushy tail. The people ate their own meager supper, hung their coats, parkas and moccasins to dry, loosened their inner clothing, and wrapped themselves in fur.

From time to time, during the night, the fire would die down. Then one of the sleepers would wake, revive it with blowing, put on more wood, crawl back into the robes and go quickly to sleep again in the renewed light and warmth.

7

On the second night of the journey, as the last piece of beaver meat was dripping grease into a pan beside the fire, the dogs broke suddenly into fierce clamor and rushed away into the darkness. Iron Feather swiftly pushed and twisted his feet into the looped snowshoe thongs. Otter Woman held out the musket to him. He took it and hurried toward the uproar, keeping to one side so that he would not be seen against the light. He-Rises, just getting back from setting snares, stopped at the edge of the shadow. The arrow notched to his bowstring was trembling a little.

For a moment the others sat rigid. Then, out there where the dogs had disappeared, they heard the sharp click of the tail of a snowshoe as it hit the wooden rim of another. The sound shot them into action.

Shanod snatched the baby. Otter Woman and Smoke Drifting scooped up armfuls of robes. Sturgeon Man lurched to his feet, bent stiffly, and picked up the axe. By the time the change in the dogs' voices announced that they had met their target everyone was ready for fight or flight.

Before the women could run into the forest a gaunt young figure appeared, pushing through the spruce boughs while he fended off the dogs. Dark skin fell away in deep hollows beneath his cheek bones. His sunken eyes gleamed at the sight of the roasting meat. He was sawing at his belly with the edge of his right hand. The forest Indians did not use the elaborate sign language of the plains, but they knew what that gesture meant.

His tattered clothing was fitted to his body in the manner of the far north. The long snowshoes were pointed at both ends and turned up sharply in front. He was speaking in a strange dialect, harsh with hissing s-sounds, but not entirely different from the language of the Anishinabeg. Clearly, he was no Abwan.

Iron Feather came back into the firelight, having circled the camp and made certain that there were no others out there in the darkness. He motioned the stranger to a place by the fire. Otter Woman gave him a cup of tea, a little dab of the bear grease, and, when it was ready, a helping of beaver. Shanod brought him a robe of caribou skin. He wrapped himself in this gratefully, and swiftly ate the food that had been given him. Then he lay back and slept.

They heard his story in the nights that followed, as they came to understand his clipped syllables and oddly accented words. He was of the Muskegag or Swampy Cree, who had migrated into the north centuries earlier. His name was Maskegwatik, the Tamarack. He was the only survivor of several families who had been wintering together. In their hunting area the rabbits had vanished as completely as the deer.

While the others of his group lay in

the lodge, conserving strength but without hope, he had stumbled south. He ate lichen from the rocks, gnawed on the inner bark of spruce, browsed at twigs like a deer, and dug down through the drifts for last fall's withered bearberries. In some places under deep snow, the ground had not frozen, and there he scrabbled up some sprouts of next spring's vegetation and a few fat crawling things from under the forest floor. A jaybird, trying to steal one of these from him, had carelessly perched within his reach and had provided several precious ounces of meat.

He had come out of the trees on the snowy summit of a rock ridge and had seen the pinpoint of fire in the valley below. Somehow he had found the strength to climb over the intervening windfalls and the luck to fumble his way through the dark maze to camp.

His hosts knew that he was a Cree almost as soon as they saw him. The rest came out later. But certain decisions had to be made on the night of his arrival.

In this country of cyclical starvation, the temptation to cannibalism could be strong. But the taboo against it was absolute. Hunting peoples don't approve of eating man. To the woods Indians, it was the unforgivable sin, never justified by any circumstances. And yet, of course, it sometimes happened.

The Anishinabeg believed that anyone who once tasted human flesh came under the the control of evil spirits who might endow him with dreadful powers and

45

supernatural guile. They had a name for such a person — windigo. Any stranger walking into winter camp might be viewed with suspicion, especially when it was surmised, correctly in this case, that he was the sole survivor of another group.

Otter Woman was worried.

"Those people from the northern swamps are different from us. Everybody knows that their magic is as dark as their skins. The men mate with their sisters. And any time the woman is a little late with dinner they start eating each other. How do you think this one kept on living when all the others died?"

Iron Feather said nothing.

His wife continued, "I could see the spittle running down his chin when he looked at the baby."

"Tonight, at least, he will be no danger to anybody," said Shanod. "He is so thin that I could easily overcome him. And he would never be able to touch Sound of Waves without waking me."

The men were inclined to agree with her. To be safe, though, it was decided that the family would take turns staying awake during the night.

Toward morning, Shanod bent over He-Rises and pressed beside his ear. It was his time to stand watch.

He sat with the old musket across his knees. He had never fired it, but he could, and would if it should be necessary. Occasionally he got up to put wood on the fire but always with the gun in one hand.

The stranger slept peacefully. When the darkness turned to gray his eyes opened. He sat up and smiled at He-Rises, taking in the situation. His right hand went up, the first two fingers together, in the sign of brotherhood.

He-Rises stared at him for a moment. Then he slowly returned the smile and answered the gesture with another, inviting the guest to come into the forest. As the other sleepers began to stir, the two young men left the shelter to follow the line of snares.

In one of these, hoisted high, they found a lanky white hare with a streak of grizzled brown along his back. Nothing more had been trapped, but on the way back to camp, Tamarack stopped, touched He-Rises' arm and pointed to another slim strip of color in a cluster of dead branches beneath a pine. The wabooz had been betrayed by his coat, changing now from winter white to gray-brown. The bow sang its short, vibrant song. Otter Woman had a little fresh meat again for her family.

There was the touch of softness in the early light as they broke camp and set off to follow Iron Feather's tracks. Chickadees were singing in the trees around them. The sun came up warm. Soon they smelled the sweet pungency of balsam poplar buds. Sounds of dripping water came from rock faces along the west side of the trail. The long-frozen country was coming back to life.

The snow began to soften, clinging to the snowshoe webbing and slowing the toboggan. The dogs pulled willingly, but they were panting hard. The women leaned against their grip on the traces and Tamarack pulled as much as his weakened state would allow. But it was slow going. They fell back a long way behind the father.

At noon the record in the snow told them that Iron Feather had struck off to the left, leaving the trail. Otter Woman smiled as her eyes followed the tracks across the muskeg toward some low hills in the east. Her man's power had not deserted him. Something good had called.

He-Rises turned the toboggan over to Tamarack and stepped out into the white pathway. For a while he was able to keep the lead. Then as the snow continued to soften, his pace slowed. The others came up close behind him in the path he had beaten, holding back a little out of politeness, but not for long.

Shanod lifted the box from her mother's back and set it on the toboggan, where Tamarack bound it in place. Otter Woman gave He-Rises the larger of her two packs, put on the trail shoes, and went ahead. He followed, bent under the tump strap, glad that he did not have to look at anyone and that none of the others could see his face. The pack seemed unbearably heavy, but he was determined not to put it down. It had been only part of his mother's load. She broke trail the rest of the day, never slowing the steady, driving rhythm of her stride.

At evening, as they were making camp, Iron Feather came down the track, dragging a dressed caribou carcass on an improvised toboggan of birch bark. They watched him approach with joy and gratitude. Gratitude to the deer who had left the long lines of his fellows, now moving across distant forest and tundra. He had walked all this way on his spreading hooves over the snow, and had shown himself to Iron Feather to feed the hungry people. Now at last, everyone would have his fill of good, fat, life-sustaining meat. And, starting tomorrow, they would eat in the morning as well as at night.

8

The next day men, women and dogs needed all the strength that the rich meat had provided. The caribou spirit had taken pity on them just in time. The bottom was dropping out of the trail.

Even Iron Feather could take only so much wallowing ahead in this kind of snow. He-Rises and Otter Woman spelled him at trail-breaking. The dogs were floundering on their bellies. Shanod and Smoke Drifting pulled continuously on the traces, breathing hard, but giggling a good deal too.

At noon they stopped where a south-sloping mass of earth and rock was emerging from the snow. They built a fire, hung their wet garments to dry, and lay on the moss for a while. But soon Iron Feather got to his feet.

"I will go now, with He-Rises and Tamarack. The grandfather and the women rest here until evening cold hardens the path that we will tread."

The three men slogged on. Each step was a grinding effort, especially for the man in front. The webbing, heavy with clinging masses of wet snow, dragged down his feet. Father and son took turns at it until Tamarack pushed in front of them, speaking in his strange dialect. Iron Feather and He-Rises were beginning to understand that choppy way of talking.

"The meat has made me strong. Now I will break the trail."

The others stepped aside for him. But he had been in the lead position only a short time when he suddenly stopped. He was staring at a pole that had been pushed into the snow at an angle beside the path. It had been partly peeled and left with the bark hanging in loose strips. From the color of the bare wood and the shape of the drift around it, they could tell that it had been standing there a long time.

It was speaking to them in language that they all understood, the Muskego as well as the Anishinabeg. It was a desperate plea for help. Somewhere out there in the direction toward which it leaned, people were, or had been, without food.

He-Rises was the first to speak.

"This sign is old. It has stood while moons have come and gone. The person who put it here is surely dead. Or he might have killed meat and gone on to the sugar camp."

The father stood looking at the stake for a while before he answered.

"If he had gone on, he would have removed the signal."

The dangling tatters stirred a little in the breeze. He-Rises

spoke again.

"The trail is softening badly. If we turn aside from it now we may not get over the Minnisabik while the ice holds. With the baby and the grandfather, we must not risk a breakthrough."

Iron Feather walked a little way in the direction where the stake pointed. He looked closely at the surface of the snow and at the condition of bushes and branches, then returned to the path.

"You two go back to the fire. Tamarack, rest there until evening. Then you and the others go on toward the river. Continue through the night. When the morning sun softens the snow, stop and sleep. He-Rises, get meat and come after me."

For the rest of the day Iron Feather searched for faint clues and old signs. A man had walked to the trail earlier in the winter, then had gone back through the forest. His tracks had long ago been obliterated but he had broken twigs and branches to point the direction he had taken.

It was slow work. Often Iron Feather had to stop and cast about to find the next twig signal, or some other trace of the passage. He-Rises waited behind his father, breathing hard. Even now, in the late afternoon, the heavy snow weighed down his steps. Searching out these fading messages seemed futile to him. The man who had left them, and his family, would surely be beyond help now. But he said nothing more.

The sun had set and it was almost too dark to go farther when they came out into a little clearing among tall pines. Protected by their shade, the drifts were still deep around the blackened top of a pikogan. There was no glow of fire, and no movement of smoke above it.

Using their snowshoes as shovels Iron Feather and He-Rises dug a shaft to the entry. Iron Feather dropped down inside. In the darkness he could see nothing.

"Get bark," he called.

While he waited he stood quiet, listening intently. He heard no sound. There was a forbidding odor, far stronger than the usual smell of a winter lodge.

The crackling birch flare showed several long, fur-wrapped bundles lying on spruce boughs around the circle of the wall. The men went from one to another, pulling back sleeping furs and clothing, finding within each wrapping only the face of death. Then He-Rises spoke.

51

"This one, I think, is alive."

He was holding up the edge of the robe as his father brought the torch. Its light flickered down on what was little more than a skull, bright where skin was stretched tight over cheek bones, shadowed in sunken eye sockets. But deep in those dark hollows he could see the gleam of life.

Bending close and shading his eyes from the torch glare, Iron Feather made out the face of a child. Dried pieces of bone were caught in the fur around her mouth and an empty bark makak lay nearby. Someone had left a little food for her, but she had long ago eaten all that.

While He-Rises went for firewood, Iron Feather cut off a small piece of venison, chewed it thoroughly, opened the tight little mouth with his fingers and eased the softened wad down into it. At first there was no response. He waited, watching. Then the jaws moved. The meat was swallowed.

He-Rises built a fire, found a kettle, and filled it with hard-packed snow from the bottom of a drift. Iron Feather sat holding the girl close to the heat. Again he cut, chewed, and fed a tiny morsel. He-Rises put meat into the kettle and more icy snow.

After a while they gave the girl a little broth. Only a little, but it was too much. Her empty stomach revolted and shot back the drink and the meat.

They let her sleep while He-Rises got more wood. Iron Feather went to each of the fur-wrapped bundles, touched the robe, and spoke to the spirit of the person within. The dead were then carried out of the lodge.

The small body that remained alive was almost as thin as they. When she was given another sip she vomited again.

"No more for a while," said Iron Feather. "Pauguk is unwilling to let her go."

Later in the evening it went better — she kept some of the soup. Iron Feather and He-Rises wrapped themselves in the furs, and slept. But during the night, Iron Feather got up at intervals to feed the girl in small quantities. By morning he was sure that she would recover. He would stay in the lodge that day to let her rest and gain strength.

He-Rises returned to the trail and followed it to the daytime camp. The fire was out but the people were lying, asleep or at ease, in the comforting warmth of the afternoon sun. He lay down beside them, but could not sleep. A snake of sorry thoughts was slithering through his head.

"If my father had continued as I urged him, taking the trail to the sugar camp instead of to the lost lodge, she would have died."

He rolled over, trying to turn away from such useless regrets, but they would not let him escape to sleep.

"I really knew that we might be leaving someone to starve. I wanted to get quickly to the sugar and the fat muskrats. But, more than that, I feared the thawing river."

In the cool of the evening the snow was firm again and they made good progress, coming down into the valley of the Minnisabik. The river would lead them south to the maple groves. At dawn they camped on its bank. Here Iron Feather caught up with them, the girl riding comfortably in a tumped sling on his back.

Shanod and Smoke Drifting were delighted. They built up the fire to warm her and to heat some stew. Her eyes stared at them blankly and she would not speak. She was able to eat, though, and the girls fed her as much as the father would allow. At last they went back to their robes with the new sister warmly wrapped between them.

But they did not sleep long. Everyone was anxious to get started on the river, which was almost free from snow. It would be a joy to walk again without snowshoes. And for the dogs, the toboggan on ice would be a feather-pull. The small weight of its new passenger would not even be noticed.

Sturgeon Man, plodding along last in the line, would like to have sat with her on the toboggan. He knew that the dogs could handle the additional load. But the ice might not.

The sun had been eating at it from above and the current from beneath, weakening it in uneven patterns. In some places it had opened into airholes. In others, long fissures had run out and were widening. Whole sections had thinned to the point where they were ready to drop into the water.

This was the part of the journey that He-Rises had feared. He knew that spring ice was less dangerous than the newly-frozen surfaces of early winter. When a man breaks through, new ice is likely to just go on giving way each time he tries to hoist his weight out of the water. He quickly becomes too chilled and exhausted to struggle further. But he usually doesn't have to break his way far through the old, worn-out ice of March to reach stronger stuff where he can get a hand-hold and climb out.

Iron Feather went ahead of the others, with an axe in his hand and a heavy pack on his back. Sometimes he would stop, feeling, listening, and tapping with the axe. He-Rises came at a cautious distance behind him, carrying a long birch sapling, ready to extend it to his father in case of a breakthrough. The others followed in single file, careful to keep in the steps of the leader but well spaced out to avoid putting too much weight on any one spot. Shanod was carrying Sound of Waves in the tikinagon. The toboggan should be safe enough at the end of this careful procession but she felt better with the baby on her back.

At times they skirted dark holes where the Minnisabik, wild with the urgency of spring, boiled up from below. Again, Iron Feather might lead them through snow along the bank rather than risk a doubtful stretch of ice. In the shade of cliffs they had to push their way through slushy drifts or wade through water between layers of snow and ice. Several times they crossed high-arching ice bridges with the river rushing beneath them.

That night Iron Feather rubbed the dogs' feet and checked each of them for ice-cuts. Otter Woman made little moccasins out of pieces of caribou hide for several injured paws.

During the morning of the second day on the river they heard the sound of rapids. The swelling stream had torn away the ice entirely, so that it was necessary to follow the portage. The trail up was shaded and so still covered with snow, but the summit, exposed to the sun, was a long expanse of bare rock. Here they cut birch saplings and laid them across the path to ease the passage. The men pushed and lifted the toboggan while dogs and women pulled. Scraping and protesting, the heavily loaded sled was forced across the stone to the sheltered down-hill slope. They circled a growing pool below the rapids and continued on the ice.

The next morning they bypassed the last rapid above the sugarbush. Here the canoes had been cached bottoms-up, wedged and bound between trees and further braced with poles. They would come back for these before the ice went out.

They passed over a lake, still frozen deep except in narrow places where river current entered and left the still water.

That afternoon they could see the maple groves standing on a line of hills and ridges that rose above the surrounding swampland. At evening they turned away from the river and climbed the grade that led to the camp.

Three other families had already arrived. He-Rises was disappointed to see that Shakes-His-Wings' people were not among them, but they might come in at any time. The women had cleared the snow away from the storage lodge and were repairing the bark utensils. They were sewing up openings with watap, the long, flexible root-strands of black spruce, and caulking leaky seams with balsam gum.

They were thin, ragged, hungry, and working with good cheer. It had been a bad winter but it was almost over now. The men and boys were out on the marshes. They would bring in some rats tonight. And soon the maple syrup would be boiling.

Iron Feather's strong and fattening people unpacked their meat and Otter Woman swiftly apportioned it. There was not a lot of food for so many, but there was some for everybody. The smell of roasting and boiling caribou venison drifted through the maples and down toward the river flats. The returning hunters, tired, soaked, chilled, and very hungry, paused, sniffing, hardly able to believe their noses.

9

Otter Woman had not distributed quite all of her venison. She hung part of a shoulder beside the lodge and set a kettle of soup close enough to the fire to stay a little warm through the night. These were not thrifty hold-outs for her own family. Her men would provide for their needs.

But she knew that those people sleeping in the lodges around her, the early comers, were the strong ones whom Wabooz and the other animal spirits had favored. Peboan would have dealt more harshly with the late arrivals and some of these might be expected at any time. She lay down and drew the robes around her without taking off her moccasins.

So she was up and out of the lodge at the sound of wood squeaking on snow and grating over bare ground. But He-Rises was ahead of her. He had not been able to sleep. He was running down to where three thin figures were painfully dragging a toboggan up the trail from the river. On it was lashed a bundle wrapped in fur, with a wisp of white hair shining in the moonlight.

He-Rises seized a trace and the sled came quickly to the door. He cut the bindings and they carried the limp form into the lodge.

Otter Woman pulled back the hood. The ancient, bony face showed strong light and dark in the firelight. There was a gasp of recognition. Smoke Drifting was the first to speak. "It's Grandmother Dawn Sailing."

In moments the old woman's lips were grasping at a spoonful of warm soup, and then another. When Iron Feather judged that she had taken enough, they laid her back on the bedding and filled bowls for the men and the woman who had brought her in.

Sturgeon Man, watching, had known who the old one was as soon as she was lifted from the toboggan. She was not Smoke Drifting's grandmother — that was just the affectionate Anishinabe way of speaking. But if events had gone a little differently, she might have been.

Memories flooded in, taking him back over the years. Back to the hurried retreat from the enemy camp on the edge of the prairie. He remembered the blanketed bundle that had been Gagonce, swinging and jolting as it was carried on the pole. He remembered the captive, hauled along by the thong around her neck and beaten with sticks whenever she failed to keep the swift pace. Her hair had not been white then. It had been heavy and glossy black. And her figure had not been emaciated, but only trim and slender.

The war party had stopped, that night, in thickening forest growth. Crooked Lightning posted scouts along the back trail and around the camp. He had the corpse washed and a grave dug in the path. Gagonce's weapons and sacred pipe were placed beside him so that their souls would go with his. A fire was built over the newly turned earth and a hasty burial feast was eaten.

The girl had been crouching, silent, in the shadows. She was an enemy, and any of the Anishinabeg might scalp or stab her at will. Now she was dragged out into the firelight. Someone tore at her gown.

Crooked Lightning became angry again. Even more angry than he had been after the battle.

"So, it comes to this. You know well how dangerous it is to sully the purity of a war party's purpose by even thinking about woman. And especially about her mysterious wound that gives life to the world and bleeds with the changing moon. The Bear-Mother guards that sacred cave. A man must not go into it before a bear hunt or a battle. To do so may bring misfortune to the enterprise and death or injury to those who take part in it.

"Do not think that such punishment must be something far away. It may already be hiding behind those bushes that shine against the edge of the darkness.

"If you have forgotten the 'Bwaneg, be sure that the 'Bwaneg have not forgotten you. At this time you should be lying in ambush

58

along the back trail, not lying with a woman."

But the young men were not listening to his stream of scold. They had stretched the girl on the ground. Three of them held her while the others, one after another lowered themselves upon her. Those who had finished went out to relieve the scouts so that they might have their turns. Even Gwekabi, carefully maneuvering his splinted arm, took his painful pleasure.

Sturgeon Man stood back at first, shaken by Crooked Lightning's words. But he forgot them as he watched the men and the girl. He had become eager, excited and a little frightened, but not of the Abwaneg. He had never entered a woman.

When his turn came he pushed aside his breech clout and came down on the raw, shuddering body. She had ceased struggling. No one had to hold her now.

His long hair fell around her face, shutting them off from the others. Her eyes, big with pain and fear, looked up at him. She winced as he clumsily prodded, not finding the opening at first. When he did find it, he emptied himself quickly and moved aside to make room for the next man.

During the following days she was treated less roughly. No one wanted to kill her. She was so stiff and sore that she was clearly unable to keep up with the men, no matter how they might jerk on her neck cord or switch her legs. So they made a blanket litter and carried her. But they took their turns with her again each night. Sturgeon Man was still eager and excited, but no longer frightened.

The war party passed through the parkland and the thickening forest, and entered the swamp country. The cached meat was only a little rotten and they ate it rather than take time to hunt. One evening the word went out that they would reach the canoes next day.

Crooked Lightning had trouble getting sentries to go out to the posts that night. The young men said that the Abwan camp had been a small one, and that even if the hunters had come in, they would be too few to attack so strong a party. The Anishinabeg had put all these days of fast travel between them and the enemy. They did not think that they need worry now about a counterattack. And they were very tired.

Sturgeon Man agreed to take a watch later in the night if he could sleep first. Soon enough the other man woke him, pointed out the way he was to go, and lay down in the vacant spot by the embers of the fire.

The moon was a slim bent bow in the sky, but there was enough light to get through that flat and thinly timbered country. Out here alone, the position didn't seem quite so secure as it had in the camp. It came to Sturgeon Man now that if the enemy were following, tonight would be their last opportunity to attack.

Sturgeon Man looked around for a rock outcropping that would conceal him and, if necessary, stop a bullet. The friendly stone that had always been so plentiful in the forest was not to be found here. He finally settled for a clump of distorted and interwoven alder trunks. The ground beneath them was dry at this season. They gave a little concealment and provided a good view of some open grassland. It was too dark to see much out there now, but he would command this natural clearing at first daylight.

He had always loaded his musket with the usual hunting measure. Now he doubled the amount of powder, and took up a handful of heavy shot. He paused, hefting the rough lead spheres and considering. He had never fired such a combination. Would it break the breech? Not if he didn't have to shoot. And if the Abwaneg did come, he wanted something that would do plenty of damage. He dropped the shot into the barrel, tamped the charge solidly home, primed the pan, and sat down in his cover.

Time passed slowly at first. Several times he thought that someone was out there in the grass, and twice he raised the musket. Each of these alarms ended when he located some night animal or realized that it was only a tree shadow that had seemed to move.

After an hour of this sitting Sturgeon Man began to feel the chill of the late summer night. He was glad that he had had the foresight to bring a thick moose-hide hunting shirt. He put it on, tying it tight with the front flaps overlapping. He felt more comfortable then and less troubled by either the cold or any possible enemies that the shadows might conceal. He may even have dozed a little.

A musket roared. Close to him, at the next post in the line of scouts. He heard someone, more than one, run past him toward the camp. He strained to see. He could make out nothing in the open before him.

He wondered whether he should shoot into the darkness for a warning. No, they would not be sleeping now.

He heard a scatter of shots from the camp, some shouting, a few more shots, and then silence. He dropped low in the sheltering brush and stared between the kinky alders.

Some gray light was opening the sky now, and he saw the Abwan as soon as he came out of the trees. He was running lightly, alert, gun muzzle swinging as he looked to the right and the left. Sturgeon Man lay silent, not moving, hardly breathing.

Still the runner must have caught some warning, some message of a hostile presence. He stopped, face and gun pointing toward the Anishinabe. He stood there, shifting his head a little, trying to make out what might be concealed in the alder thicket. Then he walked cautiously toward it.

Sturgeon Man dared not raise his musket. Any movement would give him away. The enemy, alert, ready, clearly an experienced warrior, was closing in carefully, with his finger on the trigger.

There was the sound of breaking branches behind him. A smaller person came struggling through the brush, hobbling, trying painfully to run. It was the captive. She limped across the clearing toward them, then tripped and fell.

Even a seasoned warrior can make a mistake. This one looked away, turned from the thicket, took a step back to give help or encouragement.

Sturgeon Man did not fire blindly as he had in his first fight. He rose to a kneeling position, took careful aim, and gently drew back the trigger.

The recoil from the heavy load flung him backwards. Awkwardly, painfully, he sat up and then got to his feet. He could see, through the cloud of smoke, that he had hit his mark. The fierce raider had become a bundle of torn rags and bloody meat.

The girl struggled up, looked down at the fallen man, and gave a moaning cry. She stood there a moment, her head drooping, then swung wildly about, and continued her flight.

Sturgeon Man's ears were ringing, and his shoulder ached from the jolt of the blast, but he dashed from his hiding place to cut off her escape. He was still holding the empty musket.

She tried to dodge but he seized the front of her dress with his free hand, checking her momentum and twisting the garment to force

her down.

She flung herself backward, jerking desperately, but could not break his grip. He saw something gleam in her hand. She slashed up at him like a steel-gripped lynx when the careless trapper, raising his club, leans too far forward. He felt a sharp, cold point rip his flesh and grate along a rib.

The pain and the amazing impact of the blow staggered him. Through the shock of it he felt a violent jerking. His head was being shaken backward and forward as she wrenched and pushed at a stub that projected from his reeling body.

He swung the gun barrel as hard as he could at that short distance. It caught her beside the head and she dropped. He staggered back, felt blood running down his side, but stayed on his feet.

Beside her lay part of an arrow shaft with the iron head attached. Somehow she had stolen and hidden it and honed it to a vicious edge. But the double thickness of stout moosehide had turned and slowed the point, then caught one of the barbs as she tried to withdraw it for another thrust.

She was sitting up, holding her head, when men came following her tracks from the camp. Sturgeon Man, weakened and badly shaken, but beginning to feel very proud, stood over her, ready to hit her again if she showed any more fight.

When the others had taken her by the arms and dragged her away, he walked over to the man he had shot. The Abwan's body had been torn open by the heavy load of slugs at close range. Sturgeon Man drew his knife and grasped the hair. Hacking, sawing and jerking, he got off most of the scalp. It could not be called a skilled job, or tidy. But, as he stood with the matted thing dripping in his hand, it filled him with the ecstasy of sudden, unexpected, but unchallengeable achievement.

At the camp, the healer examined his wound, sucked it, spat out blood, performed a short ceremony over it, applied a herbal poultice and bandaged it. He told Sturgeon Man that he would be able to walk without assistance but must not try to carry a pack on the trail nor paddle or portage a canoe when they got to the water.

Crooked Lightning said that the attack had been made by only a few men, probably a small party of hunters that had come back to the village before the others. They might have been following close for several days and attacked that night because it had become clear that the main body would not arrive in time to cut off the forest men from the water.

The Abwaneg had overrun and knifed down the sentry, but not before he got off the warning shot. Another of the Anishinabeg had been shot through the thigh, a serious wound but not likely to be fatal. Several of the young men believed that they had made hits, and that the Abwaneg had carried away some dead or wounded, but they could not be certain. Anyway, one enemy was dead for sure, and the rescue attempt had failed. It could have been much worse.

Crooked Lightning looked at Sturgeon Man, smiling a little.

"This one has done well. He is not one of the bush rabbits. And now he understands 'Bwan women."

10

The march had started early that morning after the Abwan raid. Sturgeon Man remembered his companions rising silently, dark forms against an opening in the timber that marked the trail east. They made no fires for cooking or to ease the predawn chill. Crooked Lightning had to speak scornfully, shaming them into taking time to bury the sentry.

The retreat, covered now by willing scouts, went on through the warming autumn day. All were happy when, in the late afternoon, they reached the shore without being attacked again. The canoes were hurriedly carried across the beach and loaded. Only when the paddles dipped and they felt the rhythm of the lake moving under them did they feel safe. The land-lubberly Abwaneg could not get at them here.

The girl's head was badly swollen but she rested in the canoe, laying back against a pack. There was less need to hurry now, and she was able to get over the portages on her own feet.

The return voyage ended at the rice camp in the moon of the shining leaf. As soon as the canoes were sighted the watchers called the people. They stared into the glare of the setting sun, counting the paddlers and counting again, wondering who the missing ones would be.

As the water distance narrowed, the names of the dead were spoken. A wail went up from the waiting crowd. But songs of victory were rising too. When the warriors stepped out of the leading canoe and carried it up the shore, dancers were already stamping.

There was a hoarse shout of triumph as the scalps came into the camp circle, bouncing and fluttering on poles. Behind them stumbled the captive with the noose around her neck again. She choked, gasping for air as eager hands jerked at the rawhide.

The woman whose son and grandchildren had been massacred was waiting with a chunk of birch firewood. She swung it at the Abwan. The girl shrank back, putting up her arm. The first blow knocked down that defense and the second struck her head, driving her to the ground. For a few moments the old woman stood over her, breathing heavily, her eyes gleaming out through the hair that had fallen across her face. Then she bent down and began to batter the unresisting figure.

She would have pounded the life out if Sturgeon Man and others of the war party had not intervened. They took the club away and held the avenger back from the flattened body.

That was not a polite thing to do. Who had a better right to kill the captive than the bereaved mother-grandmother? There were murmurs of disapproval from the crowd.

The young men felt shame. They knew that they were behaving badly, but they held the woman anyway, as gently as they could, until she gave up the struggle and sank down weeping.

Others were showing their hatred of the Abwaneg by kicking the girl and jabbing her with pointed sticks. She lay sprawled, her face pushed into the earth, and did not move.

A little boy came running up with a glowing coal in a short cleft stick and held it to her back where her dress had been torn away. That seemed to bring her to life. She raised herself a little. Her face was so caked with blood and dirt that she did not look like a person, but like some animal that had been blasted with buckshot. Out of that dark smear, the whites of her eyes gleamed wildly. Then her arms gave way and she dropped back to the ground.

This was the time when attention was shifting from the enemy to the Anishinabe fighters. The people were gathering around them, an excited audience, anxious to hear their accounts.

Sturgeon Man went to stand with the others, then stepped back to where the girl was lying. The boy was drawing a pale design on her skin, only stopping when he had to blow on the coal to keep it glowing. Fascinated with this artistic effort and soothed by the smell of scorched flesh, he had not noticed the crowd moving away.

Sturgeon Man took the stick gently from his hand and tossed it, in a shining curve, through the darkness and into the fire.

"Come, little brother. We will tell you about the war."

The story of the battle and the repulsed counterattack was acted out with brandished weapons and ferocious looks as each man described his own actions. They spoke, to the beat of the truth-demanding drum, with pride and passion, but honestly, careful not to make any false claim.

Sturgeon Man told and showed how he had killed the raider and recaptured the prisoner. The women responded with cries of pleasure, and some of them circled around him with prancing little steps. It was a magnificent moment.

The triumph ceremony went on for a long time. The drumming, dancing and singing continued. Even the smallest children insisted on handling the scalps and striking the fallen enemy. At last they all had stopped, exhausted, standing around her.

Someone bored into her back, twisting a sharpened stick. She did not move.

"I think that she is dead now."

"Let us lay her on the fire and find out."

"I will show you how to tell," said one of the older men. He bent over the girl, took an arm, slashed it with a knife, and dropped it.

"Be quiet and listen."

The people were standing around her blocking the light from the fire so that Sturgeon Man could no longer see her. But he could hear the rhythmic spurts of blood striking the dry leaves. Zit. Pause. Zit. Pause. Zit.

The man wiped his blade.

"She is alive still. But that will take care of her. There is no need to bother with her further."

"Get her legs," Sturgeon Man said to one of his friends. "You and I will carry her to the medicine woman."

"Let her lie," the knife man snarled. "They killed our people."

Sturgeon Man grasped her under the arms and tried to lift, but sharp pain struck the partly-healed wound. He let the shoulders down, and the crowd moved in. He faced them, pretending to stand strong.

Another member of the war party took his place at the girl's head and they carried her away from the fire. An indignant group followed, speaking loudly of those who loved the Abwaneg.

Keewidnok, Woman of the North Wind, put aside her sleeping

robes and got up as they carried the body into her lodge. She had watched the triumph ceremony for a while and had then gone home to bed. She was not pleased with what they had brought her.

"I didn't hit her and I don't want to have anything to do with her now. Take her somewhere else . . . . But wait."

North Wind had seen the fresh stain on Sturgeon Man's shirt.

"I don't think that's her blood."

She stepped closer and pulled the garment up.

"You need attention, young man. Take the 'Bwaneg away, you others, and I will dress this wound."

She lifted the door covering and motioned them out. The crowd made a sound like a she-bear when the hunter prods her with a pointed pole to get her out of the winter den.

"Give her to us," a woman called. "We will do with her as her people did to our people."

The bearers stopped in the doorway, looking their question at the medicine woman. Sturgeon Man lifted the girl's left arm to show the bright rhythm of the flowing blood.

"She needs your healing more than I do. And she needs to stay a little while in your lodge. Take care of her first. Then, perhaps, these people will have gone away and she can be brought somewhere else and you can see to my small hurt."

North Wind hesitated. There was more growling from outside. "Lay her here, then." She spread a robe on bough bedding.

"My husband and my daughter are away, so I will need help. You two who are whole, stand outside the door and let no one come in. You,

Cut-Side, since your hurt is little and not in a hurry to be mended, stay with me and I will tell you what to do."

She cut away the few shreds that remained of the young woman's sleeve, then took Sturgeon Man's hand and guided it to a point on the upper arm.

"Press here. . . . Harder, and not just with a finger. Use the heel of your hand."

He pushed down hard and the red fountain subsided.

The medicine woman was chanting now, but not taking time for a real healing ceremony. That surprised him, but he said nothing. She filled a kettle with water, poured something into it from a makak and hung it over the fire. She pushed a roll of tightly twisted birch bark into a split stick, dipped the bark into the flame, and put the stick into Sturgeon Man's free hand.

"Keep pressing, but hold that to light what I will do."

She knelt beside the girl and squeezed her mouth open. Her fingers searched inside and brought out some pebbles and a tooth in a smear of mud and bloody froth.

A moccasin still clung to one foot. She removed that and what clothing the crowd had left. Quickly she went over the torn and battered body. She packed another badly bleeding gash with some material that looked like dried moss, and bound a piece of soft doeskin over it. Next she turned back to the wound in the arm.

"Good. But keep pressing until I tell you to stop."

North Wind opened another bark container, this one very small and tightly sealed. From it she tapped a brown powder into the palm of her hand. She turned the woman's head to one side and held the powder under her nostrils. Sturgeon Man could smell the bitter strength rising out of it.

He saw the captive's eyelids open. She looked at the flaring torch, at North Wind's sharp knife, at the faces hanging over her, and at the long, sinister shadows that moved above them across the poles and bark of the wigwam wall. Her eyes took on a defiant intensity and her lips pressed tight together. Sturgeon Man could see that she was preparing herself for the final cutting.

The medicine woman turned to the arm again.

"The bleeding has stopped. Bring me the kettle. That torch will not burn much longer. Light another. And hold a piece of bark to keep it from shining in my eyes."

She added a little cold water to the kettle, tested it with a finger, washed the wound in the arm and bandaged it. Then she leaned over the girl and put a hand on her shoulder, speaking softly.

"You cannot understand my words but I hope you know that we are trying to keep you alive."

She spoke next with some of the sign language but mostly with her own gestures and facial expressions. Sturgeon Man was able to follow her meaning fairly well, and he could see that the Abwan understood her too. North Wind was asking the girl to let her know at which points the pain was sharpest.

Starting with the scalp she moved down, checking every part, not hurrying this time. She found the head swollen, bleeding, and lacerated but the skull not broken. She washed and stitched the torn scalp.

She watched the expansion and contraction of the chest for a few moments, then pressed in lightly from the sides. The girl flinched with sudden pain. North Wind bathed her body then, and bound the cracked ribs.

She went over the girl's belly, pressing lightly, questioning, getting murmured answers now. She squeezed down on the tops of the hip bones, very gently at first, then harder. Sturgeon Man could see that she was pleased to get no sound or shudder.

"Now take her hip and shoulder and turn her over. Roll her like a log, but slowly . . . carefully."

As Sturgeon Man turned the body, North Wind held the head, steadying it to keep it from swinging to either side. She washed the girl's back. Then her hands moved over it, palpating, searching, gently insistent. She put cold, wet, medicated compresses on the burns. She signed for fingers and toes to be wiggled against her appraising palm. She checked the bones of arms, legs, hands and feet.

Her fingers running over the right forearm stopped, went back, pressed a little. The patient said something unintelligible but agonized. North Wind investigated further.

"The bone is cracked . . . . The grandmother must have put all the strength she had into that first blow."

Sturgeon Man was told to heat a sheet of birch bark. While he held it close to the fire North Wind set the break, smeared the arm with bear grease and wrapped it in a piece of blanket. She bent the hot bark around it and had the young man hold it tight while she bound it in place. As it cooled, it formed a fitted, rigid splint. Two broken fingers were splinted with thin strips of cedar.

North Wind dressed the other wounds, stitched up the worst and bandaged them. She salved the bruises and put more cold water on the burns.

Then she spread a blanket over that patient and turned to Sturgeon Man. She treated and bandaged his injury, and handed him a little wooden figure.

"This is a sacred thing, a talisman. Touch it to your wound when you first wake, each morning for twenty mornings. During that time do not lift anything heavy. Especially, do not lift any more women. That is a necessary part of the charm. On the twenty-first day bring the talisman back to me so that it can heal others."

They heard one of the young men at the entrance speak firmly, telling someone to stand back.

"You had better leave this one here for the rest of the night. In the morning, though, you must take her away. Now go home and sleep, and the two at the door also. But first, get some other of your child-warriors to keep the noisy people away from this lodge. I will not be bothered out of my bedding again tonight."

Sturgeon Man waked others and found several willing to leave their robes. The crowd was quieter now, and some were going away from the medicine lodge. The two young men left who had stood guard first.

Sturgeon Man walked slowly past the embers of dying fires to his parents' wigwam.

11

When Sturgeon Man came came back in the morning the doctor
met him at the door opening.

"The girl had a good night. I think that she will be all right, but
she's not yet well enough to be moved. I will keep her for a few days.
The people calmed down after a while and went home to bed, so I sent
the guards away.

"How about you? Are you having any more trouble with your
little hurt? . . . Good. Blackduck got back early this morning so I won't
need any more protection."

Sturgeon Man did not want to seem too much interested in the
welfare of an Abwan, nor to bother the medicine woman more than
was necessary. But, after several days, he began to walk past her lodge
from time to time. On one of these investigative strolls he saw someone,
warmly wrapped and with a bandaged head, reclining against a backrest where the sun came through an opening in the pines. Not far away,
Blackduck was using a crooked knife to shape an axe handle from a
stick of birch. He got up quickly, putting down the knife but not the
stick, and stepped in front of the girl.

"This woman is no longer an enemy."

"I know that, uncle. I have not come to do her harm."

"Good. Some of the people have been slow to understand."
Blackduck sat down and went back to work, but kept a watchful eye
on the younger man.

Sturgeon Man turned toward the girl, closed his hands and
crossed his wrists over his chest in what he had heard was the western
sign-word for kind feelings and respect. She looked up at him and

raised a splinted hand in acknowledgment. Her eyes were good and the corner of her mouth turned up in a little smile where it was not covered by the wrappings.

This was all the communication they could manage that morning, but he stood beside her for a while until North Wind saw him and called him into the lodge to inspect his wound.

"It is healing well. So is the captive. She is still weak but she will recover. I have decided to keep her as a servant. She seems to be smart enough and I don't think that she will be dangerous. She may be useful to me."

As time passed, Sturgeon Man noted that North Wind was not disappointed. The girl did indeed turn out to be useful. As soon as she was well enough she took over the woman's work around the lodge. She picked up the language quickly, although she never lost her heavy Abwan accent. Her mistress began to assign her nursing duties and care of the sick.

The families left the rice camps for the hunting grounds, and Sturgeon Man did not see North Wind or her servant girl again that winter. When the people came together at the sugarbush in the spring he learned that she had been taken into Blackduck's family as a daughter. She had been given the name of Wabanaquayash, Dawn Sailing, in recognition of her beginning life as an Anishinabe.

North Wind's other daughter had never shown much interest in the healing work, so Dawn Sailing became increasingly important to her new mother. She grew familiar with the broad variety of *materia medica* used by the woods Indians. She learned to gather and process the plant, mineral, and animal ingredients for each of these in its proper season. Under North Wind's guidance, she made healing poultices from aspen bark and flute reed. She cut up pine bark and the inner bark of the wild cherry, then boiled and mashed them for wounds. Hemlock bark and cinquefoil or duck down stopped bleeding. Water lily roots were brewed into a tea to cure diarrhea, gargled to soothe a sore throat, or applied as a salve for boils. The leaves of fireweed were dried and crumbled to heal burns. Wild ginger and spikenard were combined to make a poultice for broken bones. Deer tendons and basswood fibers were prepared for use as sutures in surgery. Bear grease was the base for many cures and medicinal lotions — especially valued because the bear too is a healer, and can mend wounds or sores by licking them or by applying those mysterious remedies that only he understands.

In time, Dawn Sailing was able to prescribe an emetic or a medicated steam bath, let blood, pull an abscessed tooth, give an enema with a deer bladder and a hollow reed, set a broken bone or ease a difficult birth. She could open a frozen toe and rub into it the inner bark of tamarack to prevent mortification. Or, if it was too far gone to save, she would cut it off and cauterize the stump with a hot iron. Several times she helped North Wind amputate a hand, a foot, or a limb.

The old doctor did not consider herself much of a conjuror. Nursing, surgery, and healing with natural balms were done by people of either sex. Treatment of the sick with charms and ceremonies was, in most cases, carried out by a male shaman. But any physician sometimes needs supernatural help.

North Wind taught Dawn Sailing how to consult with her drum, beating it, questioning it, and listening carefully to its answer.

"Always speak respectfully to the drum. If it won't talk, don't try to force it. It usually wants to be kind to people and to help in diagnoses, but pushing an unwilling drum can bring much harm."

When Dawn Sailing became skilled and understanding in this work, she was allowed to use her mother's ancient drum stick, carved with a loon's head by some craftsman-magician of forgotten times. Later, North Wind taught her a few simple incantations that she had found effective for certain maladies.

Young men came to Dawn Sailing bringing gifts. Among them was Sturgeon Man. She looked on him with favor. He waited outside the door at night until she came out. She stood with him under his blanket and they talked in low voices until she was summoned back into the lodge by alert parental authority. If all had been well in that lodge she would probably have married him.

But North Wind was ailing now with some strange sickness. She had grown thin in a time of plenty. A sour pain burned steadily in her stomach. Lines ran out from her mouth and left deep creases in the transparent skin of her face. Neither she nor Dawn Sailing could find a remedy. The younger woman felt that she should not, at this time, leave the lodge for marriage.

Gradually Dawn Sailing was taking over the practice. This was not so profitable as it may sound. A medicine woman was respected, but was not paid much. Usually she would be rewarded for her services by a gift of food or some other small present.

The old doctor grew weaker. Often now she was wrenched by sudden, intense agony. Clearly, someone was practicing sorcery against her.

All her life North Wind had helped others. Blackduck discussed the matter with the two daughters, but they could think of no person who would wish her this misery.

They sent for a wabeno, a calm, thoughtful man with an outstanding reputation for difficult cures. For a day and a night he danced, drummed, and chanted. He tried to suck out the evil spirit through a bone tube. Then, in a low voice, he told the family that it was not in his power to draw the thing from North Wind's body and that there was nothing more to be done except to make her as comfortable as possible.

Dawn Sailing cared for the old woman, watched over her, and gave her medicines to ease the pain a little, while they waited for Pauguk. North Wind looked like him by this time and was ready to welcome him. But he seemed to feel that, now that he was sure of her, there was no need to hurry.

Months went by, a year. North Wind lay flat and silent, never stirring except when Dawn Sailing lifted her to give her drink and what little food she would take, or to clean her.

By the time death did arrive, the older daughter was married and so was Sturgeon Man. Dawn Sailing went on living in Blackduck's lodge, cooking the meat and dressing the hides of the deer and moose he brought in, and treating the sick and injured.

She was almost twenty now, rather old for a single woman in this primitive society. Eventually, though, she found the right man. Her husband was Mikinak, The Turtle — a skilled hunter who already had two capable and industrious wives.

Some Anishinabe women were beginning to take on the Saganash prejudice against polygamy, but Dawn Sailing could see its advantages. Now she would be able to devote most of her time to her patients and to a study of the darker mysteries, especially the defenses against such witchcraft as had killed her foster mother.

Several years later, at the end of the sugar season, she took her infant son on the long journey to the hunting grounds of her western relatives. She hoped to find her other parents if they were still alive, or at least her sister.

There was much gossip about this during the berry picking. The women were inclined to agree that The Turtle had been a fool to let her go. When the rice was ripe for harvest and she had still not returned they were sure that they had seen the last of Dawn Sailing. But just before the waterways froze, she came paddling back with many gifts and a big pack of healing herbs from the prairie. The baby was propped against the thwart before her in a strangely carved Abwan tikinagon.

This boy turned out to be her only child. His name was Mangozid — Loon's Foot. He grew up to be, in some ways, a disappointment to his energetic parents. He could not be called lazy, but he did not have his father's keenness at trapping nor his mother's single-minded drive toward a serious purpose. He was careless about hunting ceremonies and sometimes forgot them altogether, and then the animals were naturally unwilling to let him catch them. He could spear muskrats and shoot beaver well enough in the spring hunt, but the mink and lynx would not forgive him at any season.

He was good at tracking, though, was a capable judge of ice and weather, and drove a canoe boldly and skillfully with pole or paddle. His worst fault was an inordinate taste for ishkodewaboo, the white man's fiery drink.

While he was still very young he showed great admiration for a childhood companion, Iron Feather. The older boy seemed to like this. Or perhaps the attraction of opposites drew them together. It was a friendship that continued into later life.

When Dawn Sailing became a widow she accepted the invitation of her son's wife, Red Sky Woman, to live with them in her wigwam.

It was this couple and their son, Ashquaygons — Little Toenail — who had dragged the old woman on their loud-squeaking toboggan up the icy hill to the sugar camp.

The new arrivals took their food well that night, eating in small quantities, then resting and visiting before taking more. They were weak, but in a happy mood, especially Loon's Foot. He was a short man, and, of course, very thin now, but well set up, with sparkling eyes and a merry smile. He stopped eating long enough to wave his bowl at Iron Feather, taking care, though, not to spill anything.

"You've got a good woman, brother. I can see that she kept you fat all winter with fish and rabbits. I don't suppose you even had to go hunting.

"And that soup of hers is even better than what my wife's been serving lately. But don't get mad, Red Sky. Your spruce bark broth was excellent as long as there was a rib or two left from the dogs. And those old sleeping furs of yours were the most delicious things I ever ate."

Dawn Sailing woke, and Otter Woman spooned her more soup. She asked in a weak voice whether Sturgeon Man had lived through the winter. He bent over her and touched her shoulder. She looked up, smiled, and went back to sleep.

12

Among the men at the sugar camp, Iron Feather was known for a mysterious quality that they called manidoke. They believed that this gift was conferred on a human by the spirit world. Whether this was the case, or whether it was the result of experience and good judgment, plus luck, it did seem to be quite consistent in some people.

A man endowed with manidoke was likely to be successful in hunting, trapping, and war. He would usually be intelligent, calm, not easily angered, but ready to act quickly when action was needed. If he also knew the ceremonies, charms and incantations needed to see a reasonable distance into the future and to placate malevolent spirits, those around him would look to him for guidance in many fields.

Iron Feather was not a chief, a priest, a physician, or a judge. But he was expected to carry out the functions of each of these specialists to the extent required by a small band of independent nomads — illiterate and superstitious, but not fools and not easily taken in by fraud.

There had been no election, appointment, investiture or licensing. Rather, Iron Feather's status was established by general, silent approval. This was the man who would be best able to minimize the losses of a hard winter and direct the recovery. The people looked to him now for help and guidance.

Sturgeon Man was pleased, during the days that followed the arrival at the sugar camp, to see Dawn Sailing fill out again and regain her strength. He looked forward to sitting and talking with her in the sun. She would speak in her guttural, but somehow charming, western accent. He would smoke his pipe and she would hang a kettle over the fire for tea as had been their custom at other spring and summer camps.

She was on her feet surprisingly soon, but there was no time now for such social amenities. Pathetic little caravans continued to struggle in. These late-comers had suffered a crushing winter. Some had kept together in groups of several families and had exterminated the skimpy supply of small game. In other areas the hares had faded away. Day after day, the hunters had returned with nothing. In most cases the children had somehow been kept alive, but as shriveled little specters with big eyes and bloated bellies. They and the few surviving old people were painfully pulled through the softening snow, with those people who could still walk taking the places of the dogs. Shakes-His-Wings' family was not among them.

The duties of seer, prophet and healer were not clearly defined, and often overlapped. So Dawn Sailing and Iron Feather, working as colleagues, were applying their rituals and remedies to those still undecided whether to live or die.

They understood hunger and those other evils that accompanied it. Their patients, the product of many generations of survivors, had a remarkable ability to come back quickly from the edge of death by starvation. This spring, only one of these died — a grandfather who had been left in a pikogan. His son, as soon as he was strengthened by food, borrowed a dog team, made the long trip back to the winter camp, and brought the old man in, alive but unwilling to remain so.

The scrawny body was washed and dressed in richly beaded clothing. He-Rises helped to lay it out on a broad sheet of birch bark. He knelt beside it holding dishes of brown and vermillion coloring while Iron Feather dipped his fingers and painted the cheeks with the sacred round spots and horizontal lines. When he had finished, he straightened his back but did not rise from his squatting position. He-Rises handed him the drum. Iron Feather struck it, then spoke calmly and distinctly to the dead man.

"My father, a pouch with flint, steel and tinder is tied to your belt. Also in the pouch is tobacco and your old pipe that is carved in the shape of a squirrel. That is your manido that took you under his protection many years ago in the dream of your vision-quest. A good pair of moccasins are on your feet. Those feet are now on the road of the ghosts."

The beat of the drum is the same as a prayer. While Iron Feather gave directions for following the spirit trail, he accompanied the words with a series of drum beats. He told which turns to take and which to avoid, which spirits to trust and on which false guides the traveller must turn his back.

"Be happy in the ghost country, father, and do not fear for your children and your grandchildren. The leaves will bud in the spring

and drop in the autumn. For a long time yet geese will fly, fish will swim, and your people will hunt and live, even though you are no longer with them."

He-Rises bent the springy bark up around the body and they wrapped it and bound it tightly. With the help of the old man's son they lifted it into the branches of a birch tree. When the earth thawed, the body would be taken down and buried.

He-Rises had watched funerals before but this was the first time that he had taken an active part in one. It left him with somber thoughts about that poor, shriveled thing that had been a man and that had now been wrapped away into nothingness. Somewhere out there in the hills, Shakes-His-Wings would be lying now, unburied, stinking in the warmth that had come too late. He-Rises had failed him.

The lodges here in the spring camp were waginogans, "bent houses." These long, dome-shaped wigwams were made of saplings curved and bound together at the tops to make a rounded roof that was covered with birch bark. They were much larger than the compact, heavily reinforced winter pikogans. Each was usually occupied by fifteen or twenty people. The Iron Feather and Loon's Foot groups shared such a dwelling with two other families.

Red Sky, who had never had a daughter of her own, was much taken with the little orphan that Iron Feather and He-Rises had found in the death-lodge. The girl was gaining strength now and beginning to talk. She told Smoke Drifting that her name was Madeyn and that she was twelve years old. That surprised everyone. Her skeletal appearance had made her look ancient, but she was smaller than Smoke Drifting and all had assumed that she was younger.

It soon came to be understood that Red Sky would be her new mother. The others thought that this was a pretty good idea, except Smoke Drifting. Dawn Sailing reminded her that they would still be living in the same lodge, at least while they stayed at the sugar camp. They could go on being sisters.

13

The rough bark of the old maples, slashed by earlier generations of the Anishinabeg, was again being opened to end another long winter and bring life to the people.

Iron Feather's family worked within the boundary paths that separated its ancestral section of the grove from those of the others. They tapped the trees in sequences along routes planned for swift and efficient collection.

Otter Woman chopped each opening with just three axe strokes. Two cuts formed downward-pointing V-shaped grooves. With the third stroke, delivered carefully so as not to harm the tree, she drove in a wooden spout at the point of the V, tilted down to let the sap drip into a makak.

Red Sky and Shanod bound two heavy timbers side by side in a horizontal position, one on each side of a tree at one end, and of a strong vertical post at the other. They carried an iron caldron from the storage lodge and suspended it from a cross piece over the space between the timbers, so that it could be slid in either direction as required. Dawn Sailing and Smoke Drifting brought stout forked poles and braced both the upright post and the horizontals.

When they were finished, Otter Woman inspected the bindings and tested the structure, jerking on it, throwing her weight against it, and making several adjustments. The fall of a vat of boiling sap could have terrible consequences.

A steady fire was soon burning under the kettle and was tended day and night, most of the time by Dawn Sailing, with Sturgeon Man's assistance. They watched the boiling liquid and kept the heat where it was needed by moving the pieces of burning wood toward or away from the center of the fire or by adding more fuel as required. If the sap began to churn, threatening to boil over, Dawn Sailing would brush it with a spruce branch and it would subside long enough to give them time to reduce the heat by rearranging the fire.

Smoke Drifting and Madeyn kept up the supply of wood. When they were not needed at the fire, the girls were in the grove, minding the filling makaks, carrying in sap, and running errands for the women.

Even in the cold hunger moon the Anishinabeg joked about their trouble. In the happy sugar season, the noise of the tapping and the smell of boiling sap ran together through the woods to produce almost an intoxication of joy. Any misadventure or foolish little blunder was screamingly funny.

As Shanod was cutting a groove in a tree her foot slipped on a patch of melting ice, throwing her off balance. Her axe glanced off the tree and sliced her left hand.

The women working around her chuckled. Loon's Foot was carrying in two sap buckets. He called blithely through the trees.

"You have a fine name, the same as a Saganash lady, but that's no reason to handle your axe like one of them!"

Shanod stared at the wound and the reddening snow beneath it. Then she laughed, gave the hand a shake, and went on with the cutting.

"Your name must be Saganash too," Smoke Drifting said to Madeyn. "Because it doesn't really mean anything."

"It means something. It is French. It is the name of one of their big medicine women. Or maybe a sorceress. My grandmother was part French. She used to call me Madlan. But that is too hard to say."

Smoke Drifting put out a blocky little hand, palm down.

"Hold yours beside mine. . . .Yes, yours is lighter. Even though my sister's name is as French as yours, I don't think there is any white in us. Was the old Madeyn one of your grandmothers?"

"I don't think so. If she was, her witchcraft didn't come down to me. I think that magic may have brought your father and He-Rises to our lodge, but it wasn't any of my doing."

Sunny days and hard-freezing nights followed, perfect weather for making sugar. In the frosty mornings Smoke Drifting and Madeyn set the makaks on the snow under the spiles to catch the bright liquid that would begin to drip as the day warmed. In the afternoons they emptied them into bark pails, and the pails into large bark vessels made with strong handles.

When the men came in from the ice they carried these big buckets into camp, or pulled them in on toboggans. Then they drank the hot, sweet maple tea that Dawn Sailing had made from the boiling sap.

In the early mornings, while Otter Woman and Shanod were leaving with the collecting bowls, Red Sky and Dawn Sailing dipped out hot syrup with wooden ladles and strained it through a threadbare old blanket to get rid of twigs and bark.

The final step in the process, and the touchiest, was the "sugaring off." Dawn Sailing, Smoke Drifting and Madeyn hovered over the kettles now, or crouched beside the fire, like a senior witch with her apprentices. They made certain that the sap boiled down to exactly the proper consistency without burning. At the right moment they poured the contents of each kettle into wooden troughs. There they kept it moving with maple paddles. As it cooled, it stiffened. Loon's Foot stayed in camp to help. He stirred strongly until the syrup became sugar.

But before this happened the girls ladled some of the hot, heavy stuff from each batch into bark cones or into small wooden molds to make candy. And some they poured out on the snow where it hardened into sticky, delicious strips.

Tamarack, having come from the barren north beyond the range of maples, knew nothing of sugaring. "Bend over," Loon's Foot told him, "and listen to the tree. You will hear the sap run."

When the Muskego put his ear to the trunk, everyone shouted. It was an old trick, but funny again in the boiling moon.

Each morning the men called the dogs and walked down to one of the marshes that bordered the maple groves. The dogs' job was to sniff out the muskrats' little pushup houses hidden under the snow. The men would break into them and club or spear the inmates.

The rats had come through the winter fairly well in this area. They were plump and good eating, but the skins were too badly scarred to be of much value. They had nasty tempers and quarreled often, chewing at each other in the confinement of their winter quarters.

While the river growled and heaved below, Iron Feather, He-Rises and Tamarack dragged a specially constructed sled back to the portage and brought the canoes, one at a time, to the sugar camp. Water was flowing over the ice on both sides of the river, swirling in widening pools. The men were in and out of it, sometimes dragging the boats over a frozen area, sometimes breaking through and paddling.

Three days later the Minnisabik broke with a roar. The flood hurled down huge ice blocks and crashed them against boulders and each other, forming dams where masses of ice churned upstream and down, grinding themselves to pieces.

With the river open, a rush of smooth dark forms surged and splashed upstream, fins standing like sails above the water. Pike and suckers jumped or skittered their way over the shallows, and fanned out into the flooded swampland in a mad fury of spawning.

The people were hungry for fresh fish and the men speared all that were needed, but the frenzied swimmers were so numerous and so obsessed with procreation that they seemed not even to notice.

As open water appeared in the streams and ponds, the hunters began taking toll from the flocks of northbound waterfowl that slanted down out of the clouds to rest and feed. Like the muskrats, these birds provided fat meat that everyone craved after the lean winter.

It was good to hear again the rolling laughter of loons. Sturgeon Man said that these were Nanabush's scouts. They had stood by the hero-trickster-savior, and warned him when all the other birds and animals had joined with men to plot against him.

The annual passage from hunger into plenty was the occasion for a celebration of great joy, but not of frivolity. When the first sugar was ready, everyone in camp was invited to a feast. Sturgeon Man and the other elders were seated in a special place of honor. Tobacco was handed around, tamped into pipes, and lighted.

Iron Feather, as spiritual leader, poured out some syrup on the ground, giving it back to the earth. He offered a smoking pipe to the sky, the earth, and the four directions. In a clear, calm voice he expressed the gratitude that they all felt.

"Thank you, maples, for this delicious and life-sustaining sugar. Thank you, firewood, and you, great iron kettles, for boiling the sap. Thank you, muskrats, for your rich and early meat. Thank you, ducks, geese and loons, for returning through the air to feed us hungry ones. Thank you, pike and suckers, for coming up the streams again to our spears. Thank you, good manidog, for helping us through Peboan's cold and danger. Thank you, evil ones, for sparing so many of us.

"Help us, all the spirits, under the summer sun and moons, to gather the berries, rice, fish and meat that we will need for the next winter. We will try to keep your commandments and to observe your taboos, but forgive us our trespasses if we blunder into some forbidden acts."

The food was served with old-time formality, first to the men, then to the women, and finally to the children. Portions were carried out to the cemetery and placed before the low bark and log lodges that covered the graves and under the few burial scaffolds. Also, at this time, many gifts were given. Food, clothing, weapons and equipment were freely handed out from one person to another, and not just to friends and family.

As the last daylight faded from the spring sky, Iron Feather squatted beside the drum, bending forward from the waist. He struck it lightly and began a high, quavering chant. The sitting men joined him, their bodies swaying, their eyes closed. He thumped slowly at first, then in a quickening beat.

An old woman came out into the firelight in little hopping steps, stamping with her heels, but never taking her feet off the ground. Other dancers followed. They moved in a circle around the fire, taking the same direction as the sun in the day sky and the great bear at night, right arms on the inside, left on the out. The men stepped higher and more loosely than the women.

As the dance continued the drum was handed from one squatting figure to another. Its passionate beating rose and fell in the leaping, falling firelight. It would throb on through the night, the pulse of a thousand years, a binding together with ancestors and posterity.

He-Rises was swept up in a wave of exultation. He felt his face burning like the flame and his heart pounding with the drum. His shame and sadness were forgotten.

"Now all the people are one person," said the rhythm of the drum, the chant, and the beating feet. "We have taken this country and we have held it against fierce enemies and against cold, hunger, and sickness. None of these, nor any other evil, will destroy us or drive us out. Whatever comes, we will go on together."

14

Late winter passed swiftly into spring. Daylight came early and stayed late into the evening. Snow drifts melted from beneath, leaving overhanging edges. A dark spot appeared at the bottom of each white hollow, freezing at night but growing with the next day's sun, gnawing at the snow and ice around it. Soon these formed ponds that grew deeper and broader until they broke through to pour into the nearest marsh or stream.

The emerging patches of earth, dead leaves, moss and stone spread rapidly. Bloodroot poked up first through the leaf carpet, followed soon by arbutus, wind flowers, spring beauties and violets. Aspen, maple, and birch burst into a haze of little new leaves and were suddenly full of thrushes and warblers. They sang sweet songs and so did the frogs in the swamps and trees. There were blessed, soul-lifting smells from the growing things and from the thawing ground, brown again and alive.

As the flow of maple sap dwindled, fewer hands and hours were needed for sugaring. Some of the women began to turn to fishing, and to searching the swamps and forest for edible or otherwise useful vegetation. Leaves, fronds, roots, barks, tubers, resins, lichens, and mushrooms were gathered for soups, stews, salads, flavorings, relishes, teas, or to be made into mats, cord, clothing, toys, medicines or magical charms.

The first green shoots that came pushing out of the melting snow were especially prized. The familiar warning signs of poisonous plants were respected. Some of these hostiles were harmless and good eating when cooked while others were simply to be left alone.

For Dawn Sailing, the spring woods were a living pharmacy. This was the start of the collecting work that would continue until fall. Madeyn and Smoke Drifting searched through the hills and swampland looking for the familiar plants they knew she wanted. They brought in others, new to them, to ask about names and possible uses.

After the river opened, the ice still clung to the ponds and marshes. Until it left these still waters the spring beaver hunt could not begin. There was time for some people to do other things than gather the necessities.

Young women and men had come together at the sugar bush and would go on together to the post village and the berry camp. But nobody forgot how soon they would have to part, taking the long walk back over the ice roads to the cold, isolation, and hunger of the winter camps.

So this short season of companionship and intimacy was a time for courting. It was carried out properly with gifts, flute serenades, and formal calls at family wigwams. And less legitimately, in spite of the diligence of the older women, in the hills behind the camp, on soggy little islands in the muskeg and even in some of the lodges, where the maternal guardians were sound sleepers.

Tamarack had a pretty good idea that Shanod would not willingly refuse him. He was sure that, had she been a Muskego, they would have been sleeping together by this time. But he was at a loss to know what to do among these indirect and fastidious people of the south, with their peculiar rules for keeping lovers apart.

He had no father to arrange matters with Iron Feather. He had nothing to offer as a bride gift. He could hardly pay a noticeable courting call to a lodge of which he was already a member. And he had no hope whatever of getting under Shanod's sleeping robes without waking the vigilant Otter Woman.

Several times he had tried to maneuver Shanod into a more private and favorable situation. Each time she had hesitated, and the lack of an immediate refusal gave him joy and hope. But always she drew back with some reference to Ice Stone.

"Why are you faithful to a far away person who has done you nothing but harm and insult?"

She laughed. "You're funny. I'm not in the least faithful to that one."

Then she became serious.

"He will come again to the camp by the trading post. He is an angry man, very strong, and quick with gun or knife. I don't want him to hurt you. And his father's witchcraft could bring great harm to all of us."

There, each time, the matter ended. It made no sense to Tamarack, but he felt that further entreaties would be useless. And while he made the attempts and considered the difficulties, the days of leisure passed. The time came for beaver.

Unlike the muskrat, Amik did not snap at his fellows while they were crowded together during the winter months, so his skin was in good condition.

This refusal to become angry was only one of the virtues that led the woods Indians to consider the beaver a model animal. He was also wise, hard-working, thrifty and careful — throughout most of the year. But he did seem to become a little drunk with the joy of spring. Or perhaps he understood how much the people needed him. For a week or two at this season he put aside his usual caution. Now he could be shot as well as trapped. A grove of poles sprouted around the camp, each holding a willow hoop that encircled and stretched a dark, drying pelt.

Gradually the men and boys worked farther out into the surrounding country, avoiding ponds that they had hunted the previous year, shooting only the larger animals, and being careful not to cut down any colony to the point where it would be in danger of dying out. Most of them preferred the cheap and silent arrow to the gun.

Tamarack proved to be particularly skillful at this kind of hunting. The earliest light of each morning found him sitting in some willow thicket, as quiet as the stumps and dead trees that surround a beaver pond, watching the surface of the water for any swirl that might hint at something moving below. When the swimmer broke water his bow would be ready. Almost every time his arrow would pierce the head for a quick kill, important here because a dead beaver floats. A wounded beaver dives and may escape into the opening of a lodge or the tunnel to a bank den.

Or the two young men might hunt from a canoe at evening. He-Rises, in the stern, would turn the paddle to move edgeways through the water on each forward stroke so that there would be no sound of drops falling from the blade. Tamarack with bow and notched arrow in one hand, signalled back instructions with the other — left, right, let her run. Often they could glide silently in near the bank through the reflections and shadows of overhanging trees, and drift close to the working or feeding beavers for a sure, clean kill.

He-Rises was delighted at Tamarack's success. All could see now that this friend of his, almost his brother, was an expert hunter. He

wished that he were more worthy of such a friend.

He had failed, he told himself, not as a hunter, but in his obligations to others and to himself. Though he would soon be sixteen years old, he was not ready to move into a man's life. Most of those his age, and many much younger, had seen their visions and found their guardian manidog, but not he.

Three times, in previous years, he had gone alone to remote places in search of the dream. Each time he had fasted many days, but had found no spirit that would help him. Each time he had given up. He had simply lacked the fortitude to continue longer the thirst and hunger that bring sacred dreams. The temptation to lie had come to him, to pretend that he had found the vision. He had not done so, but even to have considered it was a disgrace. He would never tell anyone about those thoughts.

His family had welcomed him back with food and sympathy, but their kindness did not free him from the shame of failure. He could not live a man's life nor gain a man's wisdom and power until he succeeded. He wondered now whether that would ever happen.

He would try again, this time in a very sacred place, the ledge in the stone mountain above 'Tschgumi. But the sorry memories of his past attempts left him little confidence for the future.

After a few frost-free nights the catkins on the willows turned yellow, the frog choruses reached full strength, and the maple sap began to come out dark, bitter, and in diminishing quantities. A minority of eccentric connoisseurs considered this late draft the very best. Like it or not, it would be the last for this year.

And so the run ended, all the syrup boiled down to sugar, small in quantity when compared with the many heavy buckets of sap that had been carried from the trees to the fires, but nourishing, portable, storable and delicious.

It was packed safely in makaks, great riches in a small space, the first of the ramparts to be raised against hungry Peboan. These boxes were buried in bark-lined pits, ready for the late autumn return to this place, and the early winter departure from it.

The men went over the canoes, checking the seams, stitching tears and cracks, closing every opening with a heated mixture of grease, charcoal and pitch. The river was running high in the first gush of the spring rains. The stubborn ice of the big lakes would surely be breaking now. The thick black trout of 'Tschgumi would be looking for the nets. In the sacred grove above its water the tall birches would be ready to give their bark. Again, in the ancient rhythm, the time had come to move.

15

A soft spring rain was falling as Iron Feather's people left the sugar camp. The morning light was not yet strong enough to see much except the shining river. But as they carried their boats and bundles down to the bank they could hear the whistle of duck wings overhead and, from a higher level, the honking of geese.

The canoes were placed gently in the water and held, floating clear while they were loaded. Otter Woman took her place, sitting cross-legged in the bottom at the bow. Iron Feather knelt in the stern. Ma-eengun jumped into the space that had been left between the packs. He-Rises picked up one of the pups, a pretty good armful now, and set him down beside the old dog. The paddles dipped and they swept off downstream with short, quick, smooth strokes that gave the most move-ahead leverage for energy expended. It was a fast pace but one that they could hold all day.

Sturgeon Man took the stern of the second boat. His legs were no longer much good for portaging, but he could still handle a canoe on the water. He-Rises sat in the bow. Smoke Drifting and one dog fitted neatly into the cargo.

Shanod and Tamarack came next. Sound of Waves was tucked snugly in front of her mother, where the lift of the bow sheltered her from the soft but steady rain.

Dawn Sailing and Little Toenail were in the fourth canoe, then Red Sky and Loon's Foot with Madeyn. Several other families followed, trusting Iron Feather's manidoke to find the best course through the mud flats of the river and to deal with the more serious hazards that they would face later. They would follow his canoe, camp where he camped, and carry out his orders as long as they chose to do so, or until the rivers froze. But they were bound to their leader no more formally than the caribou were to theirs.

It was good to be afloat again, to be moving easily over water, away from ice-bound Peboan and into the fat curve of the summer cycle. No one was worrying about the wind-swept lakes ahead, the fierce rapids, or the spirit-haunted depths of 'Tschgumi.

For that first day and most of a second, the Minnisabik led the people in eccentric patterns through grassy savannahs bordered by cedar and tamarack swamps. Sometimes the river veered toward the hills, cutting so close to them that one bank became steep and stony. Again it would swing out into the marshland or bend back on itself sharply. Canoes a mile apart by water might pass each other at a distance of a few yards across the bog. It was quicker and easier to stay on the river than to portage across those strips of swamp.

Muskrats cut the surface to get out of the way, leaving V-shaped wakes on the still water. Worried coots swam in front of Otter Woman, heads jerking back and forth, until they could make up their minds either to take off in foot-slapping flight or to daringly double back upstream and watch the canoes go by. Squawking mallards rocketed up from the flooded grassland on both sides. Several times moose lifted their heads from feeding below the surface, stems and vegetation dangling from their mouths. There was no thought of shooting now. Small meat and fish would be taken near that night's camp.

After two days the party left the Minnisabik and followed a tributary that came in from the east. Broad at first, it quickly dwindled. In the stretches of good paddling Iron Feather was always watching the surface ahead, alert for current movements or other indications of the shifting channel. At some points the passages were just wide enough for a canoe, having been kept open, through the years, by repeated use. In the shallows the people waded, dragged the boats, joked about the discomfort of the cold water and laughed uproariously when anyone suddenly sank, clutching a gunwale hard to keep from going farther down into the mud.

Beaver dams helped, rather than hindered, the upstream progress. The canoes were swiftly unloaded, lifted over, and reloaded. Above each dam there was deep water and good paddling for a while. A series of these ponded plateaus was ascended without much effort.

Iron Feather stopped for the night at an old camp ground. A trail led up from the river into stony ridges covered with a tattered garment of earth that had been torn away, in places, to reveal cliffs, ledges, and bald, mountainous summits. This was the height of land. The water behind it flowed into the northern sea. Ahead the rivers ran into 'Tschgumi and the eastern ocean.

The route in this descending journey would be complicated by new obstacles. The edges of the great stone shield were being penetrated by railroad construction and logging operations, closely followed by settlements. Farmers were already trying, with more courage than sucess, to break the rocky pockets of earth as they had broken broader and softer fields to the south.

Iron Feather had come to believe that it was best to avoid these occupied areas, or to pass through them without stopping when there was no way around. He planned his route to bring his people to the white man that they needed, and to avoid, as far as possible, any contact with the others.

In the morning Iron Feather lashed two paddles to the thwarts of his canoe with blades close together at the center crossbar. He lifted the hull so that its rounded surface rested against his thighs, then swung it up and over with a simultaneous lift on the thwart and a boost with one knee, settling the blades on his shoulders. One hand ran out along the gunwale to steady it at an angle that allowed him to see ahead. With the canoe thus balanced, bottom up, he walked quickly up the path. Behind him, Shanod was helping the mother get her burdens on her back.

16

The flower moon was waning, but still hung slender in the brightening sky. The rain had stopped. The air smelled of new leaves, moist earth and cool, wet stone. The snow was almost gone. Coming down the trail from the divide, Iron Feather could see a few white patches through the tree trunks, but only in shaded gullies. At the lake's edge, he eased the canoe down off his shoulders and turned to lift the upper pack and box from Otter Woman's bent back.

She straightened up and lowered her tump-bound lower bundle into the boat. For a moment they stood together looking down the expanse of blue, ice-free water. Then, at the sound of He-Rises' inverted canoe being brushed and tapped by overhead branches, they took their places and paddled swiftly out on the morning-smooth surface. The others followed in an irregular line.

The hills stood steep on both sides, dark with spruce except for an occasional strip of granite where stone, earth, and trees had fallen away. At one point the canoes skimmed, as though suspended, under a precipice that rose a hundred feet above them and plunged straight down into clear depths as far as the eye could follow.

A rugged peninsula reached out to turn their course. Its pines had been so harassed by the prevailing winds that they all sloped in the same direction. As Iron Feather passed its tip, he veered sharply, running along the side of an inch-deep reef until he came to a remembered groove. It was too shallow for paddling but they poled across, reversing their paddles so as not to risk cracking the blades. A little later Iron Feather saved strokes by leading them through a narrow passage between house-size rocks tumbled into the lake from the overhang of another mountainous point.

It was raining again when they reached the end of the lake. The outlet was not deep enough to float the canoes but the portage was floored with rock and gravel, firm footing no matter how wet.

The travellers were moving steadily across the great shield now, and on the downhill grade from the divide south and east toward 'Tschgumi. The stream connecting this chain of lakes was growing so that they could usually paddle or wade the canoes through it without a carry. The lakes were of all shapes and sizes from little round ponds to many-legged, fifty-mile bodies of water. Clean, cold water that a paddler could drink by lifting his blade and tilting the drip into his mouth.

On sunny days the wind was usually from the northwest. Then the people stretched blankets between birch saplings. The woman in the bow would hold the two poles upright and they would sail swiftly down the open stretches, running with the waves, she and the stern paddler both alert for some big one that might come sneaking up from behind to surge over the gunwale.

Very seldom did they allow themselves to be kept ashore by weather on any of these inland lakes. Even when cold winds rushed down from the northeast, turning the water dark and cutting at the travellers with sheets of rain, they kept going. Iron Feather took what shelter he could find behind points and islands, looking ahead, figuring the angle and the strength of the wind, fighting across wave-hammered open water only when there was no other way.

On these exposed stretches the canoes labored in gray seas. The hulls were rocked, bow up and then stern, passing over the combers. Chilled, soaked children looked out from under the rags and pieces of hide in which their mothers had wrapped them and clung to the thwarts as they huddled, between the packs and bundles, with chilled, soaked dogs.

But the men and women were experts with the paddle. They could take their few possessions and their small families over this kind of water without much risk. And at the end of each storm-tossed day there was the luxury of hearing the rain drum harmlessly on the bark overhead and the happy surprise of being warm again, with hands and feet extended to a crackling driftwood fire. The soaking and pounding of the daylight hours never seemed to seriously damage anybody.

They left the high country on a fast-flowing river that sometimes

broadened out into island-studded lakes, but more often plunged down between constricting rock walls into rapids that continued for many miles at a stretch.

A man might venture his life and the lives of his family in rough water rather than accept a delay that would shorten the time for the fish, rice, or meat harvest, and so expose them all to the greater danger of famine. Each such risk was carefully calculated. Iron Feather knew what could and could not be done with poles and paddles. He knew the rivers and their ever-changing rapids, which varied from day to day and from hour to hour according to the volume of the flow.

These waters could be read in many ways — by the roar that might carry for miles upstream, by the condition of the river banks, by the mist rising against the trees below, by the color of the water, by the interweaving of surface currents and by the behavior of water birds. And also, perhaps, by the pull of the current as felt through the moccasins of a standing steersman, or by some other subtle signals, forgotten now, but clearly recognized then.

As Iron Feather approached each strong rapid, he rose to his feet, looking, thinking, remembering. The people rested, with paddles ready, watching his actions. If he turned his canoe toward the portage, the others followed.

If his choice was to run the rapids, the paddles flashed. With heavily loaded canoes it was necessary to build up speed greater than that of the current in order to control the steering. Otter Woman paddled hard, but at the same time watched for fast-charging rocks and looked farther ahead for the dips, humps, and swirls that came to the surface downstream from underwater boulders. At the right moment she reached out with her blade, deftly pushing or pulling the bow to right or left. For the course immediately ahead, she had become the steersman.

There was no communication by words. The water was too loud for that, and the time for response too short. Iron Feather, watching his wife's movements, swung the stern to follow her, keeping the canoe in line with the shifting rush of the current. At the same time he was holding the general course down the main chute, marked by high, stationary waves.

The others followed at spaced intervals, each crew alert to the danger, each determined to bring their boat safely through. Flying spray, white mounds of water, black rocks, and sheer escarpments hurtled past. Then suddenly the roaring river was quiet. One by one the canoes shot out into the dark, foam-flecked pool at the foot of the rapid. Several of them had shipped water and had to be bailed out, but all were soon moving downstream again. There would be worse to come.

In another rapid, Otter Woman saw a smooth horizontal break running across the surface ahead, outlined against a background of mist, where the river poured over a ledge in a low waterfall. She stopped paddling and turned, rearranging the cargo, shifting the weight toward the stern, then climbed back across the thwart and settled herself behind it. She and Iron Feather dug with their paddles. They shot across the danger-line at a low point where a notch in the flat rock allowed the greatest flow. Their speed carried them over the drop and through the white wave that rolled back below it.

He-Rises and Sturgeon Man came next, plunging their blades deep to find solid water in the frothing mass. Smoke Drifting's face, looking over the gunwale, jerked as they leveled out beneath the fall, disappeared in the spray, then showed again, wide-eyed and dripping. This was another part of her schooling. The others followed the same passage without mishap.

Loon's Foot and Red Sky came last, in the covering position, ready to help anyone who might be in trouble. Otter Woman and Iron Feather worked in silence and so did most of those who followed them. But Loon's Foot whooped triumphantly as he dodged each roaring menace.

In a particularly rough stretch, Dawn Sailing's failing eyes misjudged the depth of a submerged rock. She felt the bottom of the boat rise beneath her as it caught and ground on ragged granite.

Almost instantly her leg went over the gunwale. The canoe, in spite of Toenail's efforts, was swinging toward a dangerously broadside position. Dawn Sailing shoved with her foot and lifted, hoisting the hull clear, then reached out with her paddle to pull the bow back into line with the current. She felt water seeping in beneath her, but slowly, not a threatening rush. Cedar and birch bark are tougher than they look.

That evening, camp was made on a moss-covered ledge overlooking a pool at the foot of a rapid. He-Rises reached into the bow of his canoe and drew out a trolling line, a cord wrapped lengthwise around a flat piece of wood. He walked out on a scattering of rocks that extended into the river. Standing on the outermost of these, he carefully coiled the line in a circle on the stone at his feet. Then he swung the bright spoon at its end around his head and let it fly out over the water.

Smoke Drifting and Madeyn, watching from the shore, saw the

line tighten. They ran out, jumping from stone to stone until Smoke Drifting stood beside her brother. Madeyn was balancing on a long, narrow boulder closer to the bank.

First the white tips of fins showed through the dark water and then the metallic glint of golden scales. A heavy, round-bodied fish was struggling at the end of the line.

As He-Rises hoisted it out, Smoke Drifting caught it behind the gills, careful to keep her hand away from the sharp points of the fin along its spine. Holding tight to her violently flopping prey, she slipped the hook from its mouth and ran back, jumping from boulder to boulder, and up to the level where Shanod was waiting with a knife. Madeyn, braver now, had taken her place beside the fisherman.

More walleyes came up over the same route, carried first by one girl and then the other, from the river to the fire, where a bed of coals was beginning to glow. Loon's Foot had raked out one of these, and was applying it, in a split stick, to a wad of spruce gum. He pushed the heat-softened stuff with his thumb in along the leak in his mother's canoe. When he had finished this repair, the fish and the coals were ready for each other.

Next day there were more rapids, and steeper. The intervals of navigable water became too short to make loading and unloading worth while. Where the trees and brush did not crowd the water too closely, the canoes could be lined down. Women and children carried

as much as they could over the portages to lighten the cargo. The men worked along the bank holding the canoes with thin ropes against the pull of the current, easing them down the foaming passages.

Often the men had to scramble over glacier-rounded, slime-slippery boulders, and wade through icy water. Sometimes they fell, soaking and bruising their bodies but always clinging to the lines. When the power of the river became overwhelming they would snub the rope from one tree to another, being careful not to check the momentum of the canoe too suddenly. In a strong rapid there had to be a man with a pole in the canoe, and the jolt of a sudden stop could capsize it or throw him into the water.

Loon's Foot seemed to prefer this position of danger. He would guide the heavily loaded canoes one at a time down a bad rapid, fending off aggressive rocks with a pole and signalling instructions to the men that held the lines. After each run he would trot back to the upper portage landing where the next boat would be roped and ready. He accepted the risk as the others accepted the punishment of the bank work. Some joked, some laughed and some were silent. Nobody complained.

As the drop from the shield steepened, the river passed into a series of walled cascades that made lining impossible. The people spent most of a day carrying packs and canoes down a trail so old that it had been worn through the moss and into the granite by many moccasins.

The forest was warming now. The rains had ended, but the path was still soggy where it left the rocks. Poles had been laid down to serve as bridges over the swampy places. Here the warrior women of the mosquito tribe attacked with kill-song and sharp lances. But it was not really bad going except when someone slipped off a pole and had to flounder, full-burdened, through mud and merriment to solid ground.

Madeyn was finding it all delightfully funny. She had fully recovered from the long hunger of last spring, and was carrying almost as heavy a load as Smoke Drifting. The girls trotted across the portage with little shouts to each other and much laughter.

For Dawn Sailing it was not that much fun. Downhill travel may be harder than uphill for people with arthritic legs. She was sitting on a boulder, her tump line slack, the weight of the pack resting on the flat stone, when He-Rises, returning from downstream, paused beside her.

"I hear you breathing, grandmother. I think that you have been carrying too much weight or moving too fast. I have only a small load to carry from the upper landing. Leave the pack here. I will take it with mine on the way back."

The last portage brought them down to the river again, still several winding miles above 'Tschgumi. But as soon as they were afloat they could feel themselves being lifted and lowered by long, wind-built swells rolling up from the lake.

17

The smell of wood smoke, carried by the lake breeze, came drifting over the river, and the travellers heard a dog barking. Rounding the last bend, they saw swimmers in the water, canoes on the sand beach and nets spread to dry. Beyond, the warm brown of wigwams showed through the trees, then the bright dresses of the women as people came running down to the shore.

A sandbar stretched almost across the river's mouth and formed a lagoon that was sheltered from the lake's winds by rock ridges along both banks and by a stand of pines on the bar. The trading post stood at the base of this point on clear sand carpeted with needles. A large cabin of squared timbers, with a bark roof and a stone chimney, was the store and office. It was also the residence of Jamieson, the Saganash trader, and Willow Woman, his Anishinabe wife.

Another log building served as a warehouse. Farther inland and a little back from the beach were a cluster of waginogans and two small cabins. The Jamieson in-laws and several other Indian families lived here the year 'round. They served as retainers, bringing in fish, game, berries and firewood, and doing a little trapping on their own. The number of lodges was increasing as people came in from the hunting and sugar camps. In the summer season, sharing of lodge space was not necessary. Many incoming families would erect their own wigwams.

Several canoes were pushing out to greet the newcomers. After the hard winter, this was a moment of hope and of worry. As the boats neared the beach everyone was searching for the faces of old friends. The first questions called across the water were about those missing. Shanod was relieved to learn that Ice Stone was not present. She felt certain that he had survived, but maybe he would not come to the gathering this summer.

The exchange of news went on while many willing hands carried up the packs and bales. Wood-that-Sizzles-in-the-Fire, a brother of Willow Woman, had waded out to meet his friend Toenail and to help get the canoes out of the water. While the newcomers spread bark coverings over the lodge frames, the resident women prepared dinner for all.

Next morning at the store, Jamieson opened negotiations with gifts: a plug of tobacco and a dram of brandy to each of the men. The drink was refused by Iron Feather, and, under his stern gaze, by He-Rises. Tamarack took a cautious sip, and sputtered a little. Strange taste. Burning, incredibly vile, but somehow very good too. He took another. Sturgeon Man downed his at a gulp and so did Loon's Foot.

In earlier times, when the traders had been battling each other for beaver, a flood of rum brought ruin to the people. Iron Feather could remember the terror of one of those orgies.

As soon as the drinking had started his mother hustled him and his brother into the woods. It was as though the Abwaneg were attacking, but with a difference — the women were carrying the weapons. They gathered up guns, knives, axes, ice chisels and anything else that they thought one man might use to injure another. These were bundled into the bush and hidden.

When the revels ended, the families came cautiously back along the trail into the village. In the red glow of the dying fires, Iron Feather could see men lying about in strange positions as though they had fought to the last and gone down under overwhelming enemy numbers.

His mother stopped with a frightened little cry, then bent over a fallen figure. Coming from behind her skirt, the boy saw his father sprawled, face down, with a great split in the scalp showing through long, blood-matted hair. A broken paddle lay beside him.

At that moment, Dawn Sailing came running up, followed by little Loon's Foot. Her husband, The Turtle, drank only moderately. After some minor scuffles, he had retired to his wigwam, where his other wives had found him safe and snoring. They were tending him and putting the lodge back in order.

Dawn Sailing cleaned Sturgeon Man's gashed head, pulled the spreading edges of skin together, and stitched them with fine pieces of sinew. Sturgeon Man's wife knelt opposite her, saying nothing but watching closely, ready to protect the patient from any action that she considered harmful.

For some reason that the young Iron Feather did not understand, his mother had never been friendly toward the medicine woman. She always called her "the 'Bwan" and had spoken bitterly of certain cases where her healing had failed.

But, as the operation proceded, Iron Feather's mother was silent. Sturgeon Man's eyes opened when the sewing began. He said something that they could not understand, but lay still until the work was completed. Then, with his wife supporting him on one side and Dawn Sailing on the other, he was able to get to his feet and walk to the family lodge.

The wound healed quickly. The wife accompanied Sturgeon Man to the medicine woman's wigwam and observed the removal of the stitches as closely and quietly as she had the sewing.

Next year at the same location, Sturgeon Man found that the manager had taken it upon himself to restrict the drinking. He put his furs and his family back into the canoe and freighted them over the lakes and rivers to a distant but more accomodating post. Many of the other men did the same.

The situation was not that wild and wasteful any more. The reduced competition, the urging of respected Indians, and the self-interest of the traders limited the free booze to a round or two at the opening of a session. But a man could still get as much liquor as his pelts would buy.

While Iron Feather's people were bringing in the bales, several men and one of the women who had completed their trading were already "drinking their rats" — spending a considerable part of their fur credit for liquor.

Loon's Foot would join them when his share had been determined. The childhood experiences of drunken orgies had not affected him.

Iron Feather cut the bindings from bark-covered bales. Beaver, otter, muskrat, marten, ermine, lynx, wolf and one wolverine were spread out on the counter, and, when there was no room for more there, on the floor. Jamieson inspected, measured and recorded each. The two men had been doing business with each other for a good many years, and each had a cautious confidence in the other.

111

Iron Feather had never been able to free himself from the old Indian attitude toward trade — that dickering and hard bargaining were beneath a man's dignity. He preferred to act as though the furs and trade goods were just gifts exchanged between friends.

Otter Woman was not hampered by a need for maintaining such decorum. As soon as the serious trading began, she got up from the floor where she had been sitting with Dawn Sailing and Red Sky, and joined the discussion.

In an earlier period, this rather brazen interruption might have angered either the husband or the trader. Now it was accepted calmly by both. Anishinabe women had become conscious of the value of the furs and of the importance, to themselves and their families, of making sure that full value was received in exchange.

With Iron Feather standing silently by, his wife took over the negotiations. She remembered exactly the amounts they owed the house from the previous year. When, at one point, the post books did not agree with her recollection, the trader checked his account and found an error.

Otter Woman went through the prices inexorably, making certain that full credit was allowed for each class of fur. The pelts had been well prepared, with all the fat and flesh carefully scraped away. Jamieson found few flaws in them, but he had to fully explain and justify even the smallest deduction.

The transaction took a long time. When it was completed, Iron Feather and Otter Woman proceeded with the selection of articles to be taken in exchange. They replenished their supply of flour, oatmeal, tea, lard, rope, and fishhooks. Otter Woman, with Shanod as adviser, chose among bolts of serge and broadcloth, and selected ribbons, coarse wool stockings, thread, twine for nets, snare wire, an awl, a comb, a very small mirror, a new teakettle, and two heavy blankets. Shanod took a red woolen skirt. A few items, important for the cold season, would be too heavy or too perishable to carry through the summer's travels. These, including the winter's supply of ammunition, would be picked up later at a different trading post south of the rice country.

The shopping brought out some differences of opinion. Shanod leaned over the counter, fingering, without enthusiasm, Otter Woman's selection of beads.

"Oh my mother, nobody but bush-Indians is wearing such big awkward things any more. Those are as round and dull as moose droppings and as old-fashioned as quill work. Here, look at these new small beads of glass. See how the light shines through them!"

A never-ending succession of marvelous things were passing before Tamarack's wide eyes. The traders that he had seen had been Indian middlemen who carried only a limited supply of goods on their toboggans or in their canoes. Now he could hardly believe that such beautiful and useful articles existed. And there were other lessons for him to learn here in the white man's house.

From a display of pocket knives he selected one, opened and closed the blade several times, blew on it, tried its edge on his thumb, and found it good. He took a leather pouch from his belt, untied it and dropped the knife into it. Although this was done openly, the trader did not observe it. But Shanod did.

"Put it back! If you want it you must give skins for it."

"But see how many there are. He could never use them all. Surely he will not mind my taking one of them."

"That is not the Saganash way. He does not share the things he owns with us. They do not even share with each other, no matter how much one of them has, or how little another. If you want anything you must give skins for it."

Tamarack took out the knife, stared at it, and put it back with the others.

He did have skins, though, from the beaver hunt. When these had been laid out and sorted he got the knife and other beautiful articles. And he got still further knowledge of the white man's unusual, and sometimes savage, customs.

Slyly, carefully, taking advantage of the general concentration on commerce, one of the trader's children reached into a jar of hard candy. It was the extremity of her caution that brought downfall. She was watching her father so intently that her unseeing manipulation moved the jar to the edge of the shelf and over.

There was a crash as glass and candy spread across the floor. The trader seized the cowering girl and fetched her a swift, sharp spank. She went bawling off to be comforted by her mother while he turned back to his customers as though nothing had happened.

Tamarack was visibly shocked. He watched the incident in silence but when they had left the building he spoke to Shanod.

"A man strikes his enemies, but not his own child!"

"Whites hit children easily. Even when they are sober. They also hit their companions. I saw two of them quarrel about a piece of paper. First they spoke loud words. One of them said that the other was the son of a dog. A female dog. Of course that could not be true. But immediately that it was said, they began to strike at each other like madmen or drunks.

"After a time, for some reason that I could not understand, they stopped fighting. Neither of them had killed or badly wounded the other. They just stopped. And the next morning they were friends again."

Tamarack took a few minutes to consider that story and to try to understand its meaning.

"Maybe you heard that one speak true. Maybe they are related to dogs. They are indeed hairy and they have a strange smell. Like dogs, they will fight rather than share with each other. And that man's nose, today, did resemble the muzzle of a dog.

"Still, it is foolish to say that the mother of one of them is a dog. We know that humans are related to bears. We have a Bear Mother, but she is far in the past. It may well be that a light-skinned woman mated with a dog and became the Saganash ancestress. But such a Dog Mother is surely more than one life back.

"In any case, they are unusual people. But so are you Anishinabeg. You have fitted yourselves to their customs. In some ways you are becoming like them. That is a good thing, I suppose. But I do not understand how it has happened.

"I would like to know more about such people. And about the 'Bwaneg, too, who made war on my grandfathers before yours came in between them. I would like to know more about all of the strange people of the south."

"Then let us go and talk to the old ones," said Shanod. "Later I will take you to Jamieson's wife. She knows all about white men, of course, and she has been to the other side of 'Tschgumi."

18

Shanod, followed by Tamarack, came out on an opening in the tall pines overlooking the river mouth. Dawn Sailing and Sturgeon Man were sitting in this spot where the late afternoon sun came slanting in to warm the earth. The air was rich with the aromatic scent of resin. Shanod sat down on a springy brown carpet of needles.

"This man wants to know more about us strange people of the south. I think that you can answer many of his questions."

"I had not seen a white man before today," said Tamarack. "This one gave us many fine things for a few animal skins. You must have been happy, grandfather, when the first of them came."

"I was not yet born when the first of them came and neither was my grandfather. But I have heard that the ancestors lived better before. The animals were their friends. They talked together and were good to each other. The Anishinabeg were given the meat and furs they needed."

"But not always so easily, surely?"

"Not always. In winters when the people had become too many and the deer too few, some people had to die. Mostly the old and the weak. When the deer are too many, they have to die too. That is when the wolves are good to them. Especially to the old and the weak. It is the same with all living things. The lynx kills the wabooz, but they are not really enemies. They need each other."

"Could not the Indians deal better with those hard winters when they got guns and steel traps?"

"Much better, for a while. The people could get meat any time they wanted it. They ate several meals each day and increased in fatness and in numbers. They never could catch as much beaver as the traders wanted, but they killed many.

"After a while the moose were gone and the deer had become scarce, so we lived on white man food. It didn't taste as good as wild meat but there was plenty of it. When my father brought a bale of beaver pelts to the trading post he was given as much beans and flour as we could eat in a winter. But that is enough for me to say. Now you talk for a while."

"No grandfather, I want to hear more about those times. It seems to me that you must have needed the Saganash then more than ever."

"We did. But the time came when they no longer needed us. Because they stopped loving beaver. They wouldn't give much for even the finest fur. They went away from their post at our lake. The logs rotted and the roof fell in, but they never came back.

"After that there was only one post, a long way off. The trader there didn't seem to care whether we brought fur to him or not. No more one company trying to get the Indians away from the other. No more food and powder handed to us in autumn to be paid for in spring pelts. We had to lay the furs on the counter before they would give us anything, and a canoe-load would buy only a little food with nothing left over for traps and ammunition.

"We turned back to the bow, the snare, and the deadfall. We weren't so good with those things any more. But most of the meat animals were gone anyway. There seemed to be nothing to do but die.

"And there were new ways to do that. Now there were the spotted sickness and the coughing sickness and other sicknesses that the ancestors had never known. These killed many of us even when we were well fed, but they became much worse when the meat and the white man food were both gone.

"We believed that Pauguk would take us all and leave an empty forest. We didn't want to meet that old fellow then any more than people do now. But we learned that he is not always bad or useless. He stopped before everyone was dead. He stopped when he had brought people and animals into the right numbers so that they could live together again. With so few Indians left alive to hunt, the moose and deer began to come back to us.

"When men are starving they hunt meat, not fur. And those skins that we took, we wore. It was better to spend the time hunting than to carry pelts so far away for the few things that the whites would give for them.

"After some years the traders began to want furs again. Not so many as before. They said that they didn't need much beaver any more because their hats were being woven by worms. But they wanted some beaver and now they wanted other furs too. They would give more powder and shot and food for each skin than they had been giving us. And they would let us have these things in the fall again, so that we could trap in the winter and bring them the furs in the spring.

"A good hunter had a chance then. But only a chance. It took a lot of country to feed a family. If too many people came into any hunting ground there would not be enough meat for them all. They might get by for a year or two, or for several if they were lucky. Then would come a bad winter. The snow would be too deep to get at the beaver, or too crusty and noisy to stalk deer. Or the animals might just not be there.

"But that is how it is now, and I am telling you what you already know."

"Yes, I see how all of those things could have come about. Except the part about the worms making hats. Perhaps they meant that they used worms instead of beaver. But who would want to wear worm skins on his head!"

He turned to Dawn Sailing.

"And you, grandmother. You have lived in the west and in the east. Did it hurt your 'Bwan people when whites no longer wanted beaver?"

"When I lived in the west we always had the buffalo. We liked what the traders brought us, but we could get along without them. Before they stopped buying beaver, this man here, and his friends, visited us and persuaded me to join the Anishinabeg."

"That wasn't so hard," said Sturgeon Man. "We coaxed her with a necklace. A rawhide necklace. She couldn't resist it."

She threw a pine cone that bounced off his head. He ducked and hunched up his shoulders. Then she grew serious.

"I have gone back, though. Three times I have traveled west with Loon's Foot to visit my other relatives.

"My people were lucky. They lived north, near the medicine line, and just beyond the forest. So they did not fight the Saganashag. But they told me about the troubles of the southern and western Dakota. That was our real name, not 'Bwaneg.

119

"South in the M'nsota River country, the Americans moved in, wiped out the game and ploughed the earth. They stopped giving the food that they had promised to the Dakota.

"They should have known that warriors, still armed and mounted, would not starve to death patiently in that fat land. The Dakota rose against the whites and killed many. But the blue-coat soldiers and the wagon-guns overcame them. Some were hung with ropes around their necks. That is a bad death. Like drowning, it prevents the escape of the spirit. Others got away into the western mountains.

"The soldiers followed, attacking their camps. The men fought them and drove them off, again killing many. But the hide hunters were shooting the buffalo. They had no respect for animals and left the meat to rot. When the buffalo were gone the Dakota had no food. In the end, those that were still living gave up their horses and guns and came in to the reservations. And so did my relatives, even though they had not been in the wars."

"With us, there was nothing to fight about," said Sturgeon Man. "You don't fight somebody for leaving you. Not after he's left, anyway."

He kicked thoughtfully at the curve of a boulder that bulged up out of the moss and pine needles.

"I think that it will be a long time before the Saganashag plough this earth."

Willow Jamieson was washing the supper dishes with her back to the door, unaware that guests had entered. They stood watching her, not speaking. Even Shanod was still somewhat in awe of all this efficient splendor — the clay fireplace that drew every wisp of smoke up and away from the room, the log walls hung with shining pans and utensils, the glass window, the heavy pine table and benches, the rows of dishes and supplies standing in clean, proud, orderly obedience on wooden shelves.

When Willow Woman turned to get the drying cloth she discovered her visitors and instantly became the welcoming hostess. She insisted that they sit at the table, overcoming Tamarack's cautious reluctance to insert himself into the narrow space. She poured coffee for them and for herself.

Shanod knew it as the black medicine drink, but Tamarack had never seen it before. He sat staring into the dark liquid. Then he looked up.

"I have no more skins."

"And you need give me none. This is a small gift, like the cup of brandy. But that was in the office. In this room there is no trading."

Willow Woman spoke pleasantly of the good beaver hunt that Iron Feather's band had accomplished during the spring, as evidenced by the volume and quality of the furs. Then she began to inform Shanod of certain personal and interesting events that had taken place, or had been said to have taken place, in the village.

Tamarack, watching the sophisticated ladies, was trying, slowly and carefully, to do as they had done. He spooned sugar into his coffee, tasted it, and liked the taste. He put in more sugar, stirred it, and was amazed to see how little the level of the liquid rose. And now it tasted even better. He continued sweetening and stirring until Shanod noticed what was going on.

"Stop pouring sugar now. You are expected to leave a little in the bowl."

Willow Woman smiled.

"When I was at Chequamegon, the missionary's wife invited six of us to come into her house. We sat on the floor and I was the first in the line. She passed me a plate of little cakes. I emptied the cakes into my bag and handed the plate back to her."

She laughed. Then, getting no response from Shanod or Tamarack, she went on to explain.

"I could see that I had done something wrong. The white woman looked sad and her chin drooped so that her mouth hung open. I did not learn why until later. The cakes were not a gift to me alone. She expected me to take one and pass the rest on to the other women. But a person cannot understand such customs until she is told about them. There is plenty of sugar, Tamarack. Here, I will fill the bowl again."

"Your drink is sweet and good, my sister. It might be better if it were even sweeter, but now I am interested in hearing of these customs that you speak of. The ways of the people who live on the other side of 'Tschgumi. Will you tell us more?"

Willow Woman had traveled with her husband, by sailing ship and steamboat, to the settlements at both ends of the lake, and to trading posts on the south shore. She told about the Indians who lived in those warm latitudes.

"Are they Anishinabeg?"

"Yes, but they are different from us. Much of the country is flat there, with dark earth under foot instead of rock, gravel or swamp. They dig this earth and put big seeds into it. Strange plants grow up from these: corn, taller than a man, with ears of rich, sweet yellow grain, and squash, that runs a long way across the earth on looped vines and makes big, round fruit. And other vines that produce beans, small, but nourishing as meat. All these they dry in the sun, and store.

"Did they learn this from the Saganashag?"

"No, these plants they have always grown. But every summer a white man comes and gives them round pieces of metal. These are called money. They can trade them for anything they want.

"They don't have to move across the country as Indians do here. They live in villages and only go away for small distances and short times to the hunting grounds, the sugar bush and the rice lakes. And even in winter they are hardly ever hungry."

Tamarack set down his cup.

"This money that you speak of — is it a little gift — like the black medicine, offered without asking skins in return?"

"No skins, but the Anishinabeg have given land for it. All the land, except the places where they live. Those are called reservations, on the other side of 'Tschgumi. On this side they are reserves."

Tamarack had finished his coffee. There was a good deal of soaked sugar left at the bottom. He scooped that out with the spoon, wiped out what stuck to the cup with his fingers, and licked them. Nothing was wasted. But as he cleaned the cup he was thinking about Willow Woman's words.

"I don't understand. How can people give land in return for money? The land does not belong to them. They are just using it for a little while. The ancestors are part of it and so are those who will be born in the future. And the trees and the winds and the animals. They are all part of it."

"The ancestors and the animals get no money, but those other people will be paid after they are born."

"Did the Anishinabeg fight the Shaganashag and kill many of them, as the 'Bwaneg did, before coming to the reservations?"

"Our people have never killed whites during the times that living men remember. A few, in robberies or private quarrels, but no more than the white men kill of each other. Not even that many.

"If they had fought the blue soldiers, those that were not shot to death or hanged would be living on crowded reservations now, far away from their own country, and eating wormy biscuits and moldy salt pork. But the southern Anishinabeg live a good life. They no longer have to fight the 'Bwaneg and they don't work very hard."

She took a bark box from a shelf and set it on the table. It was rectangular in shape with vertical sides, not slanted in to a rounded rim as were the makaks of the north. The square-cornered cover was fitted perfectly. Sides and cover were beaded with gracefuly curved floral designs.

"Because they do not have to paddle or work all day the women have time to make things like this. They give these also to the whites in exchange for money."

"It is a beautiful makak," said Shanod. "I wish I could do beadwork like that. It makes ours look so plain."

"I like your plain beadwork," said Tamarack. "I like your rock, gravel, and swamp. You can't grow corn on them but neither can the Saganashag. I have come a long way south and this is good. But I have no wish to go farther."

19

Shanod looked back at Tamarack and turned away from the path to the village.

"Come, I will show you 'Tschgumi."

They walked past low-spreading juniper, and down over the sand dunes, through grasses and vines to the outer beach. The water was a pale blue-green that darkened toward the curve of the horizon. It looked as boundless as the eastern ocean of the grandfather's tales. There was no wind, but they could hear the lake moaning a little as it gently rose and dropped back across a narrow strip of wet sand.

Off to one side a pair of loons cruised — silent now, fishing, not calling. First one and then the other disappeared, leaving the sweep of the bay empty. Then they bobbed up to the surface.

Broad water brings far-reaching thoughts. Standing on this shore in the slow summer evening, Tamarack was aware of a man's unimportance. At the same time, he felt at peace with the world. The misfortunes of those rich people on the other side no longer troubled him.

And tonight, Shanod was bold.

"I'm going up the rock. Come if you think that you can climb it."

At the end of the beach a steep stone outcropping rose out of the sand. She had clambered up its forbidding face when she was a child and many times since. Now her hands and feet remembered where to find the finger- and toe-holds.

She climbed easily to a ledge and then up a slanting granite face. Just below her, his eyes close to her ankles, smelling the warm fragrance of sweat in freshly-washed calico, Tamarack felt the love magic working strongly. His hand reached up, almost without his permission, and caressed her moving buttocks, then pressed to feel the lovely, sliding action under thin cloth. She turned and smiled down at him.

When she reached a little hollow in the rocks she pulled out a dead stump, and tossed it aside. They sank into the moss together. The cries of the wheeling gulls did not disturb them. Ice Stone and Undertooth were forgotten.

Much later, walking over the beach again in the pine-scented night, they could hear drumming and a dance chant. Tamarack's great happiness was tempered, with feelings of guilt, but not for having abused Otter Woman's hospitality. Nor with any fear of revenge or sorcery. He had lain with a breast-feeding woman.

The old taboo was strong among his tribespeople of the northern swamps, an effective, if unwitting, measure for population control in a society where children were often nursed up to the ages of four or five years.

Shanod, too, was somewhat less joyful, less at ease, than the act of love should have left her. She had not intended to allow it to happen. Not, at least, until they were safely away from this village by the trading post. She stopped walking and grasped Tamarack's arm.

"Ice Stone is not yet here. He may not come at all this summer. But if he does come, do not fight with him, no matter what he says to you. Or to me. He would kill you."

"I have never seen Ice Stone," said Tamarack, "and I neither love him nor hate him, but I am sorry for him. I would not blame him if he should speak to me in anger for what he has lost and I have gained.

"I do not know whether he could kill me. I would not want that to happen, of course. So I will not fight with him."

As they came into the village the drumming had ended and the people were leaving the dance ground. Two old women eyed the guilty couple with unconcealed suspicion. They did not shout after Shanod as they might have done in a more virtuous age, but their mouths swung into strong and indignant action as soon as she was out of hearing.

In Otter Woman's wigwam, Shanod gathered up Tamarack's sleeping robes, carried them across the center space, and laid them beside her own. There had been no bride-gifts, no asking for parental approval, no marriage feast. But it was understood that she was now his wife. Tamarack had already come to be considered a member of the family, and the others welcomed this closer tie.

Love sprouted, bloomed and withered in the village as unaccountably as it does in every other place where there are men and women. But the Anishinabe wife had a greater measure of independence than either the Abwan woman of the plains or the white lady in the settlements. The forest dwelling belonged to her, and that made the difference.

During the early years of their marriage, Red Sky had accepted the fact that Loon's Foot could not be counted upon to bring in enough fur to meet the family's needs at the trading post. She had taken over much of the trapping, and had become quite expert at this difficult and demanding occupation. She had accustomed herself to letting her woman's work wait while she was following the traplines through the forest and over the frozen swampland.

The gossips thought that she probably scolded Loon's Foot fiercely for spending the credit from her furs on drink. If so, her rage must have been expressed quietly because none of them could say that they had heard her. And it had certainly not been effective.

In past years his drunkeness had been of the jovial variety, but this summer it had turned mean. He would speak loudly to his wife, like a white man. He began to break things around the lodge.

Such noisy words and actions could not be concealed from the neighbors. There was much talk, but only Iron Feather spoke to Loon's Foot about the matter. He did so in an indirect way, reminding him of the widely held opinion that men who abused their women usually died young. He named several specific cases, and Loon's Foot was both ashamed and frightened. For a week he stayed away from liquor.

Then one evening he came staggering home in a fog of brandy fumes. His usually merry face was twisted by unreasoning anger. Now he was more the white man than ever. He shouted at his wife and pushed her, then doubled up his hand to make a fist and struck her hard in the mouth.

Her head snapped back and she fell against the wall of the waginogan, shaking and cracking its structure. Her hands closed on one of the horizontal poles. She clung to it, holding herself up, staring, wide-eyed, as Loon's Foot lurched across the center space at her.

Madeyn, terrified, crouched in her place on the floor. But Dawn

Sailing got up, very swiftly for such an old woman, and threw herself at the crazed man, trying to grasp his hands. With the back of one of them he slapped her aside. She fell heavily, then scrambled to her feet and ran wailing out of the wigwam.

People were still standing or squatting outdoors in the twilight. Heads swung to follow her and then turned back to the savage sounds coming from the lodge. But no one moved to interfere. A drunken man might strike out at anyone within his reach but sustained wife beating was still comparatively new in this society. They hadn't yet figured out just what to do about it. The old tradition of minding one's own business prevailed.

Toenail and Wood-that-Sizzles were fishing on the far side of the lagoon. In the quiet evening the grandmother's voice carried across the water, clear in its terror. Quickly they drew in their lines and came paddling hard, leaving a bright wake across the dark reflections of the opposite shore.

Red Sky was lying on the floor, her knees drawn up and her arms around her head. The blows and kicks were beginning to weaken by the time the young men rushed into the lodge. Toenail pushed Loon's Foot back from his mother, while talking to him quietly. Wood-that-Sizzles, an expert wrestler, stood ready to help, but he was not needed. Loon's Foot allowed himself to be eased down into his bedding where he became suddenly very sick.

He slept late into the next morning. Then, without speaking, he left the lodge and did not return for two days. When he did come back he found that his vomit-stained sleeping robes had been washed, dried, wrapped in a neat bundle, and, with his other personal belongings, stacked outside the door. He stood looking down at them for a while, then hoisted them to his back and walked away.

Red Sky had exercised the divorce right of an Anishinabe wife.

20

The bushes above the sand beach had almost disappeared under newly-scrubbed blankets and clothing. The sun-warmed water was alive with shouting, splashing people. Farther out in the lagoon, young men raced from point to point. Others in canoes were endeavoring to upset each other. The children were swinging out over the river on ropes of basswood fiber, and diving from the cliffs upstream.

This was one of those rare and swiftly-passing times when there was no pressing duty, a few days when no great and insistent labor was demanding full-strength effort. The blueberries down the shore were fattening but they had not reached their full black ripeness.

There was plenty of work to be done every day. The lesser berry crops, strawberries and raspberries, were being harvested happily and in profusion, lugged into the village in big red-stained makaks, pressed into thin cakes, and dried in the sun.

Dawn Sailing was busy, as she was at every season except winter, searching for those medicinal plants, seeds, and roots that were ripe, at the moment, for gathering.

Firewood was brought in as needed. Hides were scraped and cured. Nets were repaired, reset, and tended. But there was also a little time now for rest and pleasure, for art and sport.

Otter Woman, Shanod, and Smoke Drifting all took part in the women's game. This rather unladylike event, called squaw hockey by the whites, was distantly related to another Indian sport, lacrosse. Instead of a ball, two chunks of wood, were tied together with a rawhide thong. The object of the game was to carry this flapping, vulnerable thing, on a stick, through flailing opposition and across the

131

goal. Once the "ball" was in play, nothing else in the world mattered except to put it over the unmarked line between the two poles at the adversaries' end of the field.

Whatever primitive ferocity was left, after two hundred years of contact with the white man, came whooping to the surface in the women's game. The swinging sticks left their marks on arms, legs, and faces. Sometimes teeth were knocked out or bones broken. It was all good fun.

Otter Woman starred in the early stages. Those powerful legs drove through all resistance. But after a while she stood, breathing hard, with the mostly male audience, watching her daughters.

Once Smoke Drifting was flung out of a swirling scrimmage to land in a heap at her mother's feet. Rolling, not coming to a full stop, she scrambled up again, stick in hand, and charged back into the crowd, a square-faced, hard-driving miniature of Otter Woman, but with more wind.

Wrestling was the favorite sport among the young men. Sometimes it would be a one-against-one match or a team might struggle against another team, sweating bodies twisting and wrapping around each other like snakes when their hollow stump is broken open in the spring.

Some years before, He-Rises had been thrown hard. So hard that, for several minutes, he could only gasp for breath. No lasting damage had been done to his body, but after that he could not bring himself to take part in the sport. This deficiency had been a source of

unhappiness to him. He had given up trying to overcome it. But he took much satisfaction from his sisters' athletic prowess, and it pleased him when Tamarack began to take an interest in wrestling.

In the Cree's experience there had been no time or opportunity for such play. He tried it now, at He-Rise's urging, and met with some success. He won several matches in succession, and the mother of one of his oppponents began to talk about Muskego magic.

Any such sorcery failed him when he grappled with Wood-that-Sizzles. Each strained against the other, searching for an advantage. Tamarack was the older and heavier. But suddenly he found himself hoisted high, arms and legs waving helplessly. He thought that he would be hurled down. But Wood lowered him gently.

Tamarack looked up laughing.

"You grew quickly tall. I thought that I was at the top of a pine tree. I don't think that anyone in the village could beat you at wrestling."

"No one now in the village. But when Ice Stone comes, I won't challenge him."

"Surely he would not use witchcraft to win a wrestling match?"

"He wouldn't need witchcraft. He is too strong, too quick, and too skillful for any of us here. I am not sure that there is a man anywhere that could overcome him."

The laugh faded out of Tamarack's face.

"You are good twice. You set me down lightly and you warn me

of coming danger. I would not want an unfriend to have me like that over his shoulder."

Tamarack was quiet for the rest of that day. He had begun to think seriously about the possibility of a confrontation with this much-feared rival.

As he walked down the path at evening to watch the moccasin game, Tamarack felt better. Ice Stone might not come at all this summer. And if he did, he would hardly attack a man who quietly avoided any argument. Let dogs and white men fight their own kind about growls and words.

The loss of Red Sky must have been a shock to Loon's Foot, but he showed no signs of depression. He was alert as ever at touch-the-moccasin. This sacred sport, played to the sound of drumming and chanting, was the only religious ceremony in which he took a real interest.

His head was bent forward but Tamarack could see him looking up slyly from under rumpled hair as he manipulated the smooth, round pebble between four moccasins laid out on a blanket.

His opponent was standing, hands gripping a stick, eyes narrowed in tense observation. He was analyzing every hint offered by movement of hand, eye and body, following in his mind the thought and strategy of the concealer, estimating the path of the pebble, on guard against any deceptive feint. It was as much a clash of wills, maybe even of intellects, as a hard-fought chess match.

Spectators crowded around the game to place small bets, lead, tobacco, fishhooks or arrows — on one man or the other. They, too, were watching Loon's Foot closely, basing their wagers on his looks and actions and on their estimates of each player's manidoke.

The stick came down with a smart rap on the sole of one of the moccasins. Loon's Foot smiled as he turned it over. There was nothing there. Tamarack heard a sigh from the audience. They must be wondering, he thought, how this man, so stupid in certain matters, could be so subtle in others.

In art, as in law, war, politics, and religion, the pressures of their environment restrained the northern Anishinabeg from the elaborate procedures carried out by Indians in more favored regions. People who must float their possessions across dangerous waters and carry them over long portages can't take much with them in the way of pictures and sculpture. Still, in their few weeks of comparative ease, they ornamented clothing, baskets, pouches, moccasins, net floats and containers with strong, meaningful, and pleasing designs.

In addition to her talents as a trapper, Red Sky had the more conventionally feminine skill of working with birch bark. She now felt that Madeyn was old enough to be entrusted with the use of the precious scissors which she carried in a little bag at her belt, refusing to lay them down elsewhere lest some careless person use them improperly and damage them.

Mother and daughter had been marking shapes on the fresh bark — animals, plants and people — and cutting them out to be used as patterns for beading. New designs had come to Red Sky in dreams during the winter and spring. Now she was hurrying to get these into more permanent form. Sometimes she would warm a very thin piece of the inner layer of the bark, fold it thoughtfully, then bite it, using her eye teeth to form a strange geometric composition that, when flattened, would draw a gasp of delight from the girl.

But she took time to help her former mother-in-law frame and cover a waginogan for herself and her son.

"Nowadays," said Dawn Sailing, "all the young people drink. He is good when he is sober. Besides, he needs me."

Red Sky did not dispute the first two of those statements and nobody could question the third. But she thought that Loon's Foot would need more help than his old mother would be able to give him. Unless he could find another woman with talents as a trapper, an unlikely possibility, prospects for his future would not be good.

The summer was passing and the village had ceased to grow. A few families were already leaving, although latecomers still continued to arrive. One of the last to come in was Ice Stone. As usual, he had had a good winter. His canoe sagged low in the water with its cargo of pelts.

When his bales were laid on the counter and opened, word ran out through the lodges that this fur from the northern hills was of unusually fine quality. Jamieson and his assistant worked all day at its evaluation, with the people crowding around to watch and sometimes to stroke the glossy pelts in admiration.

During the afternoon Shanod came into the store, drawn by a

wish to see these beautiful things and a little, perhaps, by some lingering attraction to the strong and skillful hunter. Ice Stone looked up at her and smiled across the heap of soft riches. No one had told him. Not yet.

A feast was held that night, followed by a drum-dance of thanksgiving for the abundance of fish and animals so far in this summer. On one side of the circle a group of men, including He-Rises and Tamarack, had gathered around Iron Feather, who was conducting the ceremony. Opposite them, the women sat watching.

Suddenly Ice Stone was standing in the firelight. He was silent for a moment, but a malevolent ferocity was flowing out from him, striking the people like a cold wind. The drumming and the chanting died. The dancers stopped as his searching eyes moved from one of them to the other, then turned to the seated women and came to rest on Shanod. He strode over and stood before her. He had been drinking, but his words were clear.

"I know now what you have done. You have opened your legs and let a rat come into you. A water rat that stinks of swamp slime. And that while you were giving milk to my daughter."

He looked around the circle of mute faces.

"Where are you, rat? Do not be afraid. You can come up out of the mud. I don't quarrel with rats. You will know which of her children are yours by their long and hairless tails."

Those near Tamarack looked at him, stepping apart from him a little, but he did not move or speak.

Ice Stone walked to the edge of the firelight and stood there, facing into the darkness. After a while he turned and came back to Shanod.

"You have deserted me and shamed me. I will not be one of your lovers. The rat can have you."

He paused and looked around again as though seeking the other man.

"Most of you. But I am going to take a part. A choice part. I am going to take a big, fat totosh. Since you put so little value on your milk, you can surely spare one for your husband. As a keepsake. Then I will give the rest of you back to the rat."

He bent over her and, with a powerful swinging motion, lifted her

to her feet and tore her blouse away. A knife flickered in the firelight, slashing swiftly, lightly in a half-circle, just opening the skin beside the breast. It was the preliminary incision of the skilled trapper, marking the path for the deeper cut.

Blood flowed. Shanod struggled silently, unable to break away. There was no sound except the beat of moccasins pounding on hard-packed earth as Tamarack came across the circle. The dancers were jumping out of his way. Iron Feather was running behind him, unable to keep up with him. He-Rises stood, quite still, for a moment. Then he followed. No one else moved or spoke.

Ice Stone caught the approaching sound, flung Shanod hard against the earth and turned, crouching, knife ready, point presented outwards in front of his chest. The blade was long, broad, and very keen.

Shanod rose to her knees, shaking her head to get the hair out of her eyes and the bewilderment out of her mind. She saw Tamarack bent low, without a weapon, but coming in fast.

She lunged for the hand that held the knife. She caught the wrist, hung to it, jerking, pulling Ice Stone off balance.

Tamarack's body crashed into them with a momentum that knocked man and woman to the earth. One hand came down on the trapper's face, driving his head against the ground with skull-jarring force.

He-Rises stood over them, hesitating. He could see Shanod cling-ing to Ice Stone's wrist, twisting relentlessly. Slowly the fingers opened a little, then tightened. She gave another twist that brought a grunt of pain. The knife fell to the ground.

He-Rises threw himself on the sprawling mass of bodies. He felt it heave violently beneath him as Ice Stone twisted, reaching out, trying to recover the knife. Tamarack had him by the hair now, so that he could not turn his head to see where it lay. Shanod was still clinging to his wrist. He surged against her grip, groping for the knife. His finger tips touched the haft. Shanod swept it beyond his reach.

The crowd watched in silence. There was only the heavy, relent-lessly repeated sound of the head lifted by the hair and slammed down against the earth.

After a while, Ice Stone was no longer struggling. Iron Feather had picked up the knife.

"Let him go," he said.

He-Rises looked up at his father and released his hold. Tamarack stopped the battering but kept his position, hand still gripping hair.

"Get up. He will not attack anyone again tonight."

Slowly, Tamarack obeyed.

Ice Stone lay still. The people watched, saying nothing. Dawn Sailing came and knelt beside him, her questioning fingers running over his mouth and nose. Suddenly he pushed them aside, rolled over, got to his hands and knees, and stopped there, head down, blood dripping from his nose.

Iron Feather passed the knife to He-Rises, bent over Ice Stone and helped him to his feet.

He did not speak. For perhaps a minute he stood, blankly staring at the four who had overcome and disarmed him. He took a few staggering steps, then walked more firmly into the night. Otter Woman and Dawn Sailing were already caring for Shanod.

In a little while, the watchers saw a canoe pass through the moon path, moving toward the river mouth and 'Tschgumi.

There was no more dancing or singing. The people broke up into small groups as shocked silence gave way to quiet, frightened talk.

"Oh, this is bad," whispered Red Sky. "He will go to Undertooth."

The blade was cold in He-Rises' hand. Cold with the chill of night and shining in the starlight. Its eager edge caught at the ball of his finger, reluctant to let go without tasting flesh. This was no trophy. It was a symbol of shame.

That expertly-honed edge had glided around his sister's breast, leaving a trail of parted skin and starting blood. He had stood still and watched.

"It was only for a few moments," he told himself.

"Ah, yes, but long enough. Long enough to be sure that the foreigner, the swamp man, would come to the knife first. If that had taken an hour, I would have waited. I was frozen, and not only by fear of witchcraft. That might have been more pardonable. But I also thought of this long, cold piece of steel entering my body.

"I joined the fight late. I accomplished nothing but the gesture. It was Shanod that took this knife. Shanod and Tamarack and my father. I stood and waited until the danger was over.

"But I will keep it always. I hope that it will cause me to act, if such a time for action comes again."

His fingers clenched on the handle, his eyes closed, and he felt his guts writhe within him as though they were determined to find some way out of his body, to separate themselves from so despicable a person.

"I cannot change what is past. If I could, I would now gladly accept the risk. But that opportunity is gone. I am only losing sleep and making myself sick.

"Tomorrow I will try again to find my dream. Maybe in the sacred place something will come to me and put this shame out of my thoughts."

21

Across the lagoon from the circle of lodges, a stone mountain rose over a ragged rim of lowland forest. On its far side it dropped away in sheer palisades into 'Tschgumi. A talus, a pile of broken rock, slanted down to the lake. Steep as this was, and apparently without earth, it provided enough footing for some aspiring spruce and cedar to climb a little way up the cliff. From this precarious purchase they stretched out green arms across the precipice toward similar clumps of foliage that clung to other footholds near the water level.

Looking up from a canoe you could see, perhaps two hundred feet above this dark fringe, the horizontal line of a ledge running across the face of the rock, a level shelf covered with water-rounded stones. Above this line the mountain slanted back at a somewhat easier angle that allowed files of stunted little trees to creep cautiously down.

This level strip was once a beach, the limit, for a few centuries, of a shrinking, but still enormous, glacial lake. Here, quiet ripples lapped the rock and surf roared against it until the sun, growing stronger, melted channels in the ice hundreds of miles away so that the water subsided further. Men of a more recent time, but still many generations before any living memory, had lifted some of the stones and piled them in crude walls to form a sort of hut with a doorway facing toward the lake. If they covered this structure with a roof, it must have been of brush or bark, fragile materials that had been blown away long ago.

Certainly this could never have been a place where anyone would want to live. Perhaps it was a watch post whence a sentry would send warning signals if he saw enemies coming over the lake or along the

141

shore. Or it might always have been a holy place where a young man could stand on the earth's stone base and look out over the ever-changing water while he suffered, meditated, and dreamed.

Iron Feather had led He-Rises over the moss and scrubby heather that partly covered the curve of the summit. He pushed aside some wild roses and a dwarf birch that overhung the cliff and pointed down to where a series of other clinging little trees and crevices made possible a descent to the ledge.

Below, gulls circled, their backs pale gray and white. And far below them the jagged slant of boulders, fallen from the cliff, lay stacked around its foot or shimmered up from where they had come to rest under the water.

The father walked away. He-Rises lowered himself from one hold to the next until he stood on the level rock.

His face had been blackened with charcoal and he was naked before the mysterious powers, without even moccasins or breach clout. A folded blanket and a pitch-sealed makak of water hung from his shoulder. Under the threat of sorcery, he must not fail again. This time he would stay until his vision came.

Time passed slowly that first day, and even more slowly in the days and nights that followed. He-Rises prayed and chanted. He watched the rising and setting of the sun, and the little waves below him, hidden at times by moving clouds of fog. He came to know each twisted and deformed tree that clung to life in the rocks around him.

Sometimes a gull would land on the ledge to pick at flowers that grew in the strip of moss that followed a crack across the stone floor. Or a chipmunk might sprint around his feet in cautious jerks, pausing, tail erect, a forager alert for any treachery, but finding neither crumbs nor danger.

Much of the time it was too cold for insects, but when the wind was still and the sun was hot, flies buzzed and bit, leaving small trickles of blood to dry on his body. He did not strike back. Any living thing might bring a message, or the wind might, or the clouds.

He-Rises was using very little water, taking a sip only when he felt that he could not go longer without it. But the day came when he held the makak for a long time tilted up to let the last drops drain into his mouth. When he finally lowered it, it slipped from his fingers, bounced away from his feet, and slid over the edge. He watched it flitter erratically down, tossed and lifted by the wind, until it splashed lightly. After that it grew slowly smaller, visible for a long time as it was carried over the water.

That evening the moon, which had been only a slender curve during his first night on the cliff, rose out of the lake round, heavy and warm. It was the feminine moon and He-Rises was not much surprised to see, by her light, a woman sitting at the far end of the ledge. He walked toward her. She turned a little to face him. But when he came closer, she changed into a dried-up stump and a pile of stones against the rock face.

Gradually, He-Rises' mind wandered off into some strange middle condition between sleeping and waking. When the sun came up he continued to lie on the rock, his eyes closed. And now dreams began to come, misty, dithering things that tormented more than hunger, thirst, or the cold loneliness, but did not bring him what he was seeking. They came and went through the day and into the following night, changing nothing and swiftly escaping from his memory.

When the moon rose again he was lying prone on the rock slab, and looking along its length. Yes, the woman was there again in the same place. He could see her more clearly now. Her hair was pale gray, a little green in the moonlight, the color of caribou moss. He knew that sometimes Pauguk would take the form of an old woman. That did not seem to frighten him, but he felt very weak, hardly strong enough to catch her whispered words.

"Your manido is coming."

The voice faded like the dying breeze, then rose again, faintly.

"Then you will know what to . . . ."

If she was still speaking he could no longer hear. His face sank to the stone. The spirit-dream came.

Later, he could not remember how it started. Striving, pushing back into the mists of memory, he knew that he had seen wolves gnawing at the bones of Shakes-His-Wings. The skull had spoken to him, with wisdom, not with anger. That picture was still clear, but its words had gone like snowbirds that warn of a coming blizzard and then swoop and wheel away into soft, gray air.

The next part of the vision that he could remember was listening to the sound of a drum while a little flame hopped and danced before him. Will-o-the-wisp, bounding over the muskeg, was a warning of witch-work aimed against the viewer, and of misfortune to come.

Fearfully, unwillingly, he walked toward that dreadful fire. It moved away. He found himself following it over white drifts through an endless forest. The light flickered out, but a black-masked jay bird, as big as an owl, was flapping between the tree trunks a long way ahead of him. He ran after it, desperately pursuing what he feared to overtake. The chase went on all day and into a terrible night.

The landscape of a dream can be fully remembered only in another dream. He-Rises recognized the hills that he had entered, even though he had never seen the place in his waking life. He was very tired, running heavily, bent as though under a great load, his snow-shoes sinking deep, dragging in clinging snow.

In a dream-familiar ravine, rock walls came crowding in and here the thing turned. It swooped toward him, in a sudden onslaught of vast, murderous power. He was smashed back by its hurtling weight and hammered by the flailing blows of its wings.

It had changed color, lighter now, and had taken on a human face, the face of Ice Stone, but older, creased, stained, and sagging with hatred. It was ripping at his head and body, but some other creature was fighting by his side, slashing back at the monster. He felt himself sink, torn, blinded and bleeding, into darkness. This was the end. And yet the weary struggle went on.

He woke at last, aching, but striving to remember everything, to keep what he had heard and seen from passing out of his consciousness in these first critical moments.

He had rolled off the blanket and was lying on the stone. A pink hint of dawn was glowing along the curved flatness of the lake.

He knew the importance of dreams — that their fast-fading memories are more real than life. Knew that what seemed to be reality was just a flickering of firelight. The hopeless dread that this vision had brought him was the truth, a foretaste of despair and death.

What was its true meaning? That thing that had torn him? Had it taken the form of a wolf? A jay, perhaps one of those same jays that had given him to the river so long ago? Or that symbol of relentless fate, the night-owl? But it had teeth as well as talons. Big, curved, yellow, teeth.

He would not reject the vision or pretend that it had not come to him. He would accept the punishment that it implied. Would even, he thought, welcome it as an atonement for his contemptible failures. At least he need no longer save the birth cord that Otter Woman had wrapped in bark for him. After all these years he could throw it away and proceed with his life as a man, however short that life might be.

Slowly, painfully, he climbed the face of the rock, stopping often to rest and to make sure of his way. Once he sagged under a spell of dizziness, and gripped the roots of a cedar that ran up the cliff above him. He hung there for minutes, determined not to fall.

Recovering, he crawled up the short remaining distance and out on the summit. There he lay gasping for a while, then got to his feet and staggered down through the trees in the direction of the landing.

When he found a rill of water oozing from the hillside he flattened himself against the wet earth to drink.

Iron Feather had been watching anxiously each morning. Now he came swiftly across the lagoon, bringing meat, clothing, and a steadying hand.

He who returns from a vision quest must not tell what he has seen. The family asked no questions, but they knew that the dream had not been good. Nevertheless, Otter Woman and Smoke Drifting were busy all day preparing the feast to be held that night in He-Rise's honor. Shanod helped too. Her slight wound was healing well.

Red Sky, Madeyn, and Toenail came bringing gifts, as did Dawn Sailing with Loon's Foot. There was no bitterness between the former couple, but neither was there any thought of going back.

Later in that warm night, He-Rises lay on his sleeping furs and thought again of the vision. It seemed somehow more clear in memory

145

than it had out there on the ledge. He was certain now that there had been some connection with the snarling effigy on the handle of the knife.

Again he took out the package, walked down into the open moonlight of the beach, and removed the wrappings. Was this the assailant? Or was it the mysterious being that had come to his aid, attacking his attacker in those last moments? Was this his totem, his manido? A gift from Ice Stone and from Undertooth?

He heard old feet feeling their way, cautiously, not risking a fall, through the pine shadow behind him. He knew that they were Dawn Sailing's before she spoke.

"You are unhappy, my grandson. And you are not consoled by that man's blade."

He-Rises stepped closer and spoke low.

"I fear the sorcerer and I fear this, even though it seems to be my manido. I don't know whether it will help me or destroy me. A wise dreamer might have thrown it into the lagoon. But I have kept it, because there is something in me that is worse than these fears.

"I should be a man now. But I fail in those things that men accomplish. If I had lived when Sturgeon Man was young, in war-time, I would have sat in the lodge and done nothing. I sent Shakes-His-Wings to die in the cold hills. I would have left Madeyn to starve. You must have seen, in the dance circle, how I hung back, how I was slow to come to my sister when she might have been killed. Oh, grandmother, can your medicine change me?"

"I don't think that you are less than other men. But I know that you have been much troubled. I am only a healer and not a shaman. In a few cases, though, I have been able to drive out sorcery that was causing sickness. I will make what medicine I can to help you. Let me look at your manido figure."

She took the knife, felt the edge with her thumb, then held the haft far out from her eyes, tilting her head, trying to make out the carving in the moonlight.

"No one need be ashamed of having feared to face this weapon in the strong hand of that angry man. I will keep it for a while and work with it. Maybe I can do something to turn back the witchwork that might be sent against you. But medicine cannot change He-Rises' self. You must use your own power to put these burning thoughts away."

✦ ✦ ✦

146

The days of early summer, days of frolic, friendship and love, slipped swiftly by. Too soon, like all good things, they came to an end. And this year they ended under the shadow of dark omens.

But whatever disasters might be in store for the future, preparations for Peboan must continue. The village dwindled as canoes were loaded and passed around the river bend, faded into the mists of 'Tschgumi, or disappeared behind its headlands. Soon there would remain only the trader, his family, and the post servants.

22

Early on a shining morning, Iron Feather and Otter Woman, trailed by those who chose to follow, paddled around the tip of the sandbar and out on the great, calm lake. Packs, pots, boxes, dogs and children had been loaded well back in the canoes to leave the bows light for passing over the swells.

There had been some hesitation in the village about joining this party. Examples had been cited of the terrible power of Undertooth's witchcraft. Several men and women who had opposed him, or otherwise angered him, had suffered sickness or crippling injuries and some had died sudden and painful deaths. One young hunter who had publicly defied the shaman had, just three days later, been crushed by a falling tree.

In most cases, however, the punishment had taken place months, and more often years, after the offense. Keeping these delays in mind, several families decided not to let the Ice Stone incident change their plans for following Iron Feather. It would take time for Undertooth to dream his deadly visions and then to carry out the necessary rites. They would stay with the group at least as far as the berry camp, and decide what to do at the end of that season.

The sun was already warm, but Tamarack shivered a little as the chill of the cold depths enveloped him and even seemed to strike up through the bark and thin cedar. Looking over the side, he felt as though he were floating on air. He knew that those huge rock slabs were far below him, and yet he felt that if he reached down with his paddle he could almost touch them.

Then, as his eyes moved along the shoreline, he could hardly believe the difference in its appearance when seen from the water. The weird forms taken by its escarpments confirmed the tales of powerful and malevolent beings that lived along this coast. Mountainous peaks and ridges extended out into the lake in the form of promontories, torn by storms into sheer cliffs, seacaves, and steep-sided islands. Huge, solitary boulders stood up out of the water like wading demons that had been suddenly turned to stone.

The canoes coasted to a stop before one of these, an erect pillar of granite, covered, above the water- and ice-lines, with pale-green and orange lichen. The only other vegetation was a bent and strangely contorted old cedar. Its limbs went twisting and jerking, all in the same direction, pointing toward the land, where the force of the wind had driven them. Far-searching roots, clinging to the stone, breaking through its crevices, and splitting it open with the irresistable power of growth, had somehow found enough sustenance to keep a tuft of dark green foliage alive at the top.

A breeze began to riffle the water and Otter Woman stroked a little to keep the lead canoe in place. Iron Feather looked up at the gnarled old hunchback that bent toward them from the rock. He spoke to the spirit that was known to inhabit the tree, the latent, unpredictable power and violence of the lake.

"All things come from sun, water, and stone. People change. Stone remains.

Lichen spreads. The tree lives on, as it did when our grandfathers stopped here, floating beneath it. They are gone now and we must go soon, and be forgotten.

"But through these children who are here in the canoes this morning the blood of the ancestors should go down to those who will come after. We ask you to give them and us safe passage today and in the other days and nights of the summer. Bring us to shore each evening, and protect us from any evil that an angry wabeno may send against us."

He opened his outstretched hand and the offering of tobacco fell, scattering over the waves.

The people struck up a swift stroke and moved out over the deep water. They hoped that the little ceremony, together with Iron Feather's known manidoke, and their own skill with the spruce blades, would keep them safe on this powerful, restless sea.

As the sun rose higher the wind freshened, and Iron Feather swung farther out from shore, quartering into the waves that came sweeping up from the south. He was watching the swaying surface ahead. When a thing like a fountain shot up out there, roaring through the sound of wind and water, he noted its location and changed course to stay away from that spot, where a reef lay only a little below the surface.

In windy weather, it is the shallows that are dangerous. Whether they are near the shore or far out in the lake, the water above them can change almost as suddenly as the wind. The waves there become short, steep, and angry. They slap water into a canoe as it crashes through them.

Moving easily over big swells of deep water, the Anishinabeg were not worried. This was their element. They were careful, though, and serious, feeling the rhythmic lift and plunge of the hulls, and watching, even in this honest weather, for any quick treachery by evil things that might be looking up at them from the depths.

There was not much of the customary banter. Silly talk out here might bring punishment. Throughout the long day, dogs and small children would sit quietly, content to look out over the vast distance from their little spaces between the packs.

In past years, He-Rises had taken second place to Shanod on 'Tschgumi. Now he was enjoying his new responsibility. Behind him, Smoke Drifting sat leaning against a pack, happy to be out here again.

Kneeling in the stern, Sturgeon Man had become strong and confident. He knew how to deal with waves.

Keeping time with Shanod's quick strokes, watching her lithe movements and the black hair blowing out from beneath her headscarf, Tamarack felt a joyful exhilaration. Sound of Waves, snugly stored in the bow, smiled up at her mother, pleased by the rising and falling motion.

Dawn Sailing and Loon's Foot followed, then Red Sky and Toenail, with Madeyn. Like Tamarack, she had not been on 'Tschgumi before. She sat rigid, holding tight to thwart and gunwale.

All day they followed the blue peaks, headlands, and soaring archipelagos of the shoreline, keeping their distance from it, but not too far to run for its shelter if the spirits should send a storm against them. Iron Feather was watching both sky and shore, alert for any cloud warnings and keeping in mind each bay, cove, and river mouth that would offer an escape from an angry lake. As he passed one such shelter his mind would jump along the coast to the next. Where miles of sheer cliffs offered no sanctuary, he swung farther out, as far as necessary to allow a plausible angle to the waves for flight to safety, ahead or backwards, in case of a sudden squall.

At sundown he eased in beside a table of flat rock on the sheltered side of an offshore island. The canoes were quickly unloaded. Fishermen went out in two of them. The others were bound on their sides against the stunted island trees to serve as windbreaks.

Since Tamarack's marriage, he and Otter Woman were not speaking to each other. Not that there was any anger or jealousy between them. But it would have been considered disrespectful, a gross breach of good manners, for either the mother-in-law or the son-in-law to say anything to the other.

Tamarack had simply leaned his canoe on its side against two small spruces as he would have done on an inland lake. Otter Woman inspected this arrangement and then walked past him to where Shanod was gutting the newly-caught trout.

"Tell your husband that on 'Tschgumi it is best to bind the canoe to the trees."

Later, in the darkness, the boat, seized by sudden wind, began to shake its supporting trunks. Tamarack was glad that Otter Woman had sent him the warning.

At dawn, Loon's Foot and Iron Feather made their way through the growth of twisted spruce that clung to the sheltered side of the island, and climbed over an entanglement of storm-driven flotsam, bleached stumps and driftwood that had collected at the tree line, where the stone summit flattened out before it began to slope down toward the water. No trees or shrubs could grow here — only the persistent lichens that take their food from air, rock, and sun and so have no need of earth.

Iron Feather studied the lake, looking past the heaving ridges that broke against a skirmish line of rocks, then swept around it to swirl in broad white fields over shallows and shingle. Out beyond that barrier the waves were big and powerful, but not wicked. The wind was steady.

"I think that it will be all right."

"Yes, brother, we can go on today."

They walked back to where the people waited, and carried their canoes down to the water. The others followed.

Even on this protected inner shore, loading was not easy. The high swells sweeping around the island lifted and dropped the canoes. Movements had to be timed so that each piece of cargo was set into place at the top of a rise. Everyone got thoroughly wet. But the surface water carried in by this onshore wind wasn't cold. The work was completed with joking and laughter.

The travellers were soaked again when surf broke against the bows as they came out from the shelter of the last rocky point and met the full force of the wind. Iron Feather set the course into deep water. He-Rises, next in the line, could see his parents climb high on the crest of each wave, and disappear down its other side. Then his own craft would be hoisted on the same swell and for a moment he could look far over the lake before tobogganing down between the wandering hills.

Each great wave came swiftly, sunlight glinting from its dark surface, bearing the momentum of tons of fast-moving water that could shock and overwhelm any small boat that was not properly handled. Each had to be watched, appraised, and approached at the correct angle. For a choppy crest, the stern paddler, at the last moment, would throw his weight to the downwind side, rolling up the belly of the canoe so that the threatening giant broke harmlessly against it. But some water might come in over the gunwale, no matter how skillful the steersman. When that happened, the children scooped and bailed with makaks.

The paddlers worked in silence except that Loon's Foot could not repress an occasional joyous yelp as he careened his boat over some threatening giant.

Everyone was relieved when Iron Feather led them into the unexpected shelter of a hidden cove at noon. They built a small fire, brewed tea, and heated pitch to repair seams that had opened a little under the strains of the twisting and pounding waves.

The rest was short. Soon they were out again, working their way down the coast, watching for the occasional dangerous crest. The wind went down, as it should, with the sun, but ponderous waves were still rolling as they turned again toward the land. They saw what looked like a solid line of white surf breaking on boulders before them. They swept toward it, pursued and carried by the westerly swell. Then, just as Otter Woman and Iron Feather seemed about to crash, they swerved into sudden darkness, the opening of a river mouth. The others came after them in single file but running close together, each making the sharp turn into safety.

Within the protection of the shoreline rocks, the water was still rising and falling, but its surface was smooth enough to reflect the gleam of fires. A group of people were gathered at the water's edge to help get the wet luggage ashore and spread around the heat to dry. Additional trout and mushrooms had gone into the stew kettles as soon as the approaching canoes had been sighted. The second course would be great quantities of fresh blueberries.

The newcomers were assured that the harvest would be heavy this summer. The meadow bushes had been picked clean of ripe berries now, but were loaded with small pale globes that would soon swell, turn a deep blue-black, and bend down the wiry little stems again. And in the hills the heather was dark with ready fruit. The netters were already bringing in plenty of fish for present needs of dogs and people. Big hauls for drying were expected to come later as the weather cooled.

With good food in their bellies, good prospects in their heads, and comfortably exhausted by the long day on the lake, the Iron Feather party laid out their bedding on the springy berry bushes and slept well. Neither fear nor remorse kept He-Rises awake that night.

23

He-Rises woke in the quiet that comes just before the first glow of a summer dawn. No birds were calling, no breeze stirred the leaves. The ever-restless waters of 'Tschgumi were whispering only a little.

For a while he lay inert and comfortable, his mind remaining at ease from sleep. It was still too dark to make out anything around him, but when he raised himself on an elbow he could see someone standing on the headland that separated the meadow from the lake.

Tamarack had risen early and climbed to that point for a view of the new and unfamiliar surroundings. He-Rises scrambled up the rock to join him and they stood looking out over the encampment. The first fires began to gleam in the darkness.

"This broad, flat meadow," said the Muskego, "is the only wide break I have seen in the lake's wall. And all these lodges standing in it when we have met no one since we left the trading post. It is a strange place."

"It is an old place, important to my people. This is the best harbor along the shore, and the only one where many can camp at one time. We have come here each summer that I have lived."

He pointed to where hill bracken was beginning to catch the light.

"We burn those ridges every year to hold back the forest. The bushes grow quickly after a fire and the berries there are always thicker, bigger and darker. We need them almost as much as we need meat and rice. The women dry enough of them to last through the winter except in those summers when drouth makes them scarce. When that happens there is likely to be sickness in the winter pikogans."

He turned toward the lake. "And see those lines of treetops

floating up out of the mist? They are islands that run in a long string to the west and the east. The trout come up to the reefs between them and around them. You and I will set nets out there and take many."

"Not I. That is work for young boys and women. I will bring in meat and furs, but no fish."

He-Rises lowered his voice to answer. "Fishing is not just for boys and women on 'Tschgumi. Always we must guard against his sudden attack, even when he smiles, as he does this morning.

"But it is better not to talk about these matters. We might anger the spirits of the lake. They reach up from the cold depths to drag men down for company. And on the sand beaches, even on that one right below us, you sometimes find the claw-marks of Missepishu."

"I would like to see those," said Tamarack. "When you hear that the great lynx has walked, let me know."

They went down to the camp, now awake to the new day and beginning to stir with activity. Men were launching canoes for fishing or woodgathering. Women were assembling in purposeful groups carrying bark makaks, large and small baskets of various designs and sizes, and light kettles. Boys and girls, eager with the enthusiasm of cool morning, had already completed their camp chores and were starting toward the hills, followed by a chorus of frustrated barking. The good dogs, unhappy but quiet, watched the departure, standing at the edge of the camp under firmly repeated orders. The disobedient, on leash, were loudly protesting man's inhumanity.

Otter Woman, Dawn Sailing, and Shanod were walking with some old friends and their children through the damp foliage of the meadow. Red Sky and Madeyn had gone with another group — three young women from the headwaters of the Pukaskwa, far down the coast toward the east and south. They had made the journey with their widowed father to gather the harvests of these warm uplands and cold waters.

Smoke Drifting changed the baby's diaper-moss, then took her on her back and hurried after the others. She seemed a slight figure under a large burden, but several other little girls of her age and younger were similarly loaded. As they crossed the meadow in their ankle-length skirts they looked like a procession of midget mothers bent under the weight of enormous infants.

From the top of the first hill the pickers could see row after row of craggy ridges rising above the low-hanging fog. A few jack pines came twisting up out of the berry heather and some slender birches and poplars, their leaves beginning to show the first touches of yellow.

The sun had already warmed the hillside, bringing out the fragrance of sweet fern. It warmed the women as they bent to the picking. It felt good at first. They worked with smooth efficiency. Small makaks tied around their waists were quickly filled, emptied into the large ones and filled again.

Smoke Drifting stood the tikinagon up against a spruce trunk so that the baby could watch the proceedings. That was not good enough. Sound of Waves insisted on being taken out. Liberated, she crawled after the elders with surprising speed. From time to time they got too far away, and then her aunt came back to her, put her on the cradle board and carried her to the harvest front.

The blueberry spirit was kind that gave these northern varieties, but he forgot to design them for easy picking. They grow close to the ground, enforcing a deep-stooping posture that becomes increasingly punishing as the hours pass. The fruit are biggest and most plentiful in the swampy levels between the ridges, where the sun beats down unrelieved by any breeze. The mosquitos may be letting up a little in early August, the Moon of Ripe Berries, but the flies are at the top of their wicked form. They hummed around the pickers, biting so fiercely that blood and sweat streaked their faces in almost equal quantities.

The smaller children were now working with noticeably less ardor but there was no thought of slacking off among the older workers. The women enjoyed the talk, the exchange of news, the kidding and the gossip. And they derived great satisfaction from the increasing store of dark blue riches. They paid no attention to the heat, the bites, and the bending.

They went on without a pause through the morning, milking the low bushes down one steep slope, across the flat, and up another, gradually getting farther from camp. In the afternoon, Madeyn at the far end of one of the ridges found competition. Another harvester, a bear, was working toward her. He rolled back his upper lip to show the long curved teeth, popping his jaws and huffing at her. She backed away, came up against a rock ledge, and stood terrified, unable to move farther.

Smoke Drifting hurried over to her.

"He says that he doesn't want a bunch of Indians poking around his berry patch. He isn't likely to hurt anybody but you never can be sure with bears. He'd better be gotten out of here. There will be plenty of berries for him back in the woods."

She called to her mother who was picking on the other side of the slope. Otter Woman walked up to the bear, speaking in a firm, but friendly and reasonable tone. She made a twisting motion toward him with her hand. It was a gesture that might have been used to quiet a fussing baby.

The bear had risen to his haunches as she approached, his powerful forepaws dangling against his belly. Now he dropped to all fours and shuffled off at a leisurely pace, taking a few berries as he went to make it clear that he was complying with her request of his own free will and not just being chased off. They did not see him again but the hot, strong, animal smell hung in the air for a long time.

"That is why we leave the dogs in camp," said Otter Woman. "Bears and dogs are enemies but bears and men must be friends. The men will kill a bear when we need the fur or the fat meat, but always with the proper ceremonies. When you skin one you can see that he is made like one of us. The man who kills a bear is killing his grandfather but he is also accepting a kindly and willing gift from the bear spirit. He and all who eat the meat must give thanks.

"You must never offend or annoy a bear. That is dangerous at the time, and can bring misfortune later, on the rude one or on her family."

158

The berries were spread on mats made of reeds interwoven with basswood twine to separate the stems and allow air to circulate around the berries. Children stood guard, waving sticks and shouting at any birds that came too close. Madeyn and Smoke Drifting, though, were past that age. They went on picking with the other women.

The drying process was continued until the berries shrank to a quarter of their original size and were as firm as currents. They would keep through the winter in that form, but later they might be packed in grease to make what white settlers called Indian ice cream. Or that combination could be mixed with dried, pounded meat for pemmican, a nourishing food that stored well and was compact and convenient to carry.

Whatever unpleasant things may be said about the weather on this northern coast, nobody can call it monotonous. The sunshine is as steady at this season as it ever gets. But several times Smoke Drifting and Madeyn ran to cover the drying berries from sudden thunderstorms, and once it was necessary to weight down the protecting bark with timbers and leave these in place for days while a northeaster drove sheets of cold rain across the meadow. Such interruptions were expected, and the picking and processing went on, not seriously impeded.

Tamarack, with his strongly held convictions about women's work, was suffering intense boredom. He repaired some damaged equipment and completed whatever other small jobs he could find. His only companions in the quiet camp were the dogs. The air was heavy with their smell, a rather fishy odor at this season. The ground was littered with dung and tufts of wooly hair. They scratched, snarled, fought, slept, copulated, gnawed at old bones, rolled in the dust, and snapped at flies. When the man could find no more work to do he sat with what dignity he could maintain in such company.

In the afternoon, Tamarack went back to his observation post between the camp and the lake. Way up the river, he saw a canoe appear and disappear behind the willows along the bank. It was towing a floating mass of firewood. The current was slight at this time of year, and the crew were having hard work of it to keep the clumsy raft moving and clear of points and shallows. Wood-gathering was not a job for men, either, but somehow it seemed a little more respectable than fishing. Those people could use another paddler. Perhaps he would join them on their next run.

When Tamarack turned to look out over 'Tschgumi he had to search for a while before he picked up some of the fishing fleet, bobbing in the glare of sunlight on waves. Each steersman was holding his canoe pointed into the wind to avoid shipping water while the bow man lifted the net, removed the fish from it, and returned it to the depths. That didn't look easy either, and it had a touch of danger that the wood-hauling lacked.

When the first canoes came in from the lake Tamarack helped with the processing — splitting the fish, slicing into the flesh for faster drying, and hanging them on racks over smoldering fires. This was degrading work, unworthy of any man, but better than sitting with the dogs. As long as he was here with these complacently woman-dominated Anishinabeg, he might as well do as they were doing. He hoped that it would not spoil Shanod.

As the berry pickers left camp next morning he was with He-Rises, paddling out between the stone pillars that guard the river's mouth. The mist hung low in the cool, still air, showing only the tops of the coastal range. After a while even these disappeared. The two men angled their course away from where the shore should be, looking hard into the blank whiteness until they saw a dark line of treetops that faded down into nothing. This was what they had been looking for— the first link in the chain that would lead them to their nets.

These nets had been set between rocks and barren reefs that strung together a necklace of wooded islands. The fishing was already good in the shallows and would be better when the trout began their spawning run. It would have been a rough place to work in windy weather, but now the only difficulty was finding the carved cedar floats that marked the ends of the nets. These were three feet long and fastened at one end to the upper cord so that the weight of the net stood them up above the surface. But nothing was easily found in the fog.

They paddled slowly while He-Rises studied the faint tree and rock forms that showed at times. Following these, remembering the way back, and signalling directions to Tamarack, he saw the first of the floats. He drew up the line until he reached the net, then ran it over the gunwales, across his lap, and back into the lake.

A big trout, very dark in color, was hanging quietly, wedged into the coarse mesh and caught by the gills. As it was lifted into the canoe it came violently back to life, wriggling and flopping heavily, slashing with saw-sharp teeth. He-Rises took its head firmly in his own teeth while he worked it loose from the mesh, then reached back for the short club and struck a killing blow.

Tending the nets on 'Tschgumi was slow, heavy work and hazardous. A long net, sagging with the weight of many fish, could capsize a canoe in an instant if either the net man or the paddler were careless or a little clumsy. Also, a storm might come moaning through the still air and swell to full fury in a few minutes.

He-Rises' hands moved swiftly over the meshes, steady in their place as one gunwale or the other twitched up or down. Tamarack, just coming to appreciate the difficulties of the operation, was doing his best to keep the canoe level, swinging it toward the action or away, at his partner's command, balancing it by shifting his weight and by pressing down or lifting with the flat of the paddle against the water. He wondered whether he would be able to handle this job in rough weather.

Instead of thinning to let in the sun, the fog grew denser. The top line of the net dimmed as it extended out, and disappeared into the shifting floor of water. They knew that they were not alone, and once they heard, quite close, a paddle rap against a gunwale, but they saw none of the other fishermen.

When they had finished with one net they went on to the next, some distance away.

"There is a great difference in the production of different nets," explained He-Rises. "They are jealous things and must be set far enough apart so that one of them is not disgraced by another's more bountiful catch. Otherwise the unfortunate net may refuse to catch anything, or may even tear itself in shame."

At noon they landed on an island, built a fire, and broiled trout fillets on forked sticks. The food and the heat of the flame were pleasant, and their clothes dried a little, but they were soon back in their cloud-walled circle of waves. Twice He-Rises took fish out of the nets bigger than any that Tamarack had ever seen. When the darkening fog warned that the day was ending, they struck in toward the mainland and followed the shore to the river gap with a fair load of trout and whitefish.

Iron Feather and Loon's Foot had been even more successful, and so had some of the others. Berry pickers and fishermen, working together, were tired when they finished gutting and cutting by firelight. The fat dogs sniffed at what was thrown them, ate only a little,

161

and turned away.

Not every day was that easy or that profitable. As Tamarack had feared, it took him some time to learn to steer and balance the canoe in such a way as to allow safe net handling when heavy swells were breaking over the fishing grounds. He-Rises, accustomed to expert Anishinabe fishermen, was worried. But somehow the canoe was kept right side up while he lifted the nets, removed the struggling fish and gave what instructions he thought would help. He knew that his friend was listening, watching and learning. They would soon become a fairly efficient team, although not in a class with the Iron Feather-Loon's Foot combination. Not this summer anyway.

Dawn Sailing went up into the higher hills for medicinal plants. The roots, especially, were at their best and biggest at this season.

She searched, found, said her ceremonial apologies, and dug. She worked thoughtfully and precisely, but she was thinking of other matters too. In the carefree summer season it had been easy for most of the people to forget the threat of the sorcerer. But she had not.

Often she would take time off from gathering herbs to sit with the knife and the drum, questioning them, asking their advice, then considering and interpreting the mysterious replies. Acting on their advice, she made a stout sheath of moosehide and quilled it with those old Abwan designs that she believed would be strongest, that might turn malignant magic away from the intended victim.

When it was finished she took He-Rises aside, and handed him the knife with its beautiful and sacred covering. There was gratitude in his thoughts and in his eyes, but he did not speak.

24

The summer was ending early, as summers always do on the north shore. The first changes brought a pleasant melancholy. In themselves, these changes were good. But they were also reminders of hazards and hardships to come.

By day the sun was as warm as ever, but the flies were less aggressive. The nights were suddenly cold. The skies were clear and the wind was steady in the west, good weather for fishing and for drying fish and berries. The aspens and birches were turning yellow. Seen through their branches, the lake seemed very blue.

It became necessary for Red Sky to build a little lodge of brush and bark for Madeyn. She selected a sheltered spot, well away from the berry fields and far enough from camp so that no destructive dribble would pollute the path of some innocent man. Here Madeyn waited in old, worn-out clothing, not washing, her face smeared black with soot. She could not return to the camp until the sign of the menacing moon-power had left her body.

"She is a bear now," Red Sky explained to the others, referring to the maternal principle exemplified by the Bear Mother.

Several times Smoke Drifting, thrilled by her sister-friend's accomplishment and a little envious, eluded the watchers and sneaked out to visit her, bringing "old food," broiled slices from an enormous trout and a bark dish of blueberries selected for over-ripeness. The girls talked in whispers, each careful not to touch or look directly at the other. There was still the fear that young plants, young animals, or young people might be blighted if any of their kind made contact with a menstrual novice.

When this time of segregation was completed, Madeyn returned to be honored with the new-woman ceremony, a modest little gathering, quite unlike the gala reception given after the completion of a young man's dream-quest. But it was important to her. She bathed and put on her best clothing. This was her coming-out party. She had become eligible to receive calls from young men.

The first of these visitors was He-Rises. He had qualified, rather late in life. He had proved himself an effective hunter early enough, but not until he found his vision on the ledge was he considered fit to be a suitor.

It amazed him that he should be taking such delight in bringing formal gifts to one who had recently seemed a timid little nuisance. A fortnight ago he was chatting with her easily. Now, when she stood under his blanket, he was not sure what to whisper. He could not bring himself to confess his failures. He searched for other words, found none, and remained silent.

He-Rises' opportunity for courtship was short. It was almost time to leave this pleasant encampment. At night the men and women gathered close to the fires, holding out hands that were cold and scaly from gutting fish. While they warmed themselves they watched the shimmering dance of the dead, those flames of greenish light that already rolled and flickered at evening across the northern sky.

Work patterns changed. Wood cutting and hauling continued, for the drying went on and the fires were as hungry as ever. There were still late berries to be picked, and the trout were just beginning to run really well. But the people had about as much of both now as they would be able to carry. Fishing and gathering had given way to processing.

In the morning and at evening when the air kept their work damp, the women wove mats of rushes. They spent the rest of the day working with knives and fingers to separate dried fish from the bones and pound down the crisp pieces of flesh into powder. The product that resulted was solid, heavy, and smelled strong but good. They packed many makaks tightly with it and others with dried berries, compact cargo for the return voyage.

He-Rises and Tamarack paddled down the coast to an island favored by the gulls as a rookery. They went ashore on rocks white and slippery with droppings. They had come here before for eggs. Now, while the parent birds wheeled and shrieked above them, they pursued the feathering young, not yet able to fly. Stumbling over the greasy rocks and laughing at each other's efforts, they caught many. Game had been scarce lately around the berry camp and their catch was welcomed as a change from the fish and fruit.

The two young men were still tending a net that they had left in the shallows of the archipelago to gather enough fish for this final period in the berry camp. They had intended to take it up the day after the egg hunt to dry and repair it for the journey. But they were wakened, at the end of the night, by the roar of surf on the outer shore, and they spent two days in camp waiting for the angry seas to subside. On the third day the ferocity went out of the waves, but the swells were still running high.

Late in the afternoon, Tamarack and He-Rises made their way over the heaving water to the sheltering screen of islands. He-Rises, in the stern this time, knelt as far back as he could get to balance Tamarack's greater weight in the bow. The Muskego had asked for this last opportunity of the summer to try his hand at taking in the net.

It had been tangled and torn by deadwood and stones that the storm had rolled along the bottom, but Otter Woman and Shanod would be able to mend it. Most of the fish it still held were flabby dead, fit only for the dogs.

Tamarack took a long time to remove the jetsam and the pale, washed-out trout, being careful not to damage the net any more than necessary. The waves had calmed and the sun had dropped behind the ragged fringe of island spruce as he pulled the canoe toward the last float.

Suddenly he stopped all motion, frozen by a strange cry from the stern. His eyes followed He-Rise's gaze down into the darkening water. There, just coming into sight, a human hand was grasping the mesh.

For a while, neither of them spoke or moved. Then Tamarack went on with the lifting. As the hand came up they could see that it was followed only by some dangling sinews and a piece of bone that had once been forearm.

Not easily, Tamarack loosened the stiff, crooked fingers, so tightly entangled that they seemed to grip the twine.

"Give it back to 'Tschgumi," said He-Rises.

"No. We must bring this to your father and the medicine woman."

✦ ✦ ✦

165

When Dawn Sailing stopped drumming, Iron Feather came to the fire and squatted beside her. The sad remnant from the lake lay on a folded blanket.

The people stood silent in a wide circle giving the medicine people plenty of room. Listening, trying to catch what would be said, but not hearing much except the crackle of the burning driftwood. When Dawn Sailing spoke, her words were low, intended only for the colleague.

"The drum reminds us that 'Tschgumi does not give up his dead. The ghosts of those who drown can never leave their bodies to go to the spirit country. They have no place in heaven or on earth. They stay in the deep water because there, in this lake, it is always cold. They are unwilling to come into the warm shallows where they would rot and rise.

"The drum does not say from what place or from whom this comes. The currents may have taken it away from someone out there and carried it in to the reef."

"The lake is big," said Iron Feather, "and our net is not very long."

"But nobody from the berry camp has been lost. Not this summer. Not yet."

"Perhaps some passing stranger capsized and drowned inside the islands, or just outside. The storm could have battered and ground him to pieces against the reefs."

Dawn Sailing pointed to the end of the bone.

"It is splintered, not worn down in that way. Besides, a canoe would almost surely have been seen by one of the fishermen. If not before the travellers died, then its wreckage afterward."

Iron Feather could no longer avoid the conclusion.

"I think that this has been torn from a living person far from here. The wabeno is strong with the lake spirits. They may have carried it for him through the water to our net. As a greeting."

He paused, and at that moment the mournful call of a great gray owl rolled down from the hills behind him.

Dawn Sailing leaned forward, turning her head a little, but looking, locating the sound, tracing it back with eyes and ears into the dying glow in the low sky, as the hunting owl herself tracks a murmur of movement in branches or a rustle of leaves on the forest floor.

"Kokoho answers from the ancient cleft. She says that you

166

are right."

She picked up the hand and wrapped it carefully in a piece of blanket.

"Many years ago, North Wind took me to that sacred opening in the western hills, a woman place, and a place of great power. Tomorrow, for the first time since that day, I will go back. I don't think that I could get down to it alone, and if I did, I would not be able to climb out again. I will take Smoke Drifting to help me. We will bury this dead one there, this part of him that we have. And we will ask for help against the evil.

"We cannot be sure of getting that help. You know, Iron Feather, that healing wounds and sicknesses, although often uncertain, is easier than fighting witchcraft. But we must do what we can."

They left the camp in the clean chill of the fading stars. Dawn Sailing was carrying a bark-wrapped package. Below them, as they reached the summit of the first hill, the frames of many lodges stood already bare and the river was coming alive with canoes and people.

"They are hurrying to get away from my father, my brothers and my sister. They are afraid that they will be caught in whatever trouble is sent against us. Do you think that we will be going on alone?"

"You will not be alone. Loon's Foot and I will be with you, of course. And I can see other lodges that remain standing. Some will rather risk the sorcerer's hatred than cross 'Tschgumi without your father to lead them."

She turned to push on over the ridge, but Smoke Drifting was still looking back.

"Someone is coming after us. It is Madeyn. I will wait for her and then catch up with you."

The sister-friend came running up, lifting her skirt to keep it from being soaked by the dew-wet berry bushes.

"My mother says that we will go east. She and Toenail are packing. I had been looking for you in the camp and then I saw you on the hillside. I do not want to leave you."

Smoke Drifting answered with more confidence than she felt.

"Tell Red Sky that she need not fear. We are going to the sacred opening in the earth and Grandmother Dawn Sailing will make strong medicine. Undertooth will not be able to hurt us."

Madeyn looked more unhappy than ever.

"I don't think that she is much afraid of the witch-man. That's not her big reason. She wants to go with those Pukaskwa women and their father. I don't know why. He is very old. As old as your father, I suppose, and not so wise. I like Loon's Foot better. But not all the time."

Smoke Drifting could see Dawn Sailing waiting on the ridge.

"I must go on now for the medicine. And Toenail's canoe will be loaded by the time you get back to the river. But you and I, sister, let us meet here again next summer."

"Oh, I will surely be here. And please be careful. My mother is not afraid, but I am. I am afraid for you and your family and for He-Rises."

Madeyn scudded back down the slope and Smoke Drifting turned to rejoin Dawn Sailing. They walked a long time over the rock and caribou moss of the hills, through miniature forests of gnarled and dwarfed evergreens, defiant little clumps that somehow survived on what nourishment they could suck from these hard breasts. In a few places their dark foliage was sprinkled with the yellow and gold leaves of slender birches and mountain ash.

Every so often the two women came out on some bare knob of granite where Smoke Drifting could see the blue of the lake. From one of these outcroppings, Dawn Sailing led the way down into a narrow, craggy gully. They pushed through its brush and climbed over tangled windfalls to where it suddenly fell away into a crevice, a split in the volcanic rock.

Dawn Sailing handed the package to Smoke Drifting. "Tie this to your belt. From here on I will need both of my own hands and yours too."

They let themselves down, holding to treetrunks that grew out a little at the roots and then curved sharply up into perpendiculars. Smoke Drifting found it strange to be clinging to a tree with one hand, and, with the other, to the stone face from which it grew.

Their path was steep, but the rock walls on either side of it were quite vertical. As they went farther down into the chasm, foliage came together overhead and the daylight died back into semi-darkness.

On some swiftly slanting slopes Dawn Sailing clasped Smoke Drifting's hand and slid, stiff-legged, down gravel and shifting stones while the girl scrambled beside her, the two holding to each other and managing somehow to keep their balance. In steeper drops Smoke Drifting jumped or climbed down first, to turn, take in her hands the

feet that followed and guide them into breaks in the rock.

Dawn Sailing stopped where the path fell away in a little precipice. She tested a piece of a tree trunk that had fallen long ago from above, and found it sound enough. She took a length of rope from her bag and tied one end around the wood, then wedged it firmly behind big stones. Smoke Drifting had climbed down and was waiting below. She grasped the old woman's legs, easing her weight as she let herself down the line, hand under hand, grunting with the pain of the effort.

They were standing now on flat, bare rock. Smoke Drifting saw light coming in from ahead and heard the wash of waves. Looking up she saw a boulder the size of many wigwams, caught between the walls directly above them.

"Do not fear. The stone was hanging in that place when I came here with North Wind. It will not fall until the mother gives birth again."

From here on the corridor was level except for piles of fallen rock. The two made their way over these and came to the end of the passage, where the lake rippled below. The opening was almost covered with vegetation, but enough light came through to reveal the walls that rose far above. The rock on both sides was marked with cracks, fissures, and the delicate colors of layered mineral deposits.

"Look at the lines, granddaughter. Here by the opening they are partly covered by ferns and moss, so you must follow them out thoughtfully. When you do that you will find that they form the same pattern on both sides of us."

Smoke Drifting stood with her head tilted back, studying the cracks, grooves and colored strips, first on one rock face and then on the other.

"Now I see it. But the shapes on the left side are higher than the same shapes on the right."

"If you were to light fire-bark and walk back along the passage you would find that difference all the way. Where we now stand was once solid rock. Some power split the mountain and lifted one side of it, or dropped the other.

"I do not know of any thing or any magic strong enough to do that. North Wind did not know either. But she said that it is a sacred place, and that something far below must have torn its way up through the rock, and come out into the world. She thought that a woman who came here would become wise and strong. That is all that I can tell you.

For the rest, you must look at the walls and try to understand.

"Now let us gather stones and bury the dead hand beneath them. Then I will sing and pray for the ghost of the person it came from and for protection against whatever tore it away from his body and sent it under the water to your brother's net."

25

When Dawn Sailing and Smoke Drifting got back to the camp, the dark had come in cold from the lake and the remaining families were gathered around the cooking fires.

"We have done what we could," Dawn Sailing told Iron Feather. "Now it will be for you to test the wind and the sky."

In the morning, both looked good. Heavy packs of dried fish and fish meal and bulging makaks of dried berries, all tightly wrapped to keep out water, were carried down to the beach and stowed in the boats above the household goods and equipment. Iron Feather took his place behind Otter Woman. Their paddles stroked quickly, lightly, then with increasing power. They passed between the guardian rocks and out on the lake. The others followed.

Along this coast, decisions would have to be made and risks accepted. The canoes were riding deep in the water and no one had forgotten the sorcerer's warning. But there was also and always the unrelenting pressure of the days and hours. The ripening rice, far to the west, would not wait.

Early in the afternoon the wind changed and chunks of fog came in from the northeast, moving fast over the water. They faded the colors of points and islands, bringing them all to the same gray, then thickened to hide the hills along the shore and dim the canoes from each other. No commands were given, but spacings were closed up, so that each crew could cling to the outline of the next ahead.

Iron Feather altered his course to bring them somewhat closer to shore — close enough so that he could follow the sound of the surf while keeping a safe distance away from it. At times he would hear a louder roar, and a soaring mass of rock — headland or island — would suddenly emerge, a darkening shadow, from the white mist above, its base still hidden by the denser fog along the water. These were familiar sounds and sights, each coming in proper order and each remembered from other voyages. He proceeded with confidence.

Some of the followers may have been less certain, but they were quiet and kept their places. In the afternoon, shafts of sunlight came angling down to first lighten the gray veil and then to gradually reveal the line of canoes and the high contours of the shore.

As the mists moved out of the bays and river mouths, traverses began to offer themselves, shortcuts from one point of land to another. Iron Feather considered each of these, looking at faraway peaks and at protective island formations, calculating wind strength and direction along with any signs of shifting, and always watching for squalls that could come suddenly through openings in the mountain walls. Sometimes he risked the crossing, sometimes he took the long, safe way around.

He read the weather well. When the northeaster struck, the party was safely camped in a narrow valley where a river lay quiet, barely moving through a spruce-shaded pool before rushing down into the lake.

Even in this protected place they braced their shelters and canoes with forked poles and guyed them to trees and bushes with tight-stretched lines. They brought in a good supply of firewood and were dry and comfortable for three days while the rain lashed the bark coverings and the wind tried, without success, to tear away the structures.

Tamarack, intrigued by the intensity of this coast's fast-changing moods, walked down between bending, straining tree trunks, stepping across others that had been overthrown by the wind. The lake was snatching stones from the bottom and rolling them across the cobbles that formed the beach. They came smashing into hazel brush and alder at the river mouth with the deliberate but deadly momentum of spent canon balls. He was careful to keep out of their way, and returned to camp, glad to be ashore.

The storm was followed by a day of strong and shifting winds that made travel out of the question. At evening, Iron Feather, with Sturgeon Man and Loon's Foot, stood at the end of a stony point that ran out into the lake. They studied the drifting clouds, felt the wind dying around them, listened to the sad calls of the shore birds, observed the flight of the gulls, and breathed in the cold, clean smells of wet stone, lake air, and big water. The others watched, waiting for them to decipher these messages.

Loon's Foot ended the silence. "'Tschgumi is resting. By mid-morning he will rise up and roar again. We should push on now in the dark calm, make up some lost time, and go ashore at daylight. Or sooner, of course, if he should grow angry during the night."

Sturgeon Man thought otherwise.

"My nephew is right about the wind tomorrow. And the lake has become good for travelling. But something is out there in the water and the sky that I haven't seen before. And this is not an easy coast to come to in the dark. I think that we should wait."

"The mallards are swimming among the rice stems," said Loon's Foot. "A drake reaches his bill up and tastes a kernel. 'Ah, that is good,' he tells the hens, 'and it will be better in a few days. See how the grain is growing heavy and loosening its hold on the stalk. If we leave it there much longer, it will tire of waiting, let go its hold, and sink into the water. We will start the harvest soon.'

"'But how about the Indians?' a hen asks. 'They will need their share.'

"'We can't wait for those lazy ones forever. We will leave them a little rice, but not much. They can eat something else this winter.'"

When his friend had finished speaking, Iron Feather stood looking out over the water. The lake was rolling easily in the aftermath of the storm, the waves still big, but no longer dangerous.

Not without some misgivings, he decided that he and his family would take the chance. The others could come, or, if they chose, wait for more settled weather.

That word was welcomed by the watchers. Nobody wanted any more sitting around. One of the families had already loaded their canoe. They would have gone, whatever the leader decided, and others might have followed. But they all were glad to have Iron Feather ahead as the boats slid, one after another, down the steep rush of water from the harbor to the lake.

The people were conscious of the need to keep in sight of each other, but this was not easy, with the canoes appearing and disappearing like swimming ducks in the rise and fall of the long, smooth rollers. For a time, bright moonlight revealed the flash of the paddles ahead. Later, when clouds obscured the moon, the lake had grown more tranquil so that they were able to hold a closely spaced line.

Sturgeon Man and He-Rises, with Smoke Drifting, came last. The grandfather was watching the sky uneasily. This day that had been extended into night seemed very long.

"Change sides, grandson. And change more often from now on. My arms tire to move the paddle so many times over the same path."

From the the canoe ahead of them, Dawn Sailing looked back across the swaying water. She too was feeling the weakness of age and exhaustion. But Loon's Foot sang in the stern, and sometimes gave a shout as they swung up the bulk of a passing wave to cut through the rounded crest and speed down the slope that followed.

Iron Feather was keeping a good distance from the cliffs that could be seen, from time to time, as the light dimmed and brightened. In that space between the people and the shore was the lair of Missepishu, the man-eater. The shoals that were his teeth and claws were down there, submerged now but not far below the surface, ready to slash upwards if a sudden wind should roll higher waves and deeper troughs above them.

And so the night passed, and the canoes slid smoothly over the slowly-diminishing swells. The taut strains of present danger began to ease. This was going better than anyone had expected.

Then a catspaw, a riffle of fast-driving air, darted daintily out from the shore, zigzagging at random angles to leave little cat footprints bright on the black water.

Instinctively the people turned toward the coast as the wind moaned in the distant hills, hummed in a sudden chill around them, and then struck violently like some mighty moving wall.

The smooth swells were already lifting into froth-edged ridges. The hollows between them deepened. The water lynx began to snarl, blocking the path to the land, showing white fangs above the sunken rocks. The canoes swung back, turned tail-to-wind, and ran toward the open lake.

"Good!" shrieked the storm spirits. "That is the way we want you to go. Now we will help you!"

They laid their hands on the canoes and drove them flying, white sheets curving out from the bows to right and left.

But as soon as they were well beyond the reach of Missepishu, the steersmen, acting as though on some silently communicated order, used that momentum to rudder into a sharp turn. Quartering against the wind, the paddles beat their way across its path.

The waves were growing with malevolent speed, sprouting riffles along their slopes that quickly became breaking waves themselves. Hurtling masses of water thudded against the hulls, driving spray into faces and surging in over bows and gunwales.

The flotilla hung there with paddles thrashing, laboring in the rising seas, but moving only slowly down the shore. Iron Feather was searching for a passage that he knew was there, an opening in the grinding teeth of the surf.

Otter Woman saw it first. She shouted to Iron Feather. The wind snatched away the words from her lips but he caught her look and her hand motion. Paddling hard, they turned through the white rage into a narrow path of darkness. The others struggled after them.

Each time they dropped into a trough they tensed for the stab of rock from below, but each time the canoes were lifted again, undamaged. This channel was deep.

Dawn Sailing twisted from her sitting position in the bow, turning an agonized face to her son, shouting and pointing back into the chaos behind them. Loon's Foot could hear nothing of her voice, but he understood. The canoe that should have been following them had disappeared.

The risk of turning back would be too great. Words were useless here and a hand could not be spared for gesture. Loon's Foot went on paddling. There was no other way to answer.

Red Sky shouted wildly, then reached out her blade and pulled,

177

swinging the bow toward a turn. Now the son was fighting his mother as well as the storm. A breaker crashed against the partly angled hull, drenching them both. It said what Loon's Foot had not been able to tell her. She gave up her attempt to change the course and went back to hard, straight-ahead paddling.

The grip of the wind on the bows loosened as the canoes came into the shelter of starkly rising palisades. They followed this wall, lifted high beside it on the surges and then dropped far down below its shining-wet battlements.

A broad, black opening, a breach in the cliff, appeared beside the lead canoe. Iron Feather swerved into it, searching for any way to get ashore. He found it in the form of a ledge that slanted down, almost to within reach of the top of each swell. He was able to hold the canoe parallel to this refuge for a few moments, while Otter Woman crouched, watching her chance.

Suddenly she shot up the streaming crag, nimble as a girl, hooking toes and fingers into cracks, pulling herself to sloping sanctuary.

On the next rise, Iron Feather followed, seizing her outstretched hand. As he reached the footing he turned quickly and reached back to clamp his paddle against the gunwale. He shifted the grip of his other hand to a little spruce, freeing Otter Woman, and clung there, pinning the canoe loosely with the stretched-down blade to lift and drop against the granite below.

Otter Woman caught Ma-eengun by the scruff of the neck, lifted him clear of the canoe, and tossed him up the slope. He climbed a little, then slipped back, his claws spinning on the steep, wet stone. She turned and boosted him to the point where he could make his own way.

She carried the pup to safety. After that, each time that a surge brought the canoe within her reach, she snatched out a bundle. When the hull was empty, they lifted the boat from the water, pushing and pulling it up the rounded ledge to level rock. Then Iron Feather hurried back to help his daughter and her family, waiting below. Otter Woman was paying out a line secured, at its upper end, to a tree above the rocks.

Tamarack was a strong paddler, but still not so expert as the Anishinabeg in this kind of water. For a while he was unable to hold his wildly plunging boat steady enough for unloading. Then Shanod caught Otter Woman's rope, wrapped it around one hand, and passed the baby in her tikinagon up to the anxiously waiting grandmother.

Shanod, still clinging to the line and to her paddle, got a foothold for herself. The canoe dropped away beneath her. On its next rise she hooked the gunwale with her blade and Tamarack clambered out, helped by Iron Feather's grip on his jacket.

One by one, the others came in. Children, women, men, dogs, packs, boxes and boats were dragged or handed up to safety.

Loon's Foot's canoe entered the crevice last, heavy with water. Dawn Sailing looked up helplessly from the sloshing cold. Her legs felt locked into the sitting position in that half-swamped hull. But Tamarack was already on his way down. He gripped her wrist, then clasped her under the arms as she tried to rise from the dropping canoe. Many hands were holding the rope that had been tied around his waist. Now they lifted the double weight. With his moccasins sometimes skidding, sometimes clinging, Tamarack managed to keep his balance and to hang on to the old woman as they were drawn up to the ledge.

Meanwhile, those on the high ground had been splitting driftwood to get at the dry inner sections. Soon the people, huddled around the light and heat of crackling fire, were counting, whispering, checking faces. All the canoes had come in except one. He-Rises, Smoke Drifting, and Sturgeon Man were missing.

26

Sturgeon Man was searching for another glimpse of Loon's Foot's canoe. He had been catching sight of it from time to time, a dim shape tossing in the waves ahead. But the clouds had come together to cover the sky. He could see only darkness now and the white explosions of water.

The wind was sweeping them farther down the shoreline at every stroke. If the others had found a path through the churning turmoil of the reefs, he and his grandchildren must be far past it now.

He turned back, fighting to keep that wind close to the port bow, but getting caught repeatedly by assaults from one side or the other. The search for the channel had become hopeless. The best they could do would be to hold this position, stay afloat and cling to life in the roaring violence.

But he knew that they were not holding their position. They were being carried farther out into the lake. They were losing all protection of the shore hills. The waves were swelling to nightmare proportions.

Each time the bow passed over a towering crest and slapped down on the other slope, a flare of water leaped up on the windward side, to be instantly ripped into froth and driven against He-Rise's face like a blast of fine shot. The canoe was climbing higher waves than he had ever seen, or even thought possible, and was plunging into greater depths. It seemed to shrink as the seas continued to grow — a little thing, trying to stay alive in an endless desolation, a desert of malevolent rage.

He felt a great loneliness, a need to communicate in some way with the others. The devil-wind was roaring relentlessly around his ears. If the struggle against it had left him breath to shout, it would have ripped away his words and scattered them. There was no sound from those behind him except that sometimes, when there came a sudden, momentary lull in the storm's howl, he could hear a whimper from the cringing dog and the clatter of Smoke Drifting's makak as it bumped over the boat's ribs, scooping out water.

In the solitude of that struggle, fear gripped He-Rises. A shrinking from the breaker that struck at them, swift and white and deadly as the slash of a wolf. Dread of the wild, inhuman malice that was shaking and battering them. Thoughts of those places, far beneath them, too deep and cold for any fish to swim, where dead men sprawl and toss.

As they came up out of a flying summit, a savage gust suddenly

seized the prow. It caught the high-curved nose on the lip of the wave, at that vulnerable, sky-pointed, instant when He-Rises' blade, reaching down, found no water. For that moment, below him, there was only empty air.

The sly wind, searching, probing for any weakness, saw the opportunity. This was his chance to drown Indians. In that flash of time when the bow paddle had lost touch with the wave and before the canoe could pass over the crest and drop, he hurled his whole power against them.

Sturgeon Man tried to strike back at the attacking enemy, as an old warrior should. But his arms failed him, buckled under the brutal impact. The storm-thing ripped the bow out of his control, smashed it into a sickening lurch, swung it away from the true angle, the only angle that could keep the seas from overrunning the canoe.

He-Rises swept his paddle to the downwind side. The two men struggled to regain the critical position, or, at least, to keep from being forced further around. But now all the wind spirits knew what was happening. They ceased their rending attacks from the sides and joined together in head-on force. Their war-chant swelled. Kill! Kill! Kill!

Gradually, inexorably, they overwhelmed the toiling, desperate, human strength, pried the sheltering prow aside, exposed the low center, and sent a rolling mountain of water against it.

Both passengers saw the approaching doom. The dog cowered, shrinking from the black wall that climbed and curled above them. Smoke Drifting turned and grabbled at the spare paddle behind her.

That paddle had been lashed above the cargo in such a way that Sturgeon Man, from the stern, would be able to draw it free swiftly if his own should break. But, from the center position, she had to shove it backwards with sidewise jerkings, trying to loosen it from the rawhide thongs. As she struggled to clear it, she heard the crash of the giant wave and felt the hull shudder under its impact. Then the searing cold of icy water broke over her back and flooded down around her into the hull.

The canoe stalled, broached, rolling, half-full, like a man helpless from drink. The two paddles were still thrashing but the boat was no longer fighting the wind, nor running from it. It lay broadside, at the mercy of the spirits, waiting to be capsized.

The dog, wild to get out of the invading water, scrambled up on a pack, clinging with his claws. Another battering crest swept him over the side. He swam there for a while.

Smoke Drifting had worked the paddle free from its bindings and was adding her short, strong strokes to the efforts of the men on the leeward side. For precious minutes no killer wave struck.

He-Rises could not believe that the storm spirits were taking pity. More likely it was the dog. He had disappeared. Maybe the demons were neglecting the people while they took their pleasure with him.

Smoke Drifting knew the real reason. Dawn Sailing's medicine, made in the sacred cleft, was working. It was foiling the sorcerer's allies, giving his intended victims another chance, an opportunity to regain control of their canoe.

The hull, with gunwales almost awash, offered little surface to the wind. Lifted sluggishly on a great wave, it slipped off the crest, gulped in more water, hung, for a moment, at a desperate tilt, hesitating between life and death. Then lazily, almost casually, as though not caring much one way or the other, it righted itself, still afloat, still holding up its cargo and its paddlers.

Those three, all straining on the same side, were shifting their weight, balancing against the menace of each slow, terrifying roll, but never letting up in the fight to get the canoe pointed back into the wind. Slowly and with agonizing effort they brought the heavy, sodden thing around, facing it into the gale again to split the attacking seas.

As soon as that position was achieved, Smoke Drifting tucked the paddle in beside her and seized the makak. Now that the canoe was back on course, the other two might be able to keep it there while she bailed — if those evil ones could be held off a little longer.

Her hair was whipping across her eyes but her hands moved fast, feeling for the shifting water when she could not see it. Each time the canoe pitched forward down the side of a wave, a flood from the stern dammed up before her in the space where the dog had been, forming a good pool for bailing. And as they climbed the reverse tilt, the river that flowed back from the bow deepened around her, numbing her thighs but again giving momentary depth. On these ups and downs she was bucketing an almost steady stream over the gunwale, a shining arc of life and hope.

Each breaking wave lashed her with flying spray and every so often a steeper sea would come surging into the hull. But none of them were so overwhelming as the giant that had fallen upon them while they lay wallowing in the trough. She could feel the water level falling around her and the canoe riding the waves again as it regained some of its buoyancy.

When the bucket began to come up part empty Smoke Drifting dropped it and took the paddle. Almost immediately, under an inrush from a vicious wave, she tucked it away and went back to the bailing. But then came another pause, an easing of the wild violence as the split-mountain medicine pushed the water devils back. She drove in some good strokes before she had to take up the makak again.

They had recovered some stability but they were making no headway against the wind. Sometimes they held their own for a while. Then, coming under a series of heavier blows, they were driven further back into the night.

Sturgeon Man dared not ease off from the almost head-on angle into the shock of the charging waves, lest the bow be torn away from him again. He heard the cedar frame moan, then cry out as though in pain. He wondered how long the ribs and planking could stand the strain as the bow rose high, rode across each crest and then came smashing down. And how long his old arms and back would keep on working.

His mind was dulling, his power slipping away. His breath came in gasping sobs. He could not hold this pace much longer.

Just at the thought, without any conscious lessening of effort, he felt the canoe shudder and swerve a little, under a heavy impact, then turn slowly, but with increasing speed, toward surrender and death.

The others felt it too. Somehow the three found the strength to stop the swing before it had gone too far, to hold the hull against the fury of the storm, and to force it back until the white tops of the oncoming waves were breaking on both sides again. Sturgeon Man knew that there could be no more such lapses. He would not be able to bring up another effort like that.

But 'Tschgumi is always unpredictable. The wind was relenting a little. For the moment, at least, straining hard, he could keep the bow into it.

A patch of stars came out, serene above the raging water. The wind eased further. The grandfather wondered whether the sky was beginning to lighten far off to the east. And that thickening of the darkness ahead and to the right. Was it at the water level? Or was it just a low-hanging cloud?

185

As soon as there was a little light, Iron Feather and Otter Woman climbed, painfully and at some risk, to the top of the hill behind their refuge. The great wind had ended. But the immensity of water below them revealed only the numberless lines of the swells rolling out to the horizon.

By noon these had settled enough to allow travel. Otter Woman and Shanod were keening a song for the dead. They had blackened their faces and the mother had made cuts in her arms with a sharp little knife. But there was not much time to mourn. They must go now.

All afternoon they followed the shoreline over ponderous swells, the rolling, diminishing aftermath of the storm. Iron Feather was anxious to make up lost time. They paddled late and camped high on one of a chain of islands that paralleled the coast. Everyone was quiet and very tired.

✦ ✦ ✦

Sturgeon Man, watching that place where the thinning darkness seemed to thicken, had seen it solidify into a tall island that pointed up out of the lake, a lopsided arrowhead against the approaching dawn. He turned toward it. Beyond were other islands and then the distant line of the coast.

Exhaustion was settling on his tortured shoulders, weighing down on him like a giant, impatient vulture. He knew that the grandchildren, too, were at the end of their strength. Their eyes were red, their faces swollen, their hands raw. The paddles were moving sluggishly, but with enough strength yet to keep up headway over the big swells that rolled under them, no longer attacking.

The sun was high when they came into the lee of the island. The men held the canoe with their paddles beside a flat rock. Smoke Drifting scrambled out, turned, and clutched the gunwale. He-Rises followed, and together they managed to get the old man up and out of the boat and the boat out of the water. They first spread the water-logged cargo over the slanted slabs, and then themselves, to dry and sleep in the warming sun.

When he woke, Sturgeon Man carefully examined the canoe. It had not been damaged so badly as he feared. A master craftsman had designed its light frame to withstand such a battering.

He found some dry cedar that had been washed ashore and

shaped it to reinforce several cracked members. That, with the bark and the pitch that they always carried with them, was all he needed.

Meanwhile, He-Rises and Smoke Drifting had been going over the supplies, discarding what had been ruined by the water and repacking the rest. By mid-afternoon they were ready to go. They had been blown far off their course but, if hostile spirits did not lay hands on them again; they would find the others. They pushed on into sunset and then darkness until they saw the the fire above the mist.

✦ ✦ ✦

It was a still night, with a little ice forming on the water buckets. Dawn Sailing waked cold and sad. She revived the fire, laid on more wood and then walked to the edge of a granite outcropping that fell away from her feet to the lake below. Other islands stood dark in the moonlight, their lower levels hidden in a carpet of cloud, their peaks rising softly out of it like floating mountains.

Dawn Sailing did not see the canoe coming in through the mist, but she heard the faint rasp of a paddle pushed down flat on stone to stop movement. By the time she reached the low rocks that gave entry to the island the canoe had been unloaded and was being lifted from the water. She threw her arms around Smoke Drifting, and the girl responded, saying nothing, but pressing her face hard against the old woman's shoulder.

Others had waked now with the sounds of the landing. Otter Woman came running recklessly down the dark path from camp. Soon all were gathered around one of the fires for an impromptu feast of thanksgiving to 'Tschgumi, Missepishu, and the water windigos, who had been satisfied with the sacrifice of a dog and had let the people go. And as they heard the story of the escape they gave thanks, too, for the mercy of the wind.

Smoke Drifting listened in silence for a while, then grew bold, bold enough to speak her mind.

"Out there I did not feel that anything was being merciful. It was the grandmother's medicine that held off those terrible things. They were all coming against us to carry us down. Only the power of that sacred cleft, a power that could split a mountain, was strong enough to beat them back."

Talk and ceremony ended soon. The tired people returned to their robes. The camp became silent, except for an occasional murmur from the fire as it burned down to a dull redness that finally faded into black.

The travellers were on the water early the next morning. A growing wind forced them to land again as soon as the sun was well up. But it died at sunset. Rested now, they went on through the night and entered the mouth of the river that would be their path to the west. That summer, at least, no one had left them to join those others in the depths of the great, beautiful, haunted lake.

27

For several miles the cliffs that formed the sides of the valley stood well apart from each other, giving the river room to swing in easy curves. The water was smooth except for the pulse of the lake, those long, rhythmic swells reminding travellers that they are still connected with 'Tschgumi. Upstream, the walls came gradually together and the darkening current began to swirl circles of foam past the canoes.

The travellers went ashore at a worn stone landing where the sound of rushing water came from behind a screen of cedars. Here they searched back into the forest to find straight, slender, spruce trunks. They cut these with the usual explanations to the trees, carefully trimmed off the branches, then hefted and shaved them down for perfect balance.

Each person beyond tikinagon age was fitted with one of these poles and each made lively and effective use of it in the rapids. Swiftly, efficiently, they pushed the canoe uphill against the menacing opposition of the white water.

The poles wore down quickly on the rock and gravel bottom. At the end of each day their ends were frazzled into broom shapes and had to be cut away. When a pole became too short to use, it was replaced.

But not Loon's Foot's pole — he carried a metal point that he slipped over the end. This usually held firm against slippery stone and prevented much damage to the wood.

Where the rapids were too strong for push power alone, Loon's Foot guided the canoes through them while the other men hauled on tow lines. They could hear his iron click against stone as he swung the boat around boulders and up the chutes of rushing water. Once he miscalculated, and the hull struck rock and tilted, taking in a rush of water. Swiftly he swung it clear and righted it, then gestured to acknowledge the wave of laughter that came rolling out from shore.

The travellers were moving up a flowing stairway, poling and tracking where they could, portaging around waterfalls and around rapids too strong to climb. Sometimes the trail would lead up a rock

face so steep that those carrying the canoes had to be helped with ropes pulled by others from above, a heart-pounding effort. Nobody was calling for more speed or for bigger burdens. But everybody understood the importance of getting to the rice lakes as quickly as possible. Each person, young and old, was moving as much cargo as his back could carry, and as swiftly as his breath would allow.

Returning for second loads on some of those high portages, He-Rises could see, through openings in the cliffs below, the blue horizon of the big lake. Later there were only ridges falling away behind and granite ramparts ahead. Then at last they came up out of somber depths, up and around a far-dropping waterfall, and out into the sunset's afterglow.

They were standing on the edge of a roughly level plateau. In the immediate foreground the river curved lazily past, resting before its plunge. Beyond lay hills, with pointed teeth of spruce tops sharp against the sky.

And beyond those hills were valleys, but nothing like the gigantic declivity from which they had emerged. They had climbed the side of the ancient glacial lake of which 'Tschgumi is the shrunken puddle. Tomorrow they would go far.

Some of the women went out in the twilight to gather a little food for supper. Shanod cut a long birch pole and tied a bark noose to its tip. Smoke Drifting called Ma-eengun and sent him ranging ahead as the sisters walked into the forest.

This was the season when the spring-hatched grouse had reached good eating size but still had not lost their innocence. They believed that, as long as they kept beyond reach of the women's arms, they would be safe.

When the dog flushed them they didn't bother to fly far. Several would perch in the same tree, craning their necks for a better look at the strange creatures below. Shanod reached up with her pole, gently slid the noose over the head of the lowest bird, jerked it from the branch, and swung it into Smoke Drifting's waiting hands. Small but strong hands that held the struggling bird steady against her thigh, turned the head at a right angle, and broke the neck with a quick jerk. Those above watched with interest but without alarm since the flapping victim had not passed them on its way down. The snare was already approaching the next lowest.

Several other women also had good hunting and everyone in

camp got his share. The plump little bodies were soon sending out delicious odors as their juices spattered and dripped into the coals.

In the first light of morning the canoes left their wake widening across the mirror stillness of the river, swaying the tattered remnants of faded water lilies along its edges. A heron lifted out of the mist ahead, circled the travellers, and flew with slow wing-strokes down the river. Again they were crossing the stone shield, this time near its southern edge. But now the sunrise was warming their backs instead of shining in their eyes.

The sorcerer's power over the weather seemed to have ended at the incline out of 'Tschgumi. The wind spirits and the rain were not opposing them now. The portages were firm under their feet. The lakes were long and calm. Autumn was coming in gently. They had no maps on which to measure the daily miles but they knew that they were passing swiftly over long distances.

In a few days they slid down the southern edge of the shield into a flat country of swamps, shallow lakes and quiet little rivers where the tree branches met overhead. They came out of one of these shaded streams to follow a channel that wound through marshes, broadening as other waters joined it and opening at last into a big lake. This was a sprawling body of water with sandy beaches, repeatedly broken by sloughs, bays, and the mouths of other incoming rivers. The rice grew thick in each of these backwaters and the harvest was in full swing.

The group separated here, each family turning toward its own hereditary area. All except Dawn Sailing and Loon's Foot, who were keeping with Iron Feather's party.

As they swept past the canoes working the rice beds they called back answers to questions and to friendly jeers about being late. They accepted shouted dinner invitations for the evenings ahead. But they did not stop for visiting, nor even slow their pace.

In Sturgeon Man's ancestral bay, only the waterfowl were ricing. The ducks went on with their harvest until the canoes were close, then got up heavily, flew a little way, and splashed down to continue feeding.

It was no wonder they were so bold. The kernels were big and fat, a delicious dark-ripe color, and loose on the stalk, falling into the canoes as the paddlers pushed through the rice toward the landing.

Here a double line of poles had been laid flat across the marsh. The people carried their packs and boxes over this quaking bridge and up to the crest of a hill where hardwoods glowed yellow and red above the bare bent ribs of a waginogan. Beside it stood a big vat made of cedar slabs, slanting down from a wide mouth to a narrow bottom. These old friends would get their recognition later. Now the people hurried back to the canoes, the men with long, forked poles. Each woman carried two short sticks.

Smoke Drifting stayed at the camp, first making her little niece comfortable and then checking the lodge frames. She replaced broken members, retied loosened bindings, covered the pole framework as far as her reach permitted, and laid out the materials for taller women to put in place on the upper parts of the structure. She turned, pausing in her work, to enjoy the rich autumn smells and to look out over the water. That is, she knew that she was looking over water, although she could actually see very little of it.

The bay seemed more like a pale green meadow, through which standing men glided with mysterious ease, as they poled invisible canoes. Just the heads of the women and of the grandfather appeared above the rice. They were each crouched in a stern, facing forward, bending the stalks over the gunwale with one stick, crossing over it with the other and gently tapping the grain into the bottom of the boat. The sticks moved in easy motion, striking just hard enough to dislodge the ripe kernels without disturbing those not yet ready for harvest.

Smoke Drifting noticed that one of the men was not gliding with such mysterious ease, after all. And Shanod was doing more laughing than beating. Tamarack had never seen wild rice growing, let alone poled a canoe through it. His antics were irresistably funny.

At first he pushed with the butt of his sapling, giving a good shove in what he had always considered was the proper way to pole a canoe. The birch went right down into the soft silt, with the man bent over at a ridiculous angle above it.

"Be careful," Shanod warned him, "or you'll get left behind hanging to your pole. If that happens you'll have to roost there for a while because I won't have time to come back for you until the harvest is finished.

"So I think you'd better turn that stick around and push with the forked end."

Tamarack reversed his pole but now he kept getting its crotch tangled in the mat of dead vegetation that covered the floor of the rice bed. This would instantly halt all progress. Then, straining, he would hoist up a dripping forkful of heavy, rotting stuff.

Later in the day, after an embarassingly long period of this poking and heaving, he began to get the feel of pushing the fork against the bottom without either entangling it or breaking through. The canoe moved ahead, his wife worked deftly, and he was amazed at how quickly the hull began to fill. But poling through standing rice is hard work for an inexperienced man, and he was glad when Shanod, satisfied with their cargo, laid down her beating sticks and took up the paddle.

They reached the landing as darkness was gathering. Several mallards and coots who had graciously approached the canoes during the day were already simmering in the kettle. There was a happy atmosphere around the fire that night. In spite of their late arrival this would be a good harvest.

The sun came up strong, warming the cold air of dawn — good weather for manomen. Soon, big sacks of grain were being carried up from the canoes. Dawn Sailing and Smoke Drifting spread it on sheets of birch bark. There it lay for a day and a night, exposed to sun and wind, stirred often during daylight hours so that it dried evenly.

In the next step, it was parched over slow heat. This was touchy work. The slightest delay or inattention would leave the rice scorched and ruined. Sturgeon Man alternately stoked and suppressed the little fire to provide just the right degree of heat. Dawn Sailing sat beside the kettle, which had been tilted and propped to face her. She kept a small paddle moving continuously, never letting the grain stand still on the hot metal.

Then, together, they carried each kettle of parched rice over to the the old cedar vat and poured it in. Here Smoke Drifting joined them. All three took wooden pestles and pounded the grain. But it was a gentle pounding. They just let the wood drop, never coming down hard with it. In this way they loosened the husks without breaking the kernels.

In the afternoon when the wind was steady, but not too strong, Shanod and Otter Woman took the rice in big, shallow, bark trays out into an open place, tossed it into the air, and tossed again until all the husks had fluttered away.

Then came the treading. Two heavy poles were lashed to a tree, each of them running to ground on either side of a skin-lined pit. The winnowed rice was poured into this hollow, and Iron Feather stepped out upon it. He grasped a pole in each hand, taking part of his weight off his feet, and began a rather graceful little ballet, feeling the kernels with his moccasins, bending or straightening at the waist, raising or lowering his body with his arms. All this put just the right pressure, through the soles of his feet, on the fragile, almost-finished grain, to separate the last husks and pieces of husk. The chaff remnants from this treading were carefully separated from the kernels and saved for cooking. Some of the people liked them better than the grain.

After Iron Feather, Loon's Foot took his turn, and then He-Rises. Finally, to quiet Tamarack's urgent requests, they put a little rice in the pit and let him try it.

That batch didn't turn out well.

"Those big feet of yours are too heavy," said Loon's Foot. "You have broken the rice. Here, I will show you."

He stepped into a renewed pile of grain and began again the delicately undulating dance step.

"Put more weight on your hands. You must step lightly as though you were a sandpiper on the beach. Watch me for a while and then you can get on the poles again."

Hunting, fishing and wood gathering continued, but mostly in the twilight hours. Now He-Rises was entrusted with the use of the flint-lock. The excitement was as strong in him as it is in any young hunter who has just come into the possession of a new and more effective weapon, but his methods were very different from those of a white sportsman. Shot and powder must be conserved. He could not afford to risk sporty shots at flying birds.

He moved silently through the trees at the edge of the marsh, peering out through the spruce boughs and the dense but leafless brush between the forest and the muskeg. When he saw ducks on the water he flattened down into the swamp grass and crawled toward them. At the end of the outermost cover he lay watching for a while to be sure that the birds were feeding with no signs of worry other than the erect heads of their usual sentinels. Then he slowly brought up the muzzle of the musket and waited until several of the swimmers were in line with the expanding blast zone of the flying pellets.

No matter how tightly He-Rises hugged the gun to his shoulder, the recoil of that big bore jolted him. But sometimes he hit three or four ducks at one shot. Some would be lying dead or helpless on the water while others might be sitting up, unable to fly but still capable of some lively swimming and diving.

He-Rises kept low in his ambush until he had reloaded to finish off these injured ones. Then, if the bottom was firm enough, he waded out to pick them up. Where it was too soft or too deep he waited for the wind to blow them in reach of a pole.

One of the dogs was quite good at finding any wounded birds that might be in hiding, but he was not always able to control his excitement during the stalk. He-Rises kept him tied in the woods to be released if his nose was needed to track down cripples when a shooting was over.

28

The days continued cool, dry and clear. Load after load of rice was knocked down into the canoes, carried up from the landing, dried, processed, and packed into bags. This was more than the family would be able to use, but they kept working. It was clear to Iron Feather that Dawn Sailing and Loon's Foot would be with them this winter in the spruce grove camp. Not only would extra grain be needed but also more lard, flour, powder and shot. He would take a full cargo of rice south to the American town with whatever fur might be available.

Iron Feather did not look forward to the trip with pleasure. There would be some large lakes to cross. The loads would be cumbersome, both coming and going. This late in the fall, stormy weather would be likely. Also, he would have to deal with strange white men, quite unlike Jamieson.

He had not yet decided whom to take with him. Loon's Foot knew the route and always seemed to get along well with the Americans. His skill as a canoeman would be valuable. But once they reached the settlement, he would be hard to control. Tamarack, too, was good with pole and paddle, although not the equal of Loon's Foot.

As often happens, the decision was taken out of his hands by fate, or by sorcery or by some nasty little spirit. Nobody was ever quite sure which. It happened on a hunting side-trip.

Venison, along with rice and fish, had been the mainstay of the Anishinabe diet down through the centuries, the surest defense against famine. But now caribou were seen only occasionally in this part of Canada.

Moose were not plentiful either, but were much valued for the

197

large supply of meat and fat that one kill would provide. Almost as important was the heavy hide, a necessity for good moccasin soles, snowshoes, and many other articles that required strong, long-wearing leather. The back sinew was also essential. It was used for many purposes, but especially for sewing the skin garments for winter trapping and hunting. The antlers, grease, and dried nerves were used, with appropriate charms and rituals, to cure disease.

Moose were not easy to hunt. They had learned to stay well away from the habitations of men. They moved upwind as they fed, and rested where they could keep an eye on their back track. Their big, sensitive ears were always swivelling to pick up the least sound of approaching danger.

But at this season, when the wind sighed through the empty branches of the trees on the ridge, and the down leaves made a strong, pleasant smell around the rice camp, they would be less cautious than at other seasons. This was their mating time. The bulls would be nervous, but also bold and aggressive.

The people had been eating well. The mallards were going south now, though, and the big flights of northern bluebills would not be coming in until the weather got really cold. A supply of fresh meat was needed both for present use and for the coming journeys. The hunters went back into the hills and the women set out nets again in the deeper water beyond the rice bays. He-Rises had done well with the early ducks. It seemed to Iron Feather that this would be a good time to instruct his son in another phase of the hunting mystery.

They paddled all day up a small stream and came ashore at sunset on a wooded point that ran far out into a pale waste of bog. He-Rises carried the canoe well back into the long swamp grass, where it would be out of sight, then took the gun and hurried up the grade to watch his father peel a strip of birch bark and fashion it into a cone. They sat down in a clump of alders close to the water. In the warm evening light the earth around them was bright with leaf color.

Iron Feather put the cone to the outside of his lips and spoke into it. Spoke moose. Love talk. The drawn-out moaning call of the cow and the short, throaty grunts of the bull's answer. Then a long silence.

He-Rises was listening intently. Iron Feather handed him the funnel and took the musket. A bull that comes in answer to this kind of a message is expecting to enter a triangle situation. He does not expect to be welcomed by the other male. He is looking for trouble, and the hunter had better be ready.

After a while, He-Rises spoke through the cone, play-acting, taking the parts of moose-hero and moose-heroine. He felt that he had done well on his first attempt. But the father was a sharp critic. When it was time for another call, he took the cone and demonstrated again.

The calling and coaching continued at the proper intervals while the last glow died in the west between tall stumps that leaned out over the water. But there was no response.

The two men walked to the high ground, made a little fire in the shelter of the trees, and slept. They were up again before the first light, searching their way back over trembling muskeg to their hiding place in the alders. He-Rises carried the gun, Iron Feather the horn and a dry stick.

At his second call, while the sky was still only a little light, an answer came from the rim of spruce across the river — a series of gruff grunts and the crash of antlers breaking impatiently through brush. Then there was silence. Iron Feather waited. After a while he gave a seductive feminine wail. They could hear the bull moving about. But he refused to come out into the open marsh.

Iron Feather reversed the horn, closed the mouth opening with his hand, and scooped up the bark cone full of water. For a moment he held it high. Then he let the water splash back to the surface.

The thought of that gracefully curving cascade and its adorable source was too much for the bull. They could hear him plunging through the soggy muskeg. Then, in some strange animal way, he seemed to receive a signal that something was out of order. He came to a gurgling stop behind a patch of willows.

Iron Feather was silent for several minutes, then shot out a series of challenging male snorts, and beat the bushes with his stick to make the sound of charging antlers.

That did it. The bull splashed into the river, wading and swimming toward the hunters.

They had him now. He-Rises took aim but Iron Feather reached out, touched his arm, and gave the hand sign for not yet. The butchering would be difficult if the kill were made there in the river. Let him get up and across that mud flat.

He-Rises waited through long, tense seconds. Then he was jerked around by a mighty crashing in the bushes just behind him. A huge black shape loomed over him. The old flintlock roared. The moose

went down, his antlers plowing the ground between the two men.

From beyond the river came the dying sounds of the other bull's departure.

He-Rises had been almost bowled over by the kick of the gun, but he had shot his first moose. He thought of the prophecy. The dark shape had risen threateningly. But there had been no pursuit.

Suddenly he realized that his father was waiting for him to complete the action. He reloaded the musket, stepped behind the moose, and spoke the usual words of thanks. Then he leaned forward, reaching out over the carcass, to touch the steel muzzle to the eye.

His hand shook a little, from excitement or from extending the weight of the gun. Or he might have been trembling with the exhilaration of success. The musket brushed the eyelid and struck the cheek just below the eye. It had not touched the open eye. He raised the muzzle and stepped back.

At the moment, this slight deviation from the prescribed ritual seemed of no consequence. And Iron Feather, watching each step of the ceremony, somehow failed to notice the error. He drew his knife, bent over the moose and drove the blade into the neck at the point where it joined the chest.

That was the opening of the bleeding cut. It should have been finished with a slicing thrust toward the backbone to cut the carotid artery. But the stroke was not completed.

As the knife went in, the seemingly dead animal erupted in one last spasm of life, a violent contortion of the body and a sweep of flying hoofs. The hindquarters heaved up. For a moment it seemed that the moose might actually get to its feet. Then it fell back in final collapse.

Iron Feather had been knocked into the underbrush. He came out of that rolling motion with his feet under him and snatched the flintlock from He-Rise's shaking hands. But there was no need to shoot again.

Iron Feather cut off the bull's beard and He-Rises walked up to the high ground and hung it in a tree as a sign of respect and thanks to the munificent moose. They skinned and cut up the carcass and loaded the canoe. The job went slowly, though. A pain in the upper chest, which Iron Feather had not noticed at first, became increasingly demanding. He was unable to help much with the butchering. He-Rises carried the heavy pieces of meat to the water and loaded the canoe.

Iron Feather paddled a mile or two, then felt obliged to let He-Rises take the stern. Later he gave up altogether, and tucked his paddle back in the meat.

He was still sitting in the bow when He-Rises brought the canoe in beside the log dock long after dark. For once the father's manidoke had failed him. Or else it had been overcome by a stronger power.

In her examination, Dawn Sailing found the right shoulder hanging low and a painful swelling on the chest, clearly caused by the loose ends of a broken collar bone. She bathed the injured area with warm water, applied a poultice of wild ginger and spikenard, hung the arm in a sling padded with dry moss against the body, and bound it there with another cloth to prevent movement. She warned Iron Feather not to use the arm and assured the family that no permanent harm had been done.

Even so, they all could see that the injury might have serious consequences. A temporary incapacity could be disastrous at the outset of Peboan. Iron Feather would not be shooting for some time. Worse, he would be unable to take the rice to the American town.

Nobody liked to talk about Undertooth, but the unspoken consensus was that this had been his work. Iron Feather, though, believed that it had been brought about by some lesser power, one of the many spirits that lived in the forest and always seemed to enjoy making trouble for hunters. He felt sure that if the sorcerer should strike, it would be with a more deadly blow than a little hurt to a shoulder.

He-Rises found it impossible either to forget his own responsibility for his father's injury or to speak of it to any of the others. He wondered what further evils might develop from this latest lapse.

For the present, there was plenty of food. One of the hunters had killed a bear and others had brought in two of the whitetail deer that were coming into this area as the caribou moved out. The racks over the smoky fires were heavy with meat and fish. The drying process now was not so much to preserve these. They should keep well anyway in this cool season. But it was necessary to lighten them for the coming journeys.

High-bush cranberries had been picked and hazel nuts gathered for food and medicine. The ricing would soon be ending and the women were beginning to think of other projects. Especially Smoke Drifting. Several times she had reminded her mother and her sister that one more crop had to be harvested before the freezeup — mujotabuk. That would be the kind of work that little girls enjoy and that older women would be willing to postpone. The trouble was that the longer it was put off the worse it would be.

On the morning after the last rice was processed and packed, Otter Woman and her daughters walked down to the landing. Dawn Sailing was looking after Sound of Waves. To save argument they hadn't told her where they were going. It wasn't a job for a woman of her age.

They paddled out of the rice bay and crossed the lake to enter a slow-winding little river. This widened out several miles upstream, into a series of ponds. In their still shallow water, mujotabuk — also called katniss, arrowhead, wapato, and duck potato — grew plentiful and green in the summer, its pointed leaves aiming at the sky. The leaves were gone now, but the brown stalks that remained showed where the rich little tubers would be located.

Mujotabuk was an important crop for the Anishinabeg. The tubers stored well, and were delicious boiled or roasted. But they were hard to gather. They usually lay some distance from the main plant at the ends of roots that ran out horizontally through the mud. Unless you were lucky enough to locate a muskrat hoard, the only way to get them was to feel for them with bare toes. Once loosened they would float up to the surface and could be picked up by hand. But your feet would be sinking into the soft bottom.

The women could tell from floating debris and from tracks in the mud that the river ponds had been well worked. But Otter Woman knew other good ones. They left the canoe on the bank and walked across the marsh to one of these. Here they took off their moccasins and waded in, their long skirts billowing up around them.

Smoke Drifting said that the water wasn't really cold. That remark made Shanod feel like an old woman. When she had been eleven, it hadn't been bad for her either. Now that she was nineteen it seemed very cold indeed.

The best parts of this work were the rest periods. Other harvesters would call across the marsh grass to them. Then they would come dripping out of their respective ponds and sit together in some sheltered place, pulling their dresses up to get their legs dry and warm in the sun. The company and the conversation were good. Best of all was being out of the icy water.

But this was a luxury that they could not afford for long. Soon they would get up, and each would return to her own operation.

As Otter Woman and her girls were wading in again after one of these rests they heard a cry from a nearby pool. It was not loud, but it clearly signified distress.

They raced across the intervening bog and stood on the mucky black beach. For a moment they could see no one. Then another low call brought their attention to a face at the far end of the pond, barely showing above the water. One of the harvesters had stepped into a sink-hole in the mud and had gone down to her chin. She waited for them, silent now, smiling apologetically. She was not making even the least motion, so she was going down very slowly. But she didn't have much farther to sink.

Otter Woman ran along the shore in her direction, eyes searching the swamp grass and the taller vegetation behind it. She saw what she wanted, a tall, slender spruce that had been dead long enough to be rotten at its root. She plowed into the brush, tore the trunk loose, ran along the shore to the closest point to the endangered woman, and splashed into the water. Now she moved more cautiously, testing the bottom with her foot before each step. When she judged that she was close enough she leaned forward, extending the shaggy pole. The woman gripped it.

The spirit in the swamp must have taken a fancy to her. The mud hated to let her go. Her head went under water when Otter Woman pulled hard from the other end of the pole.

But by this time Shanod and Smoke Drifting were helping. The woman hung on. Little by little they dragged her through muck, stumps and water. At last, safe on the shore, she got up on her hands and knees, gasping and covered with dark slime. They all had a good laugh and went back to the work.

The moon of freezing water was close at hand now, and the days were growing short. By mid-afternoon the sun was not providing enough warmth to continue the wet labor. They floated the canoe and carried the sacks of tubers out to it.

"That was a good day," said Smoke Drifting. "It will be sunny again tomorrow and we can come back for more."

29

Active as the Indians were in ricing, the ducks and coots managed to get their share. And in spite of the efforts of both these groups of harvesters, a considerable proportion of the grain fell into the water and sank to the oozy bottom. That would be seed for next year.

When, finally, the stalks rattled dry and empty in the wind there was a last round of feasts, with songs and dances of harvest thanksgiving, and prayers for the coming winter. Then the coverings were removed from the lodge poles and the bundles were carried down to the canoes. Quietly, without spoken farewells, but with deeply-felt hopes to meet again in the spring, the people left the harvest camps and set out for winter quarters.

Several waterways connected with the rice lakes, and each of these now flowed with streams of canoes. Loon's Foot and Tamarack took the heavy load of tightly packed sacks of rice and a bale of autumn fur down a chain of lakes and rivers south toward the medicine line, that mysterious, invisible mark across the earth, that divided the royal grandmother's country from the United States. Those going north moved in a spread-out procession clinging to the companionship, camping together for a few more nights. Well-fed now, and strong with confidence from the bountiful harvest, they followed a marshy river all the first day and part of the second, then portaged across a watershed divide, and came down again between the stony upthrusts and dark, pointed treetops of the shield. The weather was fine and clear, but each morning a rim of new ice ran well out from the shore. It was too thin to be an obstacle and disappeared quickly in the sun and the wind, but it served as a reminder that they had better keep moving.

The line of canoes grew shorter each day as one party after another turned east or west toward their winter hunting grounds. Iron Feather's people, with three other families, came back up the winding, sedge-sided river to the sugar hills. They would camp in that fertile and familiar place, taking and storing meat and fish, until the Minnisabik should change from a canoe route to an ice road.

Far to the south, Loon's Foot and Tamarack were nearing their destination. They paddled down lakes whose desolate shores had been stripped of forest. Only cut-off stumps remained, blackened and charred where fire had swept through loggers' slashings. They were meeting many canoes now, some manned by Indians and some by whites, and larger boats powered by sails or oars.

Once, coming straight at them as they rounded the curve into a windy expanse of river, they saw what looked like a gigantic, floating, charging, smoking woodpile. A whistle blew a furious blast, Loon's Foot swung the canoe hard over, and they scuttered out of the way just in time. Someone shouted a string of curses at them from the deck above. The churning ferocity of the stern paddle-wheel swept close beside them, spraying them with water. Then they were tossed, struggling, somehow staying right side up, as the wake's sudden waves broke through the heavy chop of the wind-roughened river.

This was a wood-burning steamboat, its deck piled high with fuel. It had been something quite beyond the experience of either Loon's Foot or Tamarack, but they knew that Pauguk had come close. That they had narrowly escaped another weird and dangerous creation of the white man.

The settlement served several logging camps and provided supplies for trappers, miners, prospectors and promoters. Its single street ran straight back from the lakeshore. A person walking down that deep-rutted thoroughfare might hear conversations in Swedish, Norwegian, German, Anishinabemowin or English.

On either side of the street stood a row of buildings, some of log construction, others of milled lumber in the modern style with tall false fronts that made them look much larger than they really were. There was a sawmill on the waterfront, a trading post, a blacksmith shop, a general store with post office, two lodging houses, a livery stable, and three saloons. Beyond these were new houses, their green lumber already cracking in the sun, and beyond them, several small farms in newly cleared fields.

A tote road south to larger cities had been recently cut and corduroyed — paved with timbers through the muskeg. Horse-drawn wagons were able to get over it when it was dry enough, or when it was newly frozen, and bull teams could use it any time of year except for a few weeks after the spring breakup.

Several big pine stumps stood, solidly rooted and defiant, in front of the commercial buildings. But the place had an alert, aggressive air, a feeling of confidence. This village had come to stay.

Indian Town was an untidy cluster of waginogans and tar-paper shacks in back of the sawmill. Arriving at evening, Loon's Foot and Tamarack saw the cooking fires and landed below them. They unloaded their cargo, stacked it on poles to keep it off the soggy ground, and turned the boat over it for protection from the dew. Other bark canoes lay scattered in the long grass at odd angles, bottoms up or bottoms down, as though sleeping off a drunken orgy.

Their arrival had been noted. No one came down to greet them except the outraged dogs that barked and snapped close to their heels. But many eyes were watching as they walked up to the dwellings.

These people knew something about modern times and about the value and uses of money. During the previous winter, most of the men had helped to clear the right-of-way for the road. Some did odd jobs around store buildings, or at the farms. At times there was work for them at the logging camps. When such employment was not available they might hunt, fish or trap either to provide some food for their families or to get a little additional income.

Some of the women went regularly to the town to help with the weekly wash, or to sell fish and berries. One medicine woman had several times been summoned to act as midwife for the settlers.

Prostitution was a brand new idea to the woods Indians, but they took to it readily once the monetary standard had been understood and accepted. Many of the younger women were entertaining loggers, prospectors and men from the settlement. It couldn't be said that they made a good living in this way, but just to keep themselves and their children eating regularly seemed pretty good to them. Husbands or lovers were admitted only when the paying clients did not require services.

207

The Indian quarter was littered and messy by either white or forest standards, but its residents spoke English and had learned American ways. Their white man clothing, although far from new, set them off from strangers in home-sewn broadcloth and skin garments. They were conscious of their superiority over a pair of old-fashioned rat-stabbers from the bush.

As they walked along a path between the dwellings, Tamarack was amazed at the silent stares of those who passed them or sat watching. Loon's Foot, ahead, hesitated several times before different lodges, received no encouragement, and went on. When he came to the end of the row he lifted the door covering of a waginogan and stepped inside.

"We will stay with you tonight and go to the Saganash town tomorrow."

A woman looked up from the cooking.

"There are too many of us already. We have no space for you and we have food only for ourselves. So go somewhere else now."

The man beside her looked uncomfortable.

"These are strangers, Louise, and from far away. They have nowhere else to go. We could move the boxes and make room for them."

He turned to Loon's Foot who stood in the entrance, saying nothing.

"Have you brought goods to trade with the white man?"

"We have rice and fur."

Louise Cedarstick brightened.

"You can stay, then, and I will give you some supper. But you must give money to us for these things when you sell your rice."

While his wife put more food into the kettle and went on with the cooking, Cedarstick asked about the harvest and about some relatives in the north. Loon's Foot had known those people he spoke of, but could give no recent news of them.

Tamarack wanted to know what the Saganashag were like who lived in the great square buildings.

"The Americans are hairy, quick-tempered, and sly. They talk loudly. Often they interrupt another speaker before he has finished. And they cannot control their anger. It blazes up, sudden as fire in a dead pine, sometimes against us, sometimes against each other."

His brother-in-law was of a different opinion.

"Not all of them are that way. Some are kind and helpful."

"They are all fools," said Cedarstick. "You should know that, Charlie. You were little when the 'Bwaneg made war on them in the south, but you were old enough to know what was happening. You saw them come rushing from their houses and farms and stores and huddle together in the jail. They were poking shotguns and rifles out of every window. We didn't know what they were scared of, but we stayed out of the way of the gun muzzles. And that was a good thing. Because what they were scared of was us.

"They don't trust Indians, but many of them are not to be trusted either. Some of them take your work or your fish and then don't pay.

Or if they offer you rum for them it might be half water."

He set his heel cautiously against a sizzling chunk of green popple that had fallen away and pushed it back into the fire.

"Traps and supplies always used to be safe in the bush. Now, when you go back for them, maybe they'll be there and maybe they won't."

"Somebody kept stealing from Changing Star's cabin last winter," said Charlie. "He finally caught the thief. It was He-Paddles-Away."

"I know about that. But in the old times nobody would have bothered a cache. Except to take a little food in time of famine. It was the white man that changed everything."

Tamarack thought that such people would be hard to deal with. He said so, but Loon's Foot was confident.

"Each group of men think that they are the wisest and bravest. I am half Anishinabe and half 'Bwan. I have lived in both their camps and I know what each says about the other.

"I know the Americans too. They do have strange ways. But, when you get to know them, they are just another tribe with their own good and their own bad. I can talk their language. I never have any trouble with them. In the morning we will go to the trading post and we will get all the things that are needed."

Tamarack was not entirely reassured. But then a bottle was passed around, everyone became quite jovial, and his worries dimmed. While the Muskego slept, Charlie took Loon's Foot out to show him some of civilization's more sophisticated pleasures.

30

Tamarack was wakened at dawn by a new birdsong — the crowing of a rooster. He walked carefully around the crowded wigwam, stepping clear of a broken bottle, looking at the face of each of the sleepers. Loon's Foot was not one of them.

The Muskego was feeling a little sick. He was not an experienced drinking man, and the smell of this lodge was different from the strong, fresh, working odors of a wigwam in the woods. Also he was painfully uncertain what he ought to do next.

He well understood his own inadequacy in dealing with the strange and formidable men over there in the settlement, especially since he could speak no word of their language. He was also aware of the need for haste. The weather had turned warm and there seemed to be no immediate threat of freezeup. But that could change quickly. It might be different even now in the north.

He put the canoe in the water, loaded the bale and the sacks back into it, and stood, irresolute, holding the floating boat with his paddle.

A group of children, some white and some Indian, had been playing together between the two villages. Now they came down to the beach to stare at the aborigine. He recognized the Cedarstick boy.

"Go, little brother, find the man who came with me to your wigwam last night, and bring him here."

"If I do, what will you give me?"

Tamarack was unable to think of an appropriate answer.

"Will you give me some of the money you get from the trader?"

He was still not sure what the child was talking about, but he understood that something was required in exchange for Loon's Foot and he agreed to give it. That seemed to bring the desired result. The boy spoke in English to the other kids and they hustled purposefully off.

Tamarack pulled the bow of the canoe in to rest lightly on the sandy beach, and sat on his heels beside it. The sun was warm, and a few flies, revived by the heat, buzzed around him. After a long time two of his young messengers came running. They had found their man but he would not come. That was not their fault and he must pay them as he had promised.

Reluctantly, Tamarack unloaded and stacked the cargo on its skids again, removed the canoe from the water, and followed the boys between the lodges.

"There he is."

Loon's Foot lay sleeping in the sun behind a decrepit shanty. It took a long time to get him on his feet and Tamarack had to do the reloading without much help from him. But he seemed to revive during the short paddle to the dock. When the sacks had been unloaded again he walked jauntily up to the trading post, and returned with instructions to carry the cargo to its warehouse.

After that the transaction went smoothly enough. Tamarack was surprised and impressed by his companion's fluency in American. The trader was glad to get this good supply of high grade rice. The furs, too, were of fine quality. The price paid to such a pair of obvious jackpine savages might have been a little less than the going rate, but Loon's Foot seemed well satisfied as he rolled up a wad of the green papers that were of such supreme importance to everybody in this chaotic country.

"But where is the food and the powder?"

"This is money. A lot of money. Like the round pieces of metal you heard about at the Canadian post. I will give some of it to the white man and he will give us all the food and powder we can carry. But it's too late to leave today, so we will get the supplies tomorrow. Go back to the lodge and give this to the kid and this to the woman. I will come there in a little while."

Tamarack took what was given him and did as he was told. Mrs. Cedarstick seemed pleased to get the small piece of paper, even though it was wrinkled and dirty. She fed him well again that night. But Loon's Foot did not come back for supper.

Tamarack was unable to find him in Indian Town. He poked into each of the waginogans and shanties, sometimes drawing considerable abuse from the inhabitants, many of whom were getting new aspirations to privacy and a new pride in the angry response.

After some hesitation, he made his way across the grassy stumpland that separated the two communities and came into the street of the white settlement. He stood for a while looking at those broad buildings with their warm kerosene lighting that welcomed a strolling stranger and assured him that they were open for his patronage and pleasure.

He went from one of these opulent but rather intimidating establishments to another, pressing his nose against the hard, transparent substance that covered the windows, so much larger than the opening in the wall of Willow Woman's kitchen. He could not see Loon's Foot in any of them. Finally he went up to the entrance of the largest and fumbled at the knob. After a few unsuccessful tries he heard something click and the door opened.

White men looked up from their drinks at the tables, or turned from the bar to stare at him. Their disapproval was evident. A man in a stained apron came striding across the floor.

"We don't serve Indians. Get out of here. . . . Well come on, let's go!"

He grabbed Tamarack's arm, hustled him out onto the wooden sidewalk and closed the door behind them. Then he became less hostile.

"No hard feelings, Chief, but if you want a drink, you got to go 'round to the back. Tim'll take care of you." He motioned with his thumb.

Tamarack, of course, had not understood any of the words, but the sign language was clear. He followed a well-worn path that ran the length of the building, turned its corner, and ended where a dim light showed through a small window in a door.

He was becoming knowledgeable in city ways. His hand felt in the dark below the window, found a projection, and twisted it. The door opened.

Loon's Foot was sitting at a table with several other Indians and a big white man wearing a derby hat. Each of them was holding a little fan of cards in front of him. On the table was a dark bottle, several part-full glasses, and a good many of the crumpled green papers. The white man laid his cards there, face down, and stood up.

"Come in, come in. What will you have to drink? Have you

got money?"

There was no answer.

"Well, close the door, anyway."

The man sat down and picked up his hand.

Tamarack had not seen playing cards before, but he was familiar with other gambling games. He saw Loon's Foot push several of the wrinkled green papers to the lamp light at the center of the table. Soon the dealer pulled those and others into the growing pile in front of him. Even a swamp man could understand that.

Tamarack stepped up behind Loon's Foot and spoke to him. "Come now."

The answer was given in a thickened voice and out of a tipsily placating smile.

"I can't leave yet. I've lost a little money. But it's all right. Pretty soon I'll win it back and more. Then we'll have enough for all the food, lead and powder that we can carry."

Tamarack picked up the green papers in front of Loon's Foot.

"I will take these. And give me all the others that you still have. Then you can stay."

The white man stood up again. He was holding a bottle by the neck.

"You god damn black bastard. Lay down that money and get out of here!"

Watching him, Tamarack opened his belt bag and dropped the papers into it.

For such a heavy man, Tim moved fast. He came around the table swinging the bottle above his head. Again there was no need to understand the language. Tamarack faced his assailant, knees bent, crouching a little, ready. As the bottle came down his hand shot up and caught the wrist. The bottle flew past his head and shattered on the floor.

For a minute the two stood straining against each other, their faces almost touching, the white man cursing, the Indian silent. Then, slowly, the dealer was forced back and down, with the Muskego bending above him. Tamarack got a hand free, reached back and drew the claspknife from his pocket. He gripped the blade in his teeth and snapped it open.

Then the other Indians were on him, holding his arm, pulling him up, dragging him back.

"You crazy wild man from the woods! Do you want them to put a rope around your neck? Do you want to die kicking the air with your ghost strangled in your body?"

The dealer got to his feet, still swearing, but keeping well back, his eyes seeking an escape path around the jumble of Indians. He could hardly see Tamarack under the others' bodies, but these were being shaken and tossed like wolves trying to pull down a moose.

Then the struggling mass subsided. The knife clicked shut. Tamarack allowed himself to be dragged to the door. Loon's Foot, sober now, hurried him off into the darkness. There would be no more cards for him that night and probably not for the other players either.

By the light of the wigwam fire the money was counted and counted again.

"I think," said Loon's Foot, "that there will not be enough to buy all those things that we must bring back for the winter."

The lady of the lodge had been watching. The money spread out before them, even though depleted by gambling losses, still seemed like great wealth to her. She understood the problem, and she had a solution to offer.

"I heard this afternoon that there will be work for Indians widening the road and making it better. Early tomorrow, wagons will be waiting to take all those who want to cut brush and lay corduroy. For this the white men pay well. A dollar to every man for each day that he works! It will not take you long, at that rate, to get back what you need."

And thus the two nomads from the distant north were introduced to wage labor. For six days they sweated in the warm sun of Indian summer, pleasing the foreman with their strength, staying power, and axemanship. Each night they calculated their earnings, adding mathematics to the other things they were learning in the United States. Then, at last, Loon's Foot and Louise Cedarstick, having made marks on a board with charcoal, agreed that the next day, payday, they would have the necessary total.

When the wagons brought them back on the following evening, and they had been paid by lantern light, Loon's Foot went out, presumably to celebrate. This time Tamarack kept all the money, so he was not worrying about his partner. But he was worrying about the weather. He had a strong feeling that a change was close.

The selections and negotiations at the store took a long time. Tamarack asked Louise to come with them. He let Loon's Foot conduct the deal with the shopkeeper but insisted on her confirmation of each purchase and of the total. He paid over the money only when the goods were stacked before him.

There were sacks of flour, cans of lard and other provisions, with plenty of ammunition for the winter, steel traps for Tamarack's own trapline, and various shopping list items for the others. He handed what money was left to Louise and she went back to the lodge looking happy.

They carried the supplies down to the dock and wrapped them in compact, portageable bundles. But when they were ready to start packing them into the canoe, Loon's Foot slipped away again, saying that he had forgotten something. He trotted off across the pasture to Indian Town. When he came back a woman was walking behind him.

"This is my new wife."

They put the canoe in the water and loaded it, leaving space for the passenger behind the center thwart.

"Her name is Threetit Anna."

He pronounced the title in English. Tamarack, who had picked up a few key words of that language from the road crew, looked closely and was a little disappointed to note that Anna's blouse gave no indication of covering more than the usual number of nutritive appendages.

She had a hard, tight little mouth with a front tooth missing. Her nose had been broken and a scar ran diagonally from cheekbone to chin. All the same, she was not without a certain grace. Her skin was a clear olive brown. Long, loose hair hung down her back and around her shoulders. Tamarack thought that she seemed rather old for a bride, but she was certainly younger than Loon's Foot. She was carrying a package wrapped in newspapers and wearing store clothes that might have looked quite stylish except that they were torn, dirty, and noticeably rank.

She slipped her bundle in amongst the packs and cans, took off her sharp-heeled white-woman shoes and stepped in, easing her weight neatly down from the dock so as not to risk damaging the ribs or planking. At least, Tamarack noted, she hadn't forgotten how to get into a canoe.

The men took their places. Tamarack set a quick pace. Loon's Foot matched him with short but strong strokes that got the long, heavily-loaded craft moving at an increasing speed. Soon a little wave stood up in front and whispered against the hull.

The November twilight closed in early, bringing snow dust on a wind out of the north that bit at Anna through her flimsy clothing. Loon's Foot opened a pack and got out a blanket for her. After that she sat, shrouded and silent until they finally landed in a bay between sheltering rock, outreaches.

She helped make camp and get in the firewood, but she lacked the strength, speed, and machine-like efficiency of the woodswomen. When the fire was lighted she hovered above it for a while, warming herself before she started the cooking.

She lay close to Loon's Foot that night, covered by his blanket and with his coat spread over them, but shivering. He got up several times to put wood on the fire, and, when the pile was gone, went blundering off into the darkness to find more. Tamarack slept well enough, except when he was wakened by these efforts.

As they squatted beside the morning fire, soaking up a little last warmth before they went down to the water, he looked at the chilled and bedraggled woman beside him, and spoke across her to Loon's Foot.

"We should go no farther in this direction. It is a long way to Otter Woman's winter lodge. If the weather worsens and the lakes freeze, the Anna would probably not live to reach it.

"I think that we should turn now and take her back to the settlement. That will be best for all of us. Most of all for her."

For one moment Anna's jaw hung open. Then it stormed into violent action. She thrust her face close up to Tamarack's and delivered a burst of obscenity in mixed English and Indian, with such explosive energy that he felt the spray of flying spittle.

The familiar Anishinabe words for excrement and sex, delivered with such Saganash fury, took on an overwhelming curse-power. There was no further discussion. They loaded the canoe, and continued north.

They were travelling down a broad river, helped by the current, but considerably slowed in those curves and open stretches where they were exposed to the wind. Flocks of ducks kept speeding by them, showing white bellies between flashing wings as they swerved around the canoe. The men noticed that a few late geese were also flying low. They said nothing but they both knew the meaning of that. The upper air was turning cold. Bad weather was coming.

At noon they rounded the last point at the river's mouth and faced some thirty-five miles of stormy lake. They struggled to get the boat moving against the pounding of the waves. Anna pulled the spare paddle loose from its bindings and went to work with it, reaching out on the leeward side. Loon's Foot shifted the pack in front of him to windward, balancing the weight so that she could move closer to the gunwale without tipping the hull too far. In that position she was able to help them noticeably, even though her paddle often caught water on the forward stroke and splashed.

Gradually they built up some momentum, a little headway, into the hostile wind and waves. Loon's Foot steered a watchful course, making use of each occasional bit of point or island protection along the exposed shore. But it was slow going.

At sunset the wind showed no signs of subsiding and they landed, tired, soaked, and chilled, on the sheltered side of a spruce-covered point. Anna's hands were masses of broken blisters.

They got in plenty of wood and set up a substantial windbreak. Tamarack gave Anna one of his jackets, and she was more comfortable than she had been the night before. The men slept well, but whenever one of them was waked by cold and got up to revive the fire, he could hear the wind howling in the branches overhead.

They fought against that savage power all the next day. The swift paddles blurred through the spray. The canoe bucked and pitched under the buffeting of the waves. Often these broke over the gunwales and Anna was spending as much time bailing as paddling. Lard and lead had been packed along the bottom with the more perishable things, wrapped in bark and canvas coverings, on top. So they could hope that not much damage was being done to the cargo.

In the afternoon a few flakes of snow flew by, then a heavy downfall came driving in from the north. It plastered the faces and bodies of the paddlers. It whitened the trees and boulders on the islands that, from time to time, loomed out of the whirling clouds in front of the canoe, moved slowly past it, and dropped back out of sight.

31

The maples of the sugarbush were a last northern outpost of that species, trees that had taken root in these cold hills and somehow survived. And the people camped beneath their bare branches were another final contingent, come farther north than any of the others from the rice lakes.

Iron Feather had decided to stay here until Loon's Foot and Tamarack arrived, instead of moving up the river to the rapids as had been his usual practice. With plenty of rice now on hand, they could, if necessary, store the canoes here and go on over the ice. And now, like everyone in the camp, they were waiting for that change.

Waiting, but not resting. The men were up and hunting each morning before daylight. The last waterfowl — hardy, compact, round-bodied, little ducks — had skippered off the freezing ponds of the arctic prairie and come flying south in great numbers. Many of these dropped in at daybreak to feed in the Minnisabik and in the sloughs below the hills. The ponds were dark spots now, and the river a black ribbon winding through the white expanse of snow-covered muskeg.

There was little cover for stalking but that never made much difference to these bold birds from the tundra. Like the young grouse, they thought that if they were out of reach they were safe. So this was a harvest time for both gunners and bow hunters.

The women were up early too, taking up and resetting the nets. Their name for the whitefish was adikameg, caribou of the water. And that is the way they came, like the endless herds moving across plains and forest. Some of the best flavored fish of the year. And most generous of themselves now, just before the closing of the water, when they would keep well through the winter.

Gluttony is not a sin at this season when all the forest things must prepare for Peboan. The people fattened like the bears and stored like the wood-mice.

He-Rises wondered about Loon's Foot and Tamarack. In this good weather they should have easily completed their trip. He said nothing but he noticed that Shanod and Dawn Sailing kept breaking off their work to listen or to look down toward the far bend of the river when some sound or hunch or blind hope suggested to them that the two missing ones were returning.

The nights grew colder. The swamps froze. Sound of Waves, walking a little now, watched the big children race and slide on the ponds and play elaborate games in the snow.

Then, one morning, the camp woke to find that skims of ice had run out over the river wherever a point or bay slowed the flow of the current. After another cold, still night this sheet had thickened and spread to the opposite shore. Soon the little boys were testing it, stepping out in cautious daring over the shallow places, breaking through, and running back to the fires with wet feet.

Next day a young man walked farther out, feeling the give in the ice through his moccasins, listening, and watching the cracks that ran ahead of him. He could see that they were less deep than the thickness of his little finger. Not safe yet. He turned in a cautious arc and stepped lightly back to shore, sliding his feet and keeping his weight evenly distributed between them. Others stood watching, hoping for sound ice but ready to throw a line if he should break through.

Toboggans, harness and snowshoes had been mended. Surplus ducks, fish and rice had been cached. Now it was time to get on to the winter camps. Better to make meat, bring in firewood and lay out traplines before the snow became deep.

So most of the people were happy to come out of the lodges one morning into calm, severe, cold. The river had frozen hard and deep. Bark coverings were rolled up, and toboggans loaded.

Sled dogs were still in short supply, even though many had been acquired during the summer and fall. These were mostly untrained pups, anxious to join the teams but some of them silly and overly playful. They were all being harnessed now. Any laziness or trace-tangling, youthful foolery would be straightened out by disapproving growls and nips from the old-timers, with the quick support of the whip. And whenever necessary the teams would be assisted by men and women pulling on the lines or even getting into the harness.

Soon they were moving off over the ice, some upstream, some down, each family or small band hurrying back toward its own hunting and trapping ground well away from all the others.

Only the Iron Feather group were reluctant to leave the sugar camp. But now that the ice was firm there could be no more waiting.

The thought was strong in He-Rise's mind that it had been his failure at the moose kill that had kept his father from making the trip south. If Iron Feather had been in charge the party would surely have come in long before now.

"I will come back, sister and grandmother," he told them. "I will come back with a six-dog team as soon as we are settled at the spruce grove. I will meet your men on the trail or on the Minnisabik. Or, if they are not there, I will go south and find them. I will go as far south as I have to go. But now it is time to go north."

Clearly there was nothing else to do. Loon's Foot and Tamarack were many days past due. Some minor accident could have delayed them. But everyone was aware of the hazards of bringing a heavily loaded canoe across stormy lakes and down ice-rimmed rapids in the moon of freezing water. It might be necessary to face winter without those two hunters and without the lard, flour, powder and lead that they should be bringing. The family would have to act on that grim assumption.

They left a cache of ducks, fish, snowshoes, and two caribou skin parkas, and planted a signal post on the river bank to catch the attention of the late comers. Then dog teams, sleds, and people swept down the hill from the sugar camp and out on the ice.

The two pups that had followed, unburdened, last spring were almost full grown. One of them was harnessed to Loon's Foot's toboggan behind two dogs that Iron Feather had acquired in a trade at the rice lakes. The teams moved at a fast clip over the river ice. The snow was still shallow on waterways and trails. The snowshoes, not needed yet, were riding on the toboggans. The heavy loads would have been hard pulling on the uphill grades of portages for the dogs alone, but, with help from the humans, they were quickly accomplished. The weather was what they wanted: clear and cold.

He-Rises trotted ahead with a pack and a testing pole, but they all knew that the ice was sound. Early on the third day they left the river. The going was much better than it had been in the soft warmth of spring. There was more snow in the high country but still not enough to make them put on snowshoes.

Then, as they were making camp one evening, Iron Feather said that a storm was coming in. That night the wind shifted to the northeast. So they were not surprised the next day when the velocity of that threatening wind suddenly rose to blizzard power, driving rivers of snow, sharp and abrasive as flying sand, against their faces.

Those with hide parkas pulled the hoods forward so that they were looking out through tunnels lined with wolfskin and edged with wolverine, the furs that ice least from the breath. These coverings sheltered their faces but limited their fields of vision. Iron Feather and He-Rises stepped out ahead, the son breaking the trail, the father packing it down for the team.

The women followed the toboggans, pushing the loads with poles to help the dogs. Their heads were bent under their burdens, the posture and the broad tump straps protecting their faces a little from the stinging snow. They were thinking, two of them at least, about the other men somewhere out there behind them, who, if they were still alive, were facing this same storm in thin clothing and without dogs or snowshoes.

They walked all day leaning forward against a relentless wall of flying snow. Ice clung to eyebrows and eyelashes, blurring vision. The dogs too could hardly see but persistently followed the shape of the man or the team-mate ahead.

When the pale darkness of the storm deepened into night they left the trail for the protection of a clump of pines. Here they built a strong shelter and a comforting fire. At that season, in those latitudes, and under this snow-darkened sky, night came early and stayed mercifully late. The travellers and their animals slept well, winning back strength while the wind laid long, shifting drifts around them and howled through the boughs overhead.

The next day, and the next, they made what progress they could, against the force of the storm. Then, during the night, the wind died. The fury of the blizzard gave way to intense cold that woke the still-tired travellers before dawn.

Otter Woman poked the fire, put on the last of the wood and went out into the faint light to get more. She dared not use the axe. At this temperature the steel might shatter like glass. By the light of pale, late stars she found a dead spruce, pushed it over, and dragged it to the reviving flame. Shanod was breaking off its limbs as the mother went back for another load.

Since they had left the sugar camp, He-Rises had been doing most of the men's work, helped, to the extent that they could help, by Iron Feather and Sturgeon Man. When he left the shelter to harness the dogs a jay was perched on a branch overhead, its feathers ruffled for insulation and to cover its feet, so that it looked like a gray ball. It peered down boldly at him from just overhead, refusing to move, risking attack by snare or club rather than give up its position. It was ready to grab any scrap of food that might be left behind or carelessly set aside. Or it could be a spy, watching He-Rise's movements to report every detail to the sorcerer.

His fingers were numb as he slipped the collar over Ma-eengun's head. The big dog was whimpering in that bitter cold. But when the sled was loaded he and his team mates pulled well, straining at the harness, warming themselves with the effort, so that the people had to run to keep up.

Breaking trail at this pace was hard work, with the fresh snow falling in on the webbing and weighting down each step. But He-Rises was heavier and stronger than he had been in last spring's journey. He and the team left a misty wake of vapor in the still air behind them.

They made one more camp at the base of a wooded ridge in the muskeg. The next evening, in the bitter cold of gathering darkness, they came down the familiar path through the spruce grove into the sheltered clearing.

While the men were unloading the toboggans and the two girls were shoveling out the site of the pikogan with their snowshoes, Dawn Sailing and Otter Woman were setting up the heavy poles that formed the inner frame. This was swiftly covered with bark sheets, insulated with dry moss from the cache and roofed again with more bark. The big timbers were stacked and locked over all.

He-Rises, helped by the other two men, hauled in a good supply of wood, unharnessed and fed the dogs, chopped through the lake ice and brought water. By that time, the wall mats had been hung and the sweet-smelling circle of boughs laid down. Meat was roasting beside the fire. Now they could relax, hang ice-stiffened clothing in the upper heat, and pull off moccasins and wrappings to massage feet that were aching with cold.

But busy days followed. The dogs must be rested before they began the long trip back to the river. The people did not even think of any such luxury for themselves.

Bulging sacks of rice were stacked in the ground-level cache. Frozen meat for immediate needs and a good supply of fish had come in on the toboggans. Reassuring signs of game had been noted along the trail. Iron Feather could help with the trapping, and would soon be able to hunt. But they knew better than to trifle with Peboan. If they had gained some advantage they must hold to it hard and expand it.

32

In the cold dawn, He-Rises was clearing away brush and fallen timber from an old trapline, with Iron Feather guiding, coaching, and helping as much as his mending bone would allow. Shanod was pregnant again, but she climbed to the cache platform while Smoke Drifting handed up poles and basswood cord to repair and enlarge it. Dawn Sailing was coming down one of the trails with a load of firewood on her back bigger than she was. The dogs were taking it easy.

Otter Woman and Sturgeon Man were out on the lake cutting a line of holes, the first close to shore and the last well out over deep water. When these had been completed, they pushed a long, dry pole, with a rope attached, from one hole to the next. Pulling on this line, they drew a gill net under the ice. It ran from the first hole to the last, with the stone weights on its lower line resting on the bottom and its cedar floats holding it upright beneath the surface. Otter Woman shoved poles solidly down into the mud at each end, leaving their small ends sticking up above the ice. Finally spruce boughs were laid across the two end holes and covered with snow to keep the water from freezing. Or, if the cold was too sharp for that, to keep the ice from getting any thicker than it had to be.

Later in the day a sudden wind came roaring through the forest. It tore the caked snow from the spruce boughs and hurled it in chunks at the trappers. He-Rises turned his head and shoulders to keep the drift out of his hood. He spoke loudly, to be heard above the noise of the storm.

"Unless they have reached the sugar camp they will not even have parkas. We don't know what has happened, father. Shall I start tomorrow?"

"Wait at least one more day. Then we will look at the dogs again and we will see."

That night the women did not ask about the return trip. They knew that the odds were being carefully studied and that He-Rises would start at the most favorable time. To leave sooner would reduce the chances of bringing the missing men in alive.

So work went on the next day as usual. Traps were set, fish were taken from the nets, firewood was cut and bundled in with tump lines. Late in the afternoon Iron Feather examined the dogs carefully, paying particular attention to their feet.

"They can go in the morning."

No one else spoke but there was a great feeling of gladness.

After supper, Iron Feather smoothed a patch of ground beside the fire. He-Rises, squatting beside him, watched intently as the father spoke while he made marks in the earth with a sharpened stick. This dirt drawing was not a map, but it gave directions as explicitly as the dance of the white man's fly, the honey bee, tells the other workers the location of her nectar-find.

He-Rises stared at it a long time, asking an occasional question. He had never made the trip south to the border. When he stood up, the markings were swept away unrecorded, and the boughs were replaced. But now he had the route fixed in his mind. He should be able to drive his dogs over the great expanse of frozen waterways, following the right river, finding the right bay, crossing at the right portage to arrive, if he did not find the men first, at the American town.

He started early in quiet darkness. The trail had been blown almost clear of snow. With a light load and the long train of rested and eager dogs, he travelled fast. When he turned off into the bush and made camp at the end of the day, he had covered half the distance to the Minnisabik.

In the rocky groove of the river the track of earlier passage had been buried by the storm. Here He-Rises changed from hunting shoes to trail shoes, small snowshoes that sank deep and packed a firm path just wide enough for the toboggan. He walked ahead, Ma-eengun, as lead dog, following close behind him.

Each time that He-Rises topped the crest of a portage hill or rounded a river bend, so that a new prospect opened, he hoped to see the men coming. At night he imagined that he heard the distant sound of crunching snow, and looked up from the fire, trying to catch it again, until the dead winter silence became undeniable.

When he left the river and turned up the hill to the sugar camp he had seen no other person and no tracks but those of his own north-bound family where the wind had blown away the loose snow from the ice. The cache was untouched. He bound the parkas and snowshoes on the toboggan, but left the ducks and fish. He had food enough for himself and the dogs. And for the men, if he should find them. It was good to know that this reserve would be there for the trip back.

He crossed the divide, came down into the rice lakes and passed into the unfamiliar country beyond them. With Iron Feather's tracings in mind, he had no trouble following a frozen stream down from that flat and sandy expanse until it turned into the Wawigami, a broad river that flowed north.

Its strong current had still not allowed ice to form in some of the swift places. In warmer weather these might have been a danger to one unfamiliar with the flow and channel, but now each of the openings was sending up a warning pillar of mist. The winds had a good sweep at most of the surface so that they had blown away the snow in some places and packed it hard in others. He-Rises no longer had to break trail except where it stayed soft and deep on the portages around the open rapids. But he walked ahead on the ice, thumping with a pole, circling the team around any spots that sounded thin. He was trying to mark these down mentally for the return trip, as well as the foggy openings that would not show when they had been covered by a lightly frozen crust.

At his second camp on the Wawigami he lay awake, comfortable enough by the sheltered fire, but uneasy in his mind. Where were Tamarack and Loon's Foot? No minor mishap could have delayed them this long. He had promised to go all the way to the settlement if that should be necessary to find them. He would go the distance, but he had to admit to himself that his implied assurance of success had been a gentle lie. He had really meant that he would find them if they were alive. Or some indication of their fate if they were dead.

He-Rises knew now that even that second sad alternative would not be certain. His eyes had been searching the shores for the canoe or any trace of its wreckage. But the drifts were already deep in there near the timber. Nothing that might be under them would be seen again until spring.

This swift, strong, lonely river with its ever-changing ice! Conditions were perfect for travelling over it now. But continued cold would make everything different. He might not be able to remember all those danger spots. And there would be new ones if the ice should settle under the weight of a heavy load of new snow.

The silence of the winter night was broken by a shriek like that of a baby in agony. He knew that it was the last cry of a wabooz gripped by the talons of an owl. But something about it sounded unnatural. Kokoho was a bird of ill omen and could be serving a distant master. He remembered the owl's interruption of the council at the berry camp. Was this cry another warning?

He waked as usual at the first light of the long December dawn, drawn out even longer this morning by the dimness of a heavy sky. As he led the dogs down the bank to the river a few flakes of snow were falling.

Later that day he came out on the northernmost of the big lakes that led, connected one with another in a winding chain, to the medicine line and, beyond it, to the white man's village.

By this time it was snowing hard, muffling the sound of the rapids at the outlet and fogging the view of distant points and islands. In such a blindfold there would be little hope of finding his way among those sprawling contours. Even if he did strike the right course, the men he was seeking might pass him behind the white curtains. He set up camp on the portage trail some distance back from the lakeshore. Here he would wait the weather out.

That proved to be a long wait. Sitting in his snow-banked shelter, He-Rises wondered whether he ought not to be travelling instead of lazing here by the fire. They might be lying out there on the ice now, with the snow drifting around them. He got up, waded a few steps into the storm, and knew that to go on would be futile.

Ma-eengun watched him, whining and lifting his shoulders, eager for the harness. He-Rises spoke to him and sank back into the smoky warmth. He hoped that he was doing right this time, but he could not feel at ease.

The snow continued for almost three days. After that the wind blew hard so that the way was still obscured with swirling whiteness. Not until the fifth morning was it possible to go on. And even then he had to stop often, peering to the right and the left while the gusting wind whipped loose new snow in spirals and vast somersaults around him and the waiting dogs.

It was during one of these pauses that he saw them — three dark little spots against the white landscape. They emerged from behind a snow-sculptured island far to the west, moved for a little while, and disappeared behind another.

Three. Humans, not wolves. He must talk with them. They might have word of Tamarack and Loon's Foot.

He-Rises changed his course to intercept theirs. After a long time they came out from behind the island's drifted rocks. He could see that they were moving slowly, leaning into the wind, their legs driving against it, plowing their way through the fresh snow. One of them stopped, facing towards him and pointing as the others came up behind. For a moment they stood together, a dark mass. Then they moved into single file again, coming toward him.

They had wrapped rags around their heads for protection against the cold. Where their faces showed, their brows and eyelashes were so covered with white frost from the freezing breath that they seemed to be wearing masks. But He-Rises knew, while they were still far off, that the man breaking trail was Tamarack.

The wind seized and shook them, so that the smaller traveller, behind the other two, stumbled off balance, fell in a splash of snow, and had to be helped up.

He-Rises reached them before they had come very far into the open. Without introductions or explanation, he went directly to the stumbling little figure and pulled back the face coverings. There on the brown of nose, cheeks, and ears he saw white patches of freezing flesh. He put the woman into one of the caribou parkas and onto the toboggan, tossed the snowshoes and the remaining parka to the others, and headed straight for the island.

In a break in the rock wall overhung by brush and leaning pines the men dug down to moss. He-Rises gathered resinous knots and stump wood, and built a fast, hot fire, while Tamarack and Loon's

Foot set up a shelter of boughs and snow.

Anna tried to take off the makeshift moccasins that Loon's Foot had contrived for her, but her fingers were too stiff to untie the bindings. She lay back while He-Rises cut them away and unwrapped the rags beneath them. Her feet were a loathesome mess, crusted and suppurating with frostbite sores, cut by sharp ice edges, the toes and heels rubbed raw and bloody.

He-Rises did what he could, wishing that Dawn Sailing were with them. But neither toes nor fingers seemed to be frozen beyond recovery. Later, when everyone was warm and fed, Anna assured them that she would be able to go on after a resting time.

Loon's Foot told the story of the difficult journey, and they made their plans. Tamarack and He-Rises would go back for the cargo, cached with the long canoe beside a lake that had frozen over while they slept. Loon's Foot and Anna would wait on the island, making a better pair of moccasins for her from a piece of moose hide and some sinew that Dawn Sailing had put into one of the packs for such an emergency. They would also convert a spare blanket to a hooded capote. None of the men knew much about sewing and neither did Anna, but she was sure that, however unseemly the product might appear, it would provide her with better clothing than she had had so far.

They had been walking on rough snowshoes made from branches, with bark webbing. These were poor substitutes that sank deep, caught often in the fresh snow, and continually had to be repaired.

The trip down the lakes from the canoe, with inadequate clothing, the improvised snowshoes, and frequent rests for the silently suffering woman, had been long and dismal. The run back was comparatively easy. Tamarack could hardly believe the speed with which landmarks, achieved before with slow and punishing effort, slipped past them now. They reached the cache at the end of the second day, and started north again with the food, supplies and ammunition. They would return in the spring for the canoe.

They found the couple at the island camp rested and in good spirits. Using Loon's Foot's moccasins as models, Anna had made herself quite a servicable pair. They had snared a few rabbits and she was using the skins as inner foot wrappings.

"Your wife can walk behind the toboggan on the trail shoes," said He-Rises. "We will each have a pair of real snowshoes. But the snow will be deep on the big river below. The ice will be sagging and weakened under its weight."

"Don't be afraid, little nephew. I am with you now. I will bring you safely back to your mother's lodge."

The steaming openings at the rapids were gone, frozen over and hidden under the drifts. He-Rises came second in line, tense, prepared to dodge back from any cave-in, but with rescue pole ready.

Loon's Foot, in the lead, walked slowly, thinking, remembering the course of the channel, watching the surface of the snow for clues, stopping often to thrust his stick into it and down to the ice. Sometimes he would change direction sharply or back away at some warning that the others could not read.

His manidoke, which was considered pretty effective except in trapping, was with him here. The journey down the Wawigami took four days, but was accomplished comfortably and without anyone getting wet. He-Rises relaxed as they passed through the last rock gorge and turned up the tributary from the rice lakes.

They laid over a day at the sugar camp, put the supplies that had been bought for other families into well-marked caches, and rested the dogs and themselves, enjoying the change of diet provided by the fat ducks.

The Minnisabik seemed safe and friendly, the path to home. Having driven over it twice this winter, He-Rises expected no trouble from it now. But the snow had drifted deep on the smaller, cliff-sheltered river. In some places, the ice had buckled under its weight and the water had come squirting up. Some of these flooded areas showed dark spots above them, now frozen hard. But others, covered and insulated by the deep snow, stayed wet and gave no warning.

Again, Loon's Foot was walking ahead, poking thoughtfully at the ice. Sometimes he stopped altogether, leaning on his pole while he contemplated the shoreline and the white surface in front. Then the dogs would lie down in their traces, and the two men, almost as patient, would jog in place to keep warm. Anna might say something about the cold, but no one would answer and her husband would continue his leisurely study.

The overflow was especially consistent under the deep snow close to the banks. Sometimes they had to leave the river altogether and push through the bush before coming out on the shore to try again.

That night the temperature dropped still further. When they

returned to the river in the morning everything above the flowing water was solid. Now Loon's Foot sought out and followed the dark overflows instead of avoiding them. The dogs trotted easily over the frozen slush, and snowshoes were riding again instead of carrying.

Anna could have ridden too but she preferred to run and keep warm. The fast, steady foot-travel was tiring, and she sank thankfully into any rest period. But she was sleeping well at night now. Her feet were healing. Well fed and warmly clothed, she no longer felt the overwhelming exhaustion that had gripped her during those terrible days of the journey through the new winter.

33

The reunion at the pikogan was quiet but very happy. Dawn Sailing and Shanod had prepared themselves to see He-Rises return alone.

To Loon's Foot, his wife was Threetit Anna, and that was how he introduced her. None of the others could say the strange-sounding name, but they did the best they could with it, speaking falteringly but respectfully, on the assumption that it came from a sacred dream.

They accepted Anna as a daughter or a sister from a different world, whose words and actions they could not expect to comprehend. If Loon's Foot had brought back a white bride from the settlement, the difference between her and the forest Indians would have been only a little greater.

For a few days she was a bystander, observing, but not yet accepting, the heavy and often painful work of early winter. The woodswomen went at their labor with powerful, free-swinging action, following through each stroke, push, or pull like skilled lumberjacks or mariners.

Shanod went out to check the snares as soon as the men had left for the traplines. While Smoke Drifting was doing the morning camp work, Otter Woman and Dawn Sailing carried in firewood.

Then the women would be on the lake, removing the snow and boughs from the fishing holes. In spite of these coverings, ice would usually have to be chopped away with an ice chisel, an iron bar with a sharpened end. This tool splashed less than an axe as it broke through to water — enough, though, to soon wet and chill the person who was handling it. It grew steadily heavier as layers of ice accumulated.

The net would be drawn out at the shore-side hole and fed quickly back into the water with just a small section exposed to the air at any time to avoid freezing it. In that short interval the women would run it through their hands and remove the flopping fish. Then the end would be pulled back by the line to the outer opening, both poles pushed into the bottom, and the holes covered over.

Mittens would have been instantly soaked and useless, so the work was done with teeth and bare hands. It was a nasty job even in mild weather. During intense cold it was impossible. But when fish were needed for the families, or even for the dogs, the women would put up with a good deal of punishment to get them. They knew that, when the ice got too thick, net fishing would have to stop.

The men were out through the daylight hours. Early winter was a good time to trap the water animals. The snow was not yet too deep. The fur was prime, of dark color, and not bleached by sun-glare as it would be later.

Mink, muskrat, and beaver were active at this season. The rich meat of the beaver was valued as highly as its fur. Iron Feather and Loon's Foot agreed that it was the finest of all foods. Skinned mink carcasses were only dog meat and if the dogs were not really hungry they would look up from them reproachfully, asking for something better.

But during the past trading season, mink pelts had brought twice as much as beaver. Plenty of fresh fish were coming in from the nets and there was still a good supply of dried trout in makaks and of whitefish hanging frozen in the cache. So now the trapping efforts were concentrated on the slim little killers.

Muskrats were the mink's favorite prey. The men searched the shores of the creeks, swamps and lakes for burrows and pushups. Where they found mink tracks they set traps baited with an aged and powerful concoction that included scent from muskrats. Sometimes scuffle marks and blood in the snow showed that a rat had been dragged from its shelter. From there they would follow the tracks to where the body had been cached. Traps set in such places would usually get at least one mink and sometimes several.

Coming back at evening they would hang the frozen carcasses high in the narrow upper cone of the pikogan. In that warm place they would be thawed by the time that supper was finished. Then the women would quickly cut and peel back the skins and stretch them, inside out, over tapering pieces of wood. They would scrape them clean of flesh with the sharpened leg bone of a moose. For this purpose they preferred that archaic implement to the steel knife because it allowed them to bear down hard without cutting the skin. The scraped pelts were hung, still on their wooden stretchers, back in the overhead warmth until they were completely dry, then turned right side out again, ready for the trade.

The sweat, chill, and prolonged exhaustion of woodgathering, and the scaly, bleeding fingers, half-frozen from handling the nets, were almost unbelievable to Anna. Did women really work like that without being beaten — without even complaining?

Nobody said or did anything to imply that she was expected to help. But she had been around a while and knew a few things, a few unpleasant but eternal truths. She had learned that if you want to eat you have to hurt, one way or another, at least a little and usually a lot. On reflection, she decided that she preferred the impersonal suffering delivered by the winter wilderness to the blows and curses of drunken civilization.

She began to take a part in the housekeeping work and then in the outdoor chores. Doing some of these with speed and efficiency called for skills not easily acquired after age seven. Anna was by no means a slow learner, but for a long time she could see that she was getting in the way more than she was helping.

The evening transformation of bedraggled carcasses into saleable furs was quite beyond her ability. She tried it several times under her mother-in-law's tactful supervision, but always finished with some damage to her fingers, considerably more to the pelt, and with polite but irrepressible merriment among the audience. She gave that project up and found simpler chores to do by firelight.

The moon of the little spirits dwindled to a narrow crescent and finally disappeared in softly falling snow. Late in that dark and quiet night a shrieking explosion of dog-hysteria shook the sleeping camp. In moments the men were armed and searching into the spruces. When they found nothing there, Loon's Foot ran back to the lodge and brought out a torch of burning bark.

It's flaring light showed great tracks, shaped like the prints of a man's bare feet except that they had claws. They came from under the cache. A hindquarter of moose, hung six feet high, had been torn down

237

and carried away.

The dogs were roaring and straining at the leash, but the men stood looking at the tracks, already filling with snow. Iron Feather spoke.

"We would not be able to keep up with the dogs in the darkness. One or more of them might be destroyed by the trackmaker. Or might come bleeding back to camp bringing him after them. Also, this may be something more than an ordinary bear. We had better go back into the pikogan and talk."

The family squatted around the renewed fire. The women sat on the robes in an outer circle. But in this small group and these modern times they could be expected to break boldy into the discussion whenever they felt the need to express an opinion.

Anything out of order in nature was disturbing to the Anishinabeg. They laid a sacrifice before a tree that grew out of bare rock. They worried about birds that roosted in the wrong place or a fox that stood over a rabbit that he had killed, growling and snarling, in defiance of an approaching wolverine. Such things were not good.

At this season, all bears should be sleeping, fat and comfortable, in their dens under the snow. A winter bear, so far north, was a frightening reversal of nature. It would certainly be hungry, by now a desperate and unpredictable wild animal. But much worse than that, it could be a creature of supernatural evil.

Iron Feather was the first to speak.

"I have never before seen bear tracks that big. But the claws were too long even for those paws."

"The yellow bear of the north has claws like that," said Sturgeon Man. I can remember when one of those came from the barren lands and was killed in the Wapikopa Lake country. He was twice the size of an ordinary bear. He had a hump like a moose and very long claws. A yellow bear can carry as heavy a load of lead and arrows as men can shoot into him. When he is wounded, he is not willing to die before he has killed."

"A bear is not an owl," said Loon's Foot, "to fly from the northern prairie over the land of little sticks and then the forest. Nor a caribou to walk so far. Often a black bear will give birth to a brown cub, and sometimes to one of another color. Perhaps, uncle, it was such a bear that you saw or heard of at Wapikopa."

"I don't know what color this one may be," said Otter Woman,

"but it stood and reached high like a man. It came boldly into our camp and carried away our provisions. Clearly, it is a matchi ayawish, doing the bidding of the sorcerer."

"When he tried to drown us on 'Tschgumi," said He-Rises, "the grandmother's medicine protected us. It brought us safe over the half-frozen Wawigami. It can overcome this thing, too."

There was a general murmur of agreement terminating in a cynical grunt from Anna. All faces turned toward her. For a moment she said nothing. Then she spoke firmly.

"It was my husband that brought us over the Wawigami. My husband poking with a birch pole, and listening. I don't know what happened on 'Tschgumi because I wasn't there. But I doubt that a conjuror could harm anybody a long way off and across all that water. Civilized people at the American town no longer believe those foolish Indian stories.

"As for this matchi ayawish, it is probably an old bear with worn down teeth who has to steal food because he hasn't been able to find enough to fatten himself for the winter."

For a while the fire flickered among silent people. It was not wise to talk that way about weird things and dark magic. Then Iron Feather spoke quietly.

"My sister, Teetitanna, may be right. I hope that she is. I hope that this animal has not been sent by Undertooth to starve us or to kill us. But I am not sure about it. What do you think, Dawn Sailing?"

She answered, addressing Anna.

"I will not say that you are mistaken. About these things we are none of us certain any more.

"But it is said that a powerful sorcerer can take an old fur, the skin of a wolf, a lynx or a bear, bring it back to life, fill it with his lust for revenge, and send it against his enemy.

"That is very strong medicine. Too strong. An evil wabeno would usually prefer to cause sickness or accident. Because a matchi ayawish may get out of his control.

"If a musket is fired when its muzzle is plugged with mud, it will blow back at the shooter. Just as surely, a matchi ayawish that does not destroy its intended victim will turn and rend its creator, or cause him to wither. Even its death will not stop it. Because it was already dead.

"But this sorcerer has not succeeded with lesser magic. He may be desperate in his malice. He may be taking the risk."

"If this is a matchi ayawish," said Iron Feather, "it will surely come again. And if it is not a matchi ayawish, it is still a winter bear. A big one. It had better be tracked down and killed. But I am afraid to follow this bear or ayawish into the darkness."

At first light the dogs were released. The tracks were gone, covered deep under the falling snow. For three days the hunt went on, spiraling out from the camp. Iron Feather's shoulder was well enough now to allow him to handle the musket, and the others were armed with bows, spears and arrows. They had no beartraps but along all the trails they set heavy snares, attached to toggle logs, timbers just heavy enough to follow the bear, to catch in the brush, and to drag and strangle. And they set three great deadfalls heavily weighted with rocks.

The snares stayed empty. A lynx was flattened under one of the deadfalls. The other log traps just stood where they had been placed. There was no sign of the bear, if it was a bear. Not even a footprint in the snow.

34

Shanod put a handful of small sticks on the fire and the flame leaped up. The family could indulge in some increased warmth, now that supper was over and the cooking pot had been removed, and the women would need the light for the evening work.

"He may have returned to a den," said Iron Feather. "Or he may have left the country."

The lodge was silent except for the crackling of the new kindling. Otter Woman finished the sewing, tied the knot and cut the sinew thread before she spoke.

"I don't see how he could have disappeared so suddenly and so completely without sorcery. But whatever has happened to him, you had better call off the bear hunt. Other work must be done now. And not more mink.

"The ice will soon be too thick for netting. The wabooz are still coming to the snares and we have plenty of fish in the cache but we must soon have fatter meat than fish or rabbit. Will you be able to get at the beaver in such deep snow?"

"Not beaver, but we have been seeing good moose sign — tracks, droppings, and broken willows. The moose won't be moving far now.

"The cold has been keeping the snow dry, not softened enough by day to freeze into a crust at night. So there would be no use trying to run them down with dogs. The surface is firm enough, though, to tell them when a hunter is coming, even if he takes off his snowshoes and turns his parka fur-side out. So it is not a time for stalking either. But we could drive them."

"Let us hunt together, then," said Loon's Foot. "I will take one of the young dogs and go in to where they are hiding, and chase them out. You have the musket and the manidoke. You can shoot them."

The next morning they started combing the swamps. On the second day they found the tracks of a bull leading to a wooded rise. They quietly circled it. No prints went out. As Loon's Foot turned back, Iron Feather gave whispered instructions to the others.

"The moose will avoid the open muskeg as long as he can. Then he will be likely to cross it at the narrowest place that he can find. He will look for a point of brush extending out from another wooded area and will run for that.

"So we will each stand, well hidden, to cover one of these escape ways. You, with bows, will have to be very close to yours. That clump of trees off to the north will be for He-Rises. . . . Yes, way off there beyond the far creek. Tamarack, you sit low in the brush just below the boulder that shows against the sky on the rise to the east. That will be a good possibility. Loon's Foot will be waiting until he judges that we are all in our places. He will give us plenty of time, so don't be impatient. Then he and the dog will follow the tracks, driving the moose ahead, but he will be always ready with his own bow in case it should double back. The other dogs are tied in camp because they would only alarm the animals."

It was an ancient method, still effective, but not likely to produce a quick or easy kill. This bull did not want to be caught. He-Rises saw him race off in a cloud of whirling snow beyond arrow range, taking what cover he could, appearing and disappearing in a thin string of timber that stretched off to the north. Iron Feather and Tamarack had been out of sight.

Other moose proved equally wary. Most of the islands were long and spread out, with more avenues of escape than three men could cover. In the first four days there were two narrow misses, but no meat.

The hunters took these failures calmly. Like the wolves, they knew that many attempts must be made for each kill accomplished.

On the fifth morning, Otter Woman went out with the men. She had no weapon. She would stand in plain sight at one of the get-away places, blocking that exit route and maybe turning the game toward one of the hunters.

The air was still and clear and bitterly cold. The least sound carried a long distance. The watchers could not build fires, of course, nor move about, nor even stamp the chill out of their feet. Hoods had to be worn well back so as not to limit the field of vision.

The cold stung cheeks and noses. It searched for every opening in the clothing and came in like a sharp knife. Otter Woman plugged the ends of her sleeves with mittens and drew her arms in next to her body. The hunters could not take even that small comfort because they had to be ready for instant action. But again the moose found an unguarded point with enough brush and scattered clumps of spruce to satisfy him.

They came back to the pikogan that night chilled but confident.

"At dusk," Iron Feather told Sturgeon Man, "Tamarack found the fresh tracks of a fat cow. They lead into a big island. All we need will be enough people. Would you come with us tomorrow, father? And Dawn Sailing? And Teetitanna? The long walk and the cold will not be easy but, with you to help stand guard, we think that we can get that moose."

Anna and the old people were pleased to be included.

"I will carry a bow," said Sturgeon Man. "I will stand at one of the shooting points and you may be sure that I will stop anything that tries to get by me."

Smoke Drifting spoke up, insisting that she could take a stand as well as anyone else. They hadn't thought of using her, but it was agreed that she would be able to walk at least as far as Dawn Sailing and one more guard would be that much better.

Otter Woman went on with the plan. "Snow is coming but not until morning. There is a good trail now to the hunting area. We can follow it in the dark. We will leave early enough to be on the stands at dawn."

It was understood that Shanod was getting too heavy for such an enterprise. She would have to stay in camp anyway to nurse and care for Sound of Waves. But she said that she could check the snares and take up and empty the nets alone.

The quiet of the late night, not yet early morning, was strong in the lodge when the hunters and their helpers had left. But Shanod was not inclined to go back to her sleeping robes. The fire was still bright and by its light she was weaving the webbing into a wooden snowshoe frame. From time to time she glanced up to see whether the darkness of the smoke hole had begun to fade.

This would be a busy day for her and she was anxious to get started on the snares with the first light. She would take Sound of Waves, warmly padded in the tikinagon, on her back. That girl was getting to be a considerable load, but the trail around the wabooz circuit was firm, well packed by repeated tours since the last snow.

When the frozen silence was shattered by the roaring fury of dogs, Shanod knew at once that the matchi ayawish had returned.

Maybe it was just a hungry old bear come back to steal some more food. But if it had been sent to take revenge on her for her cruelty to Ice Stone, it had come at the right time. There was no weapon in the lodge.

She heard, above the barking, the sharp sound of a cracking timber. Whatever was out there had brushed heavily against one of the cache supports. But after the last raid the remaining meat and the fish had been hung high from poles lashed to tall trees. A bear might climb one of those but he would be unable to get at the food.

Time passed. She knew by the unrelenting clamor of the dogs that the marauder had not gone away. If she had been alone she might have slipped out to unleash them. But she could not bring herself to carry her baby into that menacing darkness, and she did not dare leave her alone in the pikogan. She snatched her out of the hammock and stood waiting.

A sudden powerful blow sent the entrance planks crashing down into the firelight. The weighted bearskin that formed the inner door covering was torn away. Shanod felt the blast of cold air, smelled the musky odor, and saw eyes shine red from the darkness. She hugged the child tighter and backed against the far side of the lodge. She could have gotten through or under the wall of a warm-season waginagon, but the deep snow and the heavy timbers locked on the outside of the winter pikogan made that escape impossible. She crouched, tense, watching the bear.

He too stood for a while, cautious, sniffing, looking at her and around the lodge. Then he walked in, enormous in that small space. His legs were brown but the color of his body fur was like newly tanned buckskin.

He stepped past the dying fire, turned, and with a sweep of a paw, casually ripped away a reed mat where a pot of boiled whitefish had been placed in the cool interval between wall and hanging. He dumped it and began to eat.

Shanod crept toward the torn entrance, slowly, her eyes on the bear, her feet feeling their way in complete silence. For a moment she thought that she would be allowed to carry the baby out into the night. But Sound of Waves, perhaps sensing her mother's fear, gave a frightened whimper. At the sound, the bear whirled toward the door, then turned and faced them, snarling lip drawn back, teeth clicking. The child cried more loudly. The bear shuffled toward them.

Shanod threw herself down in the balsam bedding, covering the baby with her body. She felt the boughs flatten against the ground under the bear's weight, then the blast of his breath as he blew out to snuffle at the back of her neck.

She had heard that, in the old days, when the Abwaneg had wiped out the men of a village and were searching the forest, a mother, hidden in a bush-covered cleft in the rocks, might quiet her infant by putting the palm of her hand over its mouth and pinching its nose between the thumb and the edge of the hand. She would have to risk relaxing the hold from time to time, allowing a little air to sustain life, but she must close down again before there was enough for a cry. If the grip were held too long the child would be dead. If too much air was allowed, even a slight sound would bring the enemy.

As she lay under the bear, Shanod's hand closed over her baby's mouth and nose. The crying stopped. She felt the child fighting to breathe.

But she lacked the courage of those old-time women. She relaxed her grip too soon. A snorting, muffled, scream broke from under her hand. The bear flicked nervously at her back with his paw. It was a light touch, hardly more than a caress, but the claws ripped her dress and raked her flesh. She did not move except to tighten her grip on the baby's face. Sound of Waves subsided.

The bear walked away grumbling. She heard him tearing at the meat. When he was finished there he poked around the lodge, pulling down mats, upsetting and breaking containers, lapping up spilled food and fluids, but not finding much more of real substance. He came back to the prostrate woman.

Shanod lay rigid as he nuzzled her back. He licked a little at the blood, made another swing around the lodge, found nothing more to eat, and was gone.

She lay there for a long time, holding the baby. The dogs sub-

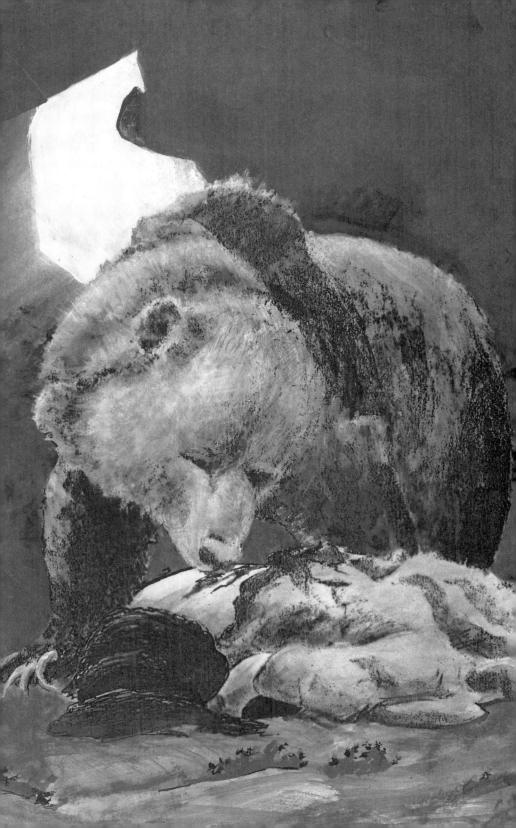

sided. Light came in and then snowflakes through the broken entrance. She was very cold, but she dared not move.

After a long time she heard the sound of approaching footsteps. The footsteps of a man, not of the animal.

One of He-Rise's snowshoes had caught between fallen timbers hidden under the snow and its frame had cracked. It would have to be spliced, soaked under the lake ice, and wrapped with wet rawhide. He had returned to leave it for this work and to get another pair.

For a few moments he stood in the doorway, dazed by the sight of the wreckage and of Shanod cowering over the child. Then he knelt beside her, made sure that neither she nor Sound of Waves were seriously injured. He looked around, uncertain what to do first.

Shanod wrapped herself and the baby in a blanket, but her continued violent shivering brought him into action. He built up the fire, bound the poles of the entrance back into position, set up the door planks, and hung what was left of the inner curtain. He bathed the lacerated back and sprinkled it with one of Dawn Sailing's herbal powders. After that he started to pick up the scattered household objects.

In the quiver at his belt, the arrows rattled a reminder. Suddenly he realized that he was wasting time, doing what could be done later by others. Wasting time purposely, maybe? The important thing now was to follow the fresh trail.

Shanod seemed to read his thoughts. "Stay here," she whispered. "It was a yellow bear."

He took a few minutes to hone the totem knife to a finer edge, then loosed the dogs. They bounded off in excited cry. He tied on a pair of snowshoes, picked up his bow, and followed.

35

Dawn brought gently falling snow and relief from the cold. As the people took their stands for the hunt they looked as though they were wearing ermine caps and mantles. Sturgeon Man came last, some distance behind Dawn Sailing.

Loon's Foot was waiting, anxious to start into the island before last night's prints were covered. In a low voice and with stick markings in the snow, he gave the instructions. The two old people were breathing hard, but they took careful note and stumped on to their assigned positions.

Tamarack stood without movement, a dark form growing white. He knew that Otter Woman was stationed on the next wooded point that ran out into the muskeg, and that Smoke Drifting was on his other side. But not the least sign of existence came from either of them.

In recent clear cold, Tamarack had been able to follow the sounds of the tracker's movements and sometimes of the quarry's as it fled. But this morning, sight and sound were cut off close around him by the falling snow. It was as though he were alone in the world.

In this silence and isolation he had no way of judging what time had passed. He began to wonder whether the hunt had taken some other direction. Perhaps he had been forgotten. But the basic rules for this kind of hunting are to stay in place, keep watching, keep listening and keep quiet. After two or three standing hours these become impossible for a white man, or a civilized man of any color, to obey. The time comes when he must take a few steps and swing his arms. That's when the animal goes streaking by.

The ermine thickened on Tamarack's head and shoulders but he did not move.

Suddenly, from beyond the gray wall of falling snow, came a clear call from Otter Woman. He swung toward the sound and drew the bowstring, one arrow notched, another held, with the bow, in his left hand.

A dark form came speeding at him, swerved sharply away into the white mist and was gone. But in that time he heard his first arrow thud hard into flesh, and then the second.

He snatched two more arrows from his quiver and ran to where the apparition had passed, but there would be no further shooting for a while. He was bending over red spots in the snow when Otter Woman came shuffling up on speedy shoes. She gave another cry, long and ululating, to summon the rest of the party. This phase of the hunt was finished.

When Iron Feather had studied the record of tracks and blood, he said that the moose had been solidly hit. He dug down to the moss and swamp grass, built a little fire, threw some of the crimson slush into the flame, and asked the moose spirit to quiet the wounded cow and keep her from running far.

The spirit would often grant this prayer. The delay for the ceremony also helped. It gave the cow more time to lie down and stiffen. Immediate pursuit might have hurried her into long and desperate flight.

Iron Feather told Sturgeon Man that he, Dawn Sailing and Anna might as well go back to the pikogan. They had done their work and would not be needed further. The old people, very tired, were glad to take the advice, but Anna said that she would go on with the hunt.

She could follow, then, and help with the butchering. Even if the bleeding stopped, tracking would not be difficult in the fresh snow. And yes, Smoke Drifting could come too.

He-Rises was still running after the frantic war cry of the dogs. This bear refused either to climb a tree or to come to bay. As the chase went on he led the pack through the densest thickets that could be found, and over the highest and most tangled windfalls. He seemed to know just which obstacles would be the toughest for a man on snowshoes.

Often He-Rises would come to an exhausted stop, heart pounding, breath rasping, and terror gripping at his thoughts. But he did not stand long. The recessional of the barking choir summoned him on. His stupidly brave legs seemed to keep on rushing him ahead even though his cautious mind demanded that they turn and take him back.

They were carrying him into a strangely familiar landscape, up through low hills and down into a long deep ravine with rock walls rising along both sides. Just as they had in the dream.

He-Rises knew now that Anna had been wrong. The thing out there leading them over this terrible course was no ordinary bear. It was the vision-evil.

As the pale, sunless daylight began to darken, there was a change in the sounds of the pack. The baying of pursuit had sharpened into the high-pitched staccato of combat. He-Rises stopped, listening. Then he summoned what strength he had left and raced on toward the clamor.

The cliffs came close together and the gully between them was criss-crossed with bleached timber, the gesturing and embracing skeletons of trees. In the gathering darkness the bear had chosen this place to make his stand.

Where the tracks entered the tangle, He-Rises came to a sudden stop, staring down. One of the young dogs lay sprawled there, still gasping a little, its entrails fanned out in a red design over the snow.

Fear, that had squeezed He-Rises as he followed the chase, sickened him now, shook his bones.

He stood a moment listening to the sounds of the fight, then twisted out of the snowshoes and climbed into the thicket of snags. He was holding bow and two arrows in one hand while with the other he felt his way, hoisting his body over level and angled tree trunks, and swinging it through the resisting hostility of stiff branches.

He stopped again when he saw a blond shape ahead, shifting and swinging, sometimes revealed, and again hidden, by the snow-covered timbers and the bounding, dodging dogs.

He heard the thud of a crushing blow as one of them was knocked, flying, loose-legged, out of the circle.

He-Rise's legs moved, carried him closer. He found himself standing just outside the whirl of the fight. The dogs were doing their work. It was time for the man to do his.

He notched an arrow and pulled hard on the cord, drawing the shaft back to its razor-edged head. The bear faced him, ignoring the dogs for a moment, then whirled back as one of them seized a hind leg.

He-Rises stepped in close, almost touching the hairy mass. His grip tightened on the bow. Aiming just behind the shoulder, he drove the arrow in. Right to the feathers. But a little too far back.

The bear turned, rising on hind legs, biting at the projecting stub, then dropped to all fours and came at the man as he notched and drew again.

It met the second arrow with a grunt, and suddenly swelled huge before He-Rises. It smashed him down into the snow between the timbers. Instinctively he drew up knees and feet, covering his belly for a moment from the raking claws.

The bear snapped at a foot, caught the moccasin, jerked it off. Shook it savagely then dropped it and came at He-Rises again, crushing down his protecting legs.

He had drawn the totem knife and was stabbing into the heavy fur. He saw yellow-toothed jaws opening before his face. He drove his left forearm into them, felt them grind down on his wrist and hand, heard the bones crunch.

He struck again with his right hand, stabbing with the desperate strength of pain and terror, driving the long blade through matted hair, then flesh, gristle, and bone, breaking or penetrating each living barrier.

The bear's jaws had seized the man's head. As the steel went in they let go to give a bellow of bewildered agony. He-Rises smelled the musky odor of animal fury, felt blood rush hot over his fingers. As he sawed and shoved with the knife it seemed to take on a life of its own, dragging his hand with it, widening the wound, forcing its way in deeper. Bear against bear. Witchcraft attacking deadly witchcraft.

Ma-eengun, panting hard and streaming with blood, slashed at the enemy's flank. But it had forgotten dogs in the blind rage for revenge against the man. An avalanche of gouges, blows and teeth tore He-Rises' body and drove it down between the timbers, through the wooden meshes of their network and into a slush of suddenly blood-soaked snow.

He twisted and rolled, striving to reach cover as frantically as a wood-mouse that has been hit and wounded, but not yet clutched, burrows into the forest floor while the owl turns, swooping back with eager talons.

A snarl of fallen timbers tilted dizzily above He-Rises. He struggled toward their shelter, pushing with torn flesh and broken bones. He came hard against unrelenting rock, could move no farther, and waited for the death stroke.

It did not come. The fierce persistence of Ma-eengun's teeth had won back the bear's attention. The noise of the fight dimmed in He-Rises' ears and then faded out.

✦ ✦ ✦

The chill and the great pain began to intrude, prodding He-Rises, forcing him out of unconsciousness.

He knew that everything was bad, but not, at first, where he was or what had happened. There was no sound for a long time. Then he heard the distant call of a wolf.

The snow had stopped and moonlight was filtering down through the tracery of trunks and branches. It was not very cold for a clear night in the subarctic winter, but cold enough. Cold enough to kill a badly injured man without fire, if his wounds should fail to do that, before morning.

He-Rises opened his left eye. Looking from under a flap of skin and through blood-clotted hair he could make out the mangled length of the arm. At the end of it he found a mass of flesh, with some limp fingers attached.

He wondered whether they were his. He willed them to move. They did not respond.

With his other hand he plucked at the clothing that had been torn from his body, trying to cover himself against the cold.

To live, he must have heat. His fire-pouch lay twisted beneath him. He must raise himself enough to get to it, must draw out flint, steel and tinder.

He reached with the good right hand and gripped a branch that stretched down from a tree trunk above him. He tried to lift his body, failed, lay back, resting. On the second attempt he got clear of the ground. His left elbow, dragging the wreckage of the hand, felt for the pouch, found it, nudged it toward one side. Just a little more. . . . He must lift himself a little higher. . . .

The branch broke. His weight crashed down on the injured hand. He rolled off it and lay, unable to move. Again the whirling brush and treetrunks faded around him.

The delay and the burning of the moose blood had been only partially effective. The cow was still able to get to her feet when she heard the approach of the hunters. They saw her go running stiffly off across the open muskeg, well beyond range. But they could also see the arrows in her side catch in the brush as she entered a thicket, throwing her out of her stride. She might be able to run a long distance, but she would not escape.

When Iron Feather calculated that she would have slowed, they swung wide of her course, and managed to turn her in the general direction of the lodge. Later in the day the tracks showed where she had faltered, and finally paused to blow and bleed.

She would be likely to lie down where she could watch her back trail and catch any scent that might come from the pursuers. Iron Feather and Tamarack left the tracks again to circle in from downwind on the place where they thought that she would be resting. Loon's Foot followed the tracks, walking slowly. He waited, and walked again. The women cleared the snow from a log, made a little fire beside it, and sat in the gracious warmth until they heard the distant roar of the old musket.

Instantly, Smoke Drifting's toes were pushing into the rawhide straps and she was on her way, trotting down the trail. Anna followed. Otter Woman came last, the axe on her shoulder.

The moose was quickly gutted and skinned. In the hands of those expert anatomists, axe and knives found their way swiftly to the weak spots in the bone frame, cutting off the head, quartering the carcass, and separating the ribs from the backbone. The arrowheads and the musket ball were quickly located and removed for reuse. But when the butchering was finished, the short day was almost over.

Iron Feather thought that they could not be far from their outgoing trail. They started off in its direction, dragging the meat on sheets of bark. This was heavy going in the fresh snow, and when they came to a sheltered spot in a swamp island they built a fire and settled down for the night.

✦ ✦ ✦

Sturgeon Man and Dawn Sailing listened to Shanod's account, rested on the bedding for a short time, then made up two light packs, with blankets and a little meat from the cache. Watching the old woman's movements, Shanod did not believe that she could go much farther.

"You are so tired. Rest here tonight with Sound of Waves. I will go with my grandfather to find He-Rises."

"He has followed a matchi ayawish. If he has found it and is still alive, he will need me. Stay here and take care of your baby and of the other one that will come. Send your father and Loon's Foot when they get in. Our trail may be covered by that time, but Iron Feather will find us."

Dawn Sailing had packed her remedies, surgical equipment, and medicine bag. Sturgeon Man had his bow and a light axe. They put their snowshoes back on their feet and started in He-Rises' tracks.

These had been filling in with snow but could still be followed through the forest. In the open wind-swept places they were either gone entirely or stood up only a little above the surface. Sturgeon Man had often to stop and cast about to find them.

When darkness closed in, he made a fire and slept beside it until Dawn Sailing woke him and told him that the moon had come out. By its light they were able to follow the trail again.

Sturgeon Man poked at the tuft of fur with the tip of his bow, then pried it up. The frozen paw and leg of a dog emerged stiffly from the drift. He ceased all movement and stood listening for any sound, his eyes running over the confusion of uprooted tree forms ahead. He saw the shape of a snowshoe outlined in white where it had been caught and held on the stub of a broken branch. He motioned Dawn Sailing to stand back.

His arrow was ready, but he wondered whether he would be able to draw it to the head. He worked his way over the timbers, following the depressions in their crests of snow where He-Rises had crossed earlier. When he saw the crumpled figure under the tree trunks he stopped again, not going to it directly but exploring the battle-ground and the surrounding woods.

He found big, bloodstained, barefoot prints, then the broken body of Ma-eengun, and finally the mound of the great carcass lying on its back. The snarling handle of the manido knife, smeared with hair and frozen blood, stood up out of it. The two bears were of the same color.

When he had satisfied himself that the ayawish was dead he called to Dawn Sailing. She came, running stiffly, from where she had been waiting in the back trail. She bent over He-Rises and gave a little trill of sorrow.

Sturgeon Man lit a twisted bark torch and held it, shading the flame from Dawn Sailing's eyes as she pressed and bound the mangled flesh.

The remembered duty and the sweet smoke of the burning birch took him back to that other time when he had held light to another torn

and battered young body. North Wind's skill had kept the life in her. But she had been savaged only by the fury of human malice.

He-Rises was holding back, unwilling to leave the cold dark for firelight and agony.

"Let me alone," he tried to say. "Let me stay with Pauguk."

He was in a weird and terrible place, and under torture by fierce enemies. They were trying to drag him back into life so that they could keep on hurting him. He was fighting feebly against cruel old hands that were holding him, cutting him with a sharp blade, searing him with red-hot iron, sewing him with sinew. Dimly he heard a familiar voice. "Quiet! You must lie quiet. Oh, there comes the blood again!"

A stick was pushed into his mouth.

"Bite on that, grandson, and do not move. Let the medicine woman finish her work."

As he had once risen from the deep, cold restfulness of the Minnisabik to Otter Woman's intrusive hands, so he came up now to Dawn Sailing's. He lay still, sinking his teeth in, crushing the yielding cedar, shaking a little, but no longer struggling.

36

It was the usual landscape for an Indian reservation of the nineteen fifties. The road was two winding, sandy tracks through jackpines and patches of young aspens standing up out of burned areas and low brush. My little car scrambled up over bone-rattling boulders on the hills and then raced down, building up speed to bounce and splash through the deeply rutted mudholes that bottomed each depression.

And not always through. Twice I had to jack up a wheel, push stones under it, then jack again until there was room enough to build a small highway of rocks out through the ooze in front of that wheel. In Canada or the United States, you can usually count on plenty of good, serviceable stone close at hand in any place that a thoughtful government has set aside for Indians.

The afternoon was getting on when the trail curved around a dump and came out on a village of log cabins and shanties. There were a few waginogans, too, covered with tar paper now instead of birch bark. On one side of the street the markers and little fenced enclosures of a graveyard were tilting or already fallen before the onslaught of wind and decay. On the other side lay a strip of dun-colored marsh and then the sparkling blue of a lake.

I found He-Rises sitting in the sun on a wooden box in front of a cabin. Wrapped in a blanket and wearing a fur cap, he looked more the traditional Indian than he ever had in his guiding days.

Several dogs advanced barking fiercely, but slunk away when I bent to pick up a stone. A skinny little boy with tousled hair and a runny nose peeked cautiously at me from the doorway. No one else was in sight. The old man turned his face up to meet me with a blank stare.

"You look pretty good, Mwashkamagad. Only you should be wearing some feathers with that outfit."

A smile of recognition started on the good side of his face and ran on across the caved-in section. He held out a hand, white man fashion.

"I had not expected to see you again. I am glad that you have come."

I sat on the rusty fender of a truck that was parked beside the cabin. It must have been there for some time. The tires, shrunken and knobby as old arms, had sunk into the earth until the car had come to rest on its running boards. An aspen had sprouted between bumper and radiator and was thickening out of saplinghood into a sizeable tree.

We talked about the old days in the woods and on the water. About swift rapids, steep portages, big fish, and good men. Then there was a pause, the kind of lengthening quiet that distresses a white person but doesn't bother an Indian. The races have different rules about the requirements of polite conversation.

There was plenty that I wanted to know. When I had been a boy I had learned about He-Rises' early life leading up to his injuries. Now, in middle age, I had come to hear the sequel. But I felt that it would be best not to move too quickly into personal matters.

I asked about the rice harvest.

"It's a good year for manomen. Lots of it, with big, clean kernels. Most of the people are on the rice lakes now. But they don't camp there for the season any more. They go in Model T's, with the canoes tied to the sides, and they come home every night.

"I'm too old to pole. But Smoke Drifting will bring us all the rice we need. She's with her daughter and two grandsons. She can still go out with either one of those boys and beat the canoe full. She'll get plenty for Sound of Waves too."

"Doesn't Sound of Waves go ricing?"

"She hasn't lived here for a long time. She and her brother stayed with Madeyn and me when their mother went away. But those two wanted to go to the Indian school. We couldn't stop them."

"Why did you want to stop them?"

"None of the other kids would go. Their parents didn't want them to either. They cut their hair off short at school and took away their moccasins and made them wear hard shoes. They washed their mouths out with soap if they spoke Indian. So the people used to keep the kids at home. But Sound of Waves kept on begging until we said she could go. And then little Tom got the idea too.

"That was before we moved in to the reserve. We used to leave them there before ricing started and pick them up as soon as leaves came on the birches.

"When Sound of Waves finished school she went to the city and worked for the whites. She married a city Indian. She still comes back for visits. Her car is too low to get over the rocks in our road and too long to get around the curves. But her nephews meet her at the highway."

"You said that Shanod went away. Are she and Tamarack still living?"

"I don't know about her. The last I heard of her was that she and her husband were leaving to trap in the western mountains. My mother went with them. But that was a long time ago. 'Tschgumi took Tamarack."

"You mean he was drowned?"

"My father, too. That was while I was still lying in the berry camp, with Dawn Sailing looking after me. My father said that a big storm was coming. A big one that would tear the nets. So they went out to take them up. Maybe they judged the wind wrong. Or it could have been witchwork.

"Undertooth was alive then, ailing, but still strong with the water things.

"They said that the morning after I was hurt there was the skin of a yellow bear beside his door. It had blood on it. He took sick then and died the next winter. At the end, they said, toads and snakes came out of him and crawled off into the snow. When the people saw those, they threw his body on the fire."

"Shanod married again, then?"

"She married Ice Stone."

"But why him?"

"He asked her. She said that she was afraid not to. Said she wasn't going to bring any more trouble on us than she already had. That was part of the reason. But I think that she had always wanted him a little."

"It must have been a terrible marriage for her."

"He didn't hurt her any more. He was a good hunter. She and her children ate good.

"When Ice Stone and I had got to be brothers-in-law, he said that he never told his father about the fight in the camp circle. I think that was true. But I suppose a wabeno would know anyway."

"How did Anna and Loon's Foot get along at the trading post camp? Did he beat her often?"

"Not ever. She knew how to handle a drinking man. She never let him get near a bottle. It wasn't easy. But she had a tongue like a cornered carcajou.

"I think that if Red Sky had spoken to him the way Anna did, things would have been different. The woodswomen didn't talk like that. Not in those days, anyway.

"Loon's Foot and Anna stayed with us through the next two winters. Then, when I was able to hunt again, they went to a Saganash town. Not the one she came from. He got a job in a sawmill. Every payday he gave her the check and she took care of the money. She kept it in a box and had a lot of it. Just like white people.

"We paddled down to visit them one autumn after ricing, Madeyn and me and the children. That was a good winter.

"One time I went to the mill with Loon's Foot. I watched him for a while and then I left. He worked there all day doing the same thing over and over, or whatever the head man told him to do. Every day except Sunday. Then he did what Anna told him to do. He never got to holler any more the way he used to in the white water. I knew I wouldn't ever want to be him. Not for any amount of meat or money.

"They fed us good, though. Madeyn got as big as Anna. And they showed us many strange sights in the town. But when the ice went out of the river Anna told us that it was time for us to go home. Just like white people."

"What became of that boy of Shanod's that you spoke of? The little brother that stayed with you when she went away?"

"He's still here. Tom Stone. When he grew up he cut away the Ice to make it a white man name. But he's not little any more. Biggest man on the reserve."

"How do you mean, big?"

"Big every direction. Tall like his father, but with a big belly. And big other ways. The white men like him too much. The Indians do what he tells them. They don't want to get him mad."

I had to know more about this grandson of Iron Feather and Undertooth, this resultant of two powerful and opposite manidokes.

He-Rises disapproved of many of the nephew's actions but took pride in some of his exploits.

"He did good at the school. He did pretty good just not to die there. A lot of kids did. The Saganashag said that was because Indians were sickly and had no will to live. But Tom didn't die. He didn't even get sick much. He learned to talk white man talk, then to write and to figure. Then he came back here.

"When the agent went out to pay the treaty dollars he took Tom along to help him. They read over the lists together and decided who got money and who didn't. And, later, who got food and blankets and seeds.

"We wanted the food and the blankets. We didn't care much about the seeds. The frost comes too early for those plants here. They went with the other stuff and we were supposed to take them. We gave up on trying to plant them but some of them were pretty good boiled.

"When the welfare people began to come they would ask Tom who was working the way they wanted us to work, and who was keeping their shacks clean, and who got drunk too often and fought, and who had too many wives and who were hiding their kids when the school man came around. All those things could make a difference in what they gave people.

"The white men made him chief. That means head Indian. And he gets paid money. He has a big house now and an old wife. Built of sawed lumber. And a lot of kids. Two of his boys work with the Saganashag just like he does. The trader and the nurse and the missionary are friends of theirs.

"When the beaver-boss comes, Tom tells him how he should settle arguments about traplines. Some say that he tells the game warden who's been jacklighting deer. I don't think he ever did that.

"But he might tell who is sick and pretending not to be. Then if they still won't go, the police come and take them away to the hospital. That is not a good place to die. You are not buried with your own people.

"So the Indians began to treat Tom pretty good and give him presents. They vote him for chief every election. Like with Shanod, they're scared not to. Some of them think he's got the same power as Undertooth.

"I don't think he's that way. He wouldn't call on a tree or animal to kill anybody. I doubt if he'd even wish a crick into somebody's back

265

or spoil a man's trapping season. I don't know, though. Anybody goes against him, he don't do so good.

"Except Joe Mashkegwatik. That's Joe Tamarack in your language. Tom's brother. Since he came back from the German war he's got other ideas. Sometimes he stands up to Tom in meeting. Once he called him a government Indian. But Tom doesn't get mad at him. He just lets him talk. Then he tells the people how it will be best to vote, and they vote that way. He never did Joe any harm or anything to get even.

"Last week three strange white men came in a plane. They went to Tom's house and stayed there all afternoon. Since then he has been saying that it will be good to let them dam the river. It won't hurt the fishing much and there will be jobs and money for the Indians. Joe says that we must not let them drown the rapids. But the people will go along with Tom. The river stinks so from the pulp mill I guess it won't make much difference."

"Would you rather be living here than in the bush?"

He-Rises laughed. "If we'd stayed out there I wouldn't be living. By now, in some hungry winter, it would have been my time to walk out.

"That seems crazy here. Nobody has to starve any more. Except babies, sometimes, when the parents are on a binge.

"You vote for Tom and you get flour and beans and salt pork. And of course we still make rice for ourselves, and sugar in the spring, and venison when we can get it, and pick berries.

"But we can't talk to the animals. Those old-time Indians could. And to the rocks and the trees. And to us. I believed everything they told me. I still do. We trusted each other then. A big man would have been ashamed to have a lot when others had little.

"But it doesn't matter which way was better. We couldn't go back now. There are too many of us. Too many Indians and not enough animals."

He looked at me slyly.

"Your people thought we'd disappear. For a while it looked like they were right. But not any more."

"Do you still have the manido knife?"

He reached back under the blanket and handed it to me. Time and sweat had darkened the sheath, but the fine quills from the porcupine's belly, flattened between Dawn Sailing's teeth and sewed on with sinew instead of thread, were still firm and bright in that relentlessly geometric design. And the creature in the handle glared up at me, defiant and mysterious as ever.

I drew out the long blade. It caught the light of the setting sun and glowed red. It was thinner now, from many honings, but it looked efficient. I touched the edge and maybe I slipped my finger a little along it. Anyway I felt it lift a slim peeling of skin.

"You haven't let it get dull. And you keep it handy. Are you expecting another matchi ayawish?"

"We don't have those around any more. But I still want it sharp and with me. Now and later. Never know what you might meet on that road."

A breeze plucked a shower of bright leaves from branches and swirled them around us. In a little while a matronly young woman came out of the cabin. She was carrying a worn piece of maple cut off at the swelling of the root to form a cane. The boy, close behind her, was watching me, but she looked only at He-Rises.

"It's getting cold, grandfather. You'd better come in now."

He took the stick from her and grasped it with both hands. She crooked her arm strongly under his elbow. With a well-timed mutual effort they got him to his feet. He smiled goodbye and limped beside her into the cabin. The boy went ahead of them, still keeping his eyes on me.

I walked back to the car and stood there for a while looking out over the lake. Beyond its blue, the aspens were a smoky gold in the late sunlight. A loon called. I could see him flap his wings, almost lifting himself out of the water. He would be going south soon. Nanabush's friend.